SNAKE
ON
SATURDAYS

Jean Gill

First Impression—2001

ISBN 1 85902 981 7

© Jean Gill

This book is published with the support of the
Arts Council of Wales.

Printed in Wales at
Gomer Press, Llandysul, Ceredigion

for John

Acknowledgements

Lyrics by Francis Cabrel on pp. 10 and 11 courtesy of Sony Music, France. The reference to the 'iridescence on a pigeon's neck' on p. 19 borrows Sheenagh Pugh's image from 'Do you think we'll get to Earth, Sir?', *Selected Poems* (Seren, 1990). The quotation on p. 229 is taken from *The Harem Within: Tales of a Moroccan Girlhood* (Transworld), by Fatima Memissi.

1

'Behind the bike shed.'

'Hardly counts, it's so predictable. In an Astra . . . a Cortina . . . a Renault . . .'

'OK, OK, cars . . . I get the idea. In a rowing boat on the Loughor.'

She thought for a minute. 'On a pine needle bed in a squirrel-filled wood.'

He regarded her narrowly. 'Squirrels don't live in coniferous forest.'

'Well, obviously, it was a mixed forest. I didn't say all the trees were pines, did I?'

'And it was *full* of squirrels, which presumably made themselves known to you at your moment of passion.'

'Stop quibbling. You're just playing for time.'

'In a changing room at the swimming pool.'

'Very romantic.' Another pause for thought. One of the prints on the wall caught her eye. 'In a mountain stream where the currents mixed the coldness of snow with the warmth of summer.'

'No doubt the stream was full of fish. Was there a camera team filming a cigarette advert at the time?'

She smirked. 'We all have our treasured memories.'

He rolled on his back and put his hands behind his head, relaxed. 'On the top bunk of a sleeper car on the Orient Express, just as it was entering Venice. Symbolic, don't you think?'

'You and your films. Cary Grant, *North by Northwest,* with more than a little of Dai's imagination.'

'Perhaps it was the Flying Scotsman then. So easy to lose track of place and time at such moments, don't you find?'

But she'd turned serious and he could see from the frown of concentration that an idea was arriving. This was a pity, as he enjoyed the suspended time when they lay together, with no urgency to the circling caresses. She was lying upside down, head against his feet, and to look at her expression he had to raise up from the pillow, straining his neck muscles. He gave up and waited with resignation. Ideas could be very uncomfortable and – worse still – a response was expected. He had given up aiming to please with his response and was less often treated to a silence of affectionate contempt.

'It's probably different for men,' (one of her least attractive opening gambits); 'I've found that crazy places were exciting but not that satisfying. With the possible exception of the squirrels.' She threw him what would have been a sideways glance had she been the right way up, but his eyes were closed as he listened. If he was listening. 'And the same is true about a new man. You know, it's exciting, but not the best.'

'No doubt there was an exception to that too. . .'

'Yes actually, now you come to mention it. . . So where is it best for you?'

He knew the answer to that one. 'Here. In your bed. With you.'

She felt the disappointment of having forced him, but also the warmth of knowing it was true.

'Il a fait tout l'amour de la terre, Il n'a pas trouvé mieux.'

'I love it when you talk dirty.'

'It means "he travelled all around the world to find out home is best," but it sounds better in French.'

They lay back in contented silence, but time was ticking back into the evening.

'Dance with me,' she demanded suddenly. 'No,' she

10

stopped him reaching for his clothes, 'as we are.' He laughed and shook his head but conceded, watching as she put one of her shameful secrets on the CD player. Every now and then she confessed a 'shameful secret' to him, making him promise not to tell. No one was to know that she licked the cream out of custard cream biscuits before eating the outside; no one was to know she slept with a one-eyed toy dog called Heathcliff; no one was to know she had a compilation album of popular love songs.

As the lugubrious notes of the CD oozed into the room she took his hand. He shambled to his feet and held her, shifting to the rhythm with as much grace and dignity as he could muster with a rash of goose pimples and a horribly new awareness of the way his body was assembled. For a few seconds he lost the self-consciousness, held her eyes, and this time his murmured 'love you' was unforced. Then the laughter took over, as both of them complained about bits bobbling.

There was a slight awkwardness in the air as they dressed, and she knew it was time.

'Helen.'

She just looked at him, poised, waiting.

'It's time to go . . .'

The end of his sentence hung in the air . . . 'home.'

She kissed him, and though he looked for signs that she minded, he saw none bar a hint of coolness. But then that's how she was.

'À bientôt.' She smiled at him as she closed the door, trying to shut out the echoes in her mind,

'Il n'a pas trouvé mieux.'

She muttered her personal litany, 'Liberty, autonomy and space for me.' She had plenty of space to be herself, and it was only at moments like this that the word 'empty' emerged from the silence.

11

When she woke, she glimpsed through the curtains that particular shade of grey which indicated a dull summer day. She found it impossible to enthuse about Llanelli's mild climate and retained her immigrant's awe at the varieties of rain possible. She had once started a rain lexicon, inspired by the knowledge that there were forty? sixty? one hundred Inuit words for snow, and was disappointed that this was not the case in Welsh. Her attempt to fill the gap in English, at least, had reached twenty categories before the project was abandoned, defeated by the apathy which watching rain induced in her. Sheet rain, drizzle, the torrent, the downpour and picking rain were among the more obvious; she was best pleased by 'the kettle spout' (the type of rain which drenches one specific location – usually you – and steams upwards from the pavement), 'the devil's miracle' (which falls steadily from a cloudless blue sky) and 'gloop' (the drops having a gelatinous quality). The project had not been encouraged by friends, who explained carefully to her that she must work to the key phrase 'Look at that "___" !' While 'gloop' met this requirement, the fact that no one else understood the word did inhibit conversation, which could usually continue comfortably for several minutes on the subject of the weather.

However, the weather had not really been a consideration five years ago when Helen had moved to Llanelli. She had wanted somewhere rural by the sea, with cheap rents for business and accommodation, and as far away from Leeds as possible. No one had objected to the last point; not that she had discussed the decision with anyone else. While browsing through a daily paper, the headline *Pembrey flagged as Britain's best beach* caught her eye. The description of miles of milky white sands had captured her imagination. When she looked out of the bus window and saw one lad puking, another peeing against someone's

12

garden wall and a third kicking a plastic bottle in drifts of old newspaper, her mind was made up. The magic word *Llanelli* was her one-way ticket out of this. Although there had been some readjustment to the reality of Llanelli as a large town with more than its fair share of rough lads and unemployment, there was also the magic. The sea itself, even from Llanelli's warehouse-ridden grey beach, was a source of wonder to her. Local stories told of youngsters and visitors cut off on sandbanks by the deceptive speed of the estuary tides. Even the much-touted Pembrey Beach (for which she preferred the tidal flow of the Welsh name Cefn Sidan) was famous among the old 'uns for its lethal currents.

Her first visit to Cefn Sidan had inevitably been a disappointment. In her innocence she had not checked bus times or tides and had suffered a long wait to catch the former and a long walk to catch the latter. Her entry point to the beach, trying to avoid people, gave her a trek across sand dunes on a wooden path. Convinced that she would see the sea after rounding the last hillock, she was daunted by the vast stretch of sand which met her view. Clean white sand, certainly, but where was the sea? Adjusting to another walk, she aimed for the horizon, which really wasn't that far away. Or so she thought. After ten minutes walking, the sea looked no nearer and she continued with gritted teeth. When she finally reached the sea, she kicked it repeatedly with her bare feet and vented her feelings verbally. Thoroughly drenched and pausing for breath she heard it, that silence which is full of nature's sounds; the distinctive two-tone note of the curlew and the food squabbles of gulls. She looked across the sea to the Gower Peninsula, its muted shades of green, and the long, low outline of Worm's Head blurry at the edges. Fired up by a sudden determination, she had told the Worm's Head that she was here to stay and that there were dragons in the north of England too.

13

On this particular grey summer day, Helen kept to her working routine. A short walk from her rented house on the Pembrey Road took her to the centre of town, where she opened up shop. The window display, with its summer sale prices on nubbly cotton tops would soon have to be changed for the Christmas hard sell, even though it was only August. She hated the way that working in a shop made the year disappear, and yet she could only meet orders if she did work well in advance. There were always customers who thought she could design and handknit a garment by someone's birthday 'tomorrow' and who took it as a personal affront when she explained that it would take longer. Luckily, she had a growing number of regular customers, as well as some passing tourist trade.

Tuesday was generally quiet, with smaller shops still closing for the traditional half-day, so she settled to some design work after a quick and moderately depressing updating of the accounts. Takings were just high enough to keep her life ticking over, but there was no margin for safety or luxury. Once a year, in January when trade was slack, she treated herself to one of her own designer jumpers, but generally she couldn't afford time off from the day-to-day work of meeting orders and adding to stock. Each item was unique and she'd lost count of the number of times she'd patiently rejected customers' insistence that they wanted 'one exactly like that one'. Her high standards were beginning to pay off, though, and she was risking more imaginative designs and mixed textures, with some success.

Sucking her pencil and plotting the stitches on graph paper, Helen sketched a batwing jumper, fashionably cropped, with variants of traditional fair-isle motifs in two vertical bands. She looked through her samples box with a miser's greed, savouring colours and textures, imagining

14

different combinations. Rejecting the impracticality of pure mohair, she chose an olive mohair/acrylic mix with a tawny twisted silk yarn for the motifs. She'd have to be careful with the stranding on the inside, but she was sure that the design would work. This was a design that would glow, would beg to be bought, and would attract the interest of visiting royalty. She would be the Norman Hartnell of woolly couture. She would out-Fasset Kaffe. Better still, a visiting foreign delegate would see The Jumper and realise that the interests of international trade would be best served by a joint trading venture that would make M&S look like a penny bazaar again. Lost in these visions, she was disturbed by the alarm clock, which told her it was lunch and Tuesday closing time.

Not one customer all morning and yet she was satisfied with her half-day's work. The latest creation was on its way, with some intricate cable in the ribbing and the pattern set. She knew perfectly well that this design was meant for her, the colours to suit the dark red of her long, unruly hair and the freckled cream of her skin. She also knew that she would sell the jumper to someone else, hopefully after a long enough spell in the shop window to attract orders. It was difficult to balance immediate sales against orders and she was grateful when customers allowed her to display sold items for an extra week or two. Even with the piece-work provided by Sian and Glenys, Christmas was crazy, and she really could not afford to take on more workers. If only she could have a year off to build up stock, then she could cope with the Christmas rush.

It had been two weeks before Christmas that she had met Dai. He had waited patiently behind three other customers, who all wanted to agonize in turn over which character from *The Lion King* or *Pocohontas* should be in what pose, on a jumper of which colour and size, for little Bethan or

15

Ian or Emma. Noticing that it was quarter to six – well after closing time – she flipped the sign in the door to CLOSED / AR GAU and turned the key in the lock as a further precaution, excusing herself to her last customer. Finally, she turned her attention to the stocky man in jeans and shabby weatherproof jacket.

Her smile was still bright but a little weary as she asked, 'Is it *The Lion King* or *Pocohontas*?'

'Neither, I'm afraid. If people weren't encouraged to see animals as cute entertainment, my job would be a lot easier.' He smiled ruefully, softening the bitterness of the remark. 'I'm sorry. It's been a hard day and vets don't look forward to Christmas.'

'I hate Christmas too,' came spontaneously from her, to her chagrin as she would have to give some reason why, and the truth was something she didn't even tell herself any more, never mind a total stranger. She rushed to pre-empt the question. 'It's so commercialised,' and she kicked herself for the cliché. He must think her boring. Then she kicked herself for even considering what he might think of her.

'I'd like some kind of fluffy jumper in tasteful colours for my wife's Christmas present. She's about your size.'

She pulled her professional self together, showed a selection of jumpers, using rather more exact descriptions of yarn than 'fluffy' but he seemed to lose interest, told her to choose for him and said, 'Yes that will do fine,' as he crumpled up a cream Angora tunic with seed pearls sewn into the shoulder cabling detail.

Helen packed the jumper with exaggerated care but the point seemed to be lost as he was quite openly scrutinizing her face.

'I don't usually find redheads attractive, but you look like a Botticelli angel,' he announced, as if this were a mere statement of fact.

16

'That's me, fat and virtuous. I don't usually find married men attractive, especially arrogant ones, and you're no exception,' she retorted, with the colour in her cheeks fuelling the spark of her temper.

He seemed unmoved and merely asked her politely for his credit card back. She realised that his Visacard was clutched tightly in her hand and had been waved in the air to illustrate her feelings. Both card and package containing the jumper were dumped gracelessly on the counter, retrieved by the man, who thanked her and would have left if the door had not been locked. She had recovered her poise, enjoyed watching him re-arranging his bags to turn the key, and timed her intervention so as to help him as little as possible, while being the one who actually unlocked the door. They had wished each other a Merry Christmas and she had not expected to see him again, although he had made enough of an impression for her to notice from his credit receipt that he was D. R. Evans.

His name always seemed a mystery to her, even when she knew him well. David Richard Evans, known as Dai. The essential Welshness of 'Dai Evans, the vet' worried at her prejudices. The ones she'd been sure she didn't have. Why was it impossible to take someone called Dai seriously? Why was it so difficult to accept that a 'Dai' was more than a match for her intelligence? Why did Evans sound like a pseudonym for an illicit weekend? It was characteristic of him that he accepted himself as Dai, although he joked that his parents had named him D. R. in the hope that he would rise to the level of medical doctor. Her favourite, special name for him was Dafydd; she loved the Celtic sound of it and the way it suggested all the strangeness of him.

She had survived Christmas, using all the defensive rituals she had developed, automatically destroying unopened Christmas mail from the few people from pre-Llanelli days who still made a token gesture at contact. Friends made more recently knew that she didn't celebrate Christmas, and if anyone pestered her on the subject, she ended any discussion by saying that her dead parents had been Jehovah's Witnesses and that this was the only article of faith she observed out of respect for them. Her parents, in their three-bedroomed suburban Leeds semi, would have been distressed but not surprised by her story of their demise. Theirs was one of the cards destroyed each Christmas, despite the plea on the back of the envelope 'Helen, please get in touch. We love you.'

On a slack day in January, he had appeared again, lugging a bag of medicine, syringes and plastic gloves, all jammed in and bulging over the top.

'I don't suppose there's any chance of a coffee? The police called me to a road victim and then I did my town visits. There's a Persian next door to you, the flat above the shop, horrific eczema and stupid owners. Half the problem is diet and it's an indoor cat so there's no chance of it foraging to add roughage to its *haute cuisine*. They're more likely to give caviar to the cat than coffee to the vet so I remembered there was a friendly face close by and I wondered . . .'

She had continued knitting, without looking up, although she was perfectly capable of following a complex design and watching television at the same time, so this was from choice not necessity. There was silence until she reached the end of the row, pushed the needles through the three balls of wool she was working with, stretched and stood up.

'How did your wife like her Christmas present?' Helen asked.

'She loved it,' he replied, holding her gaze steadily. And then they had coffee. And talked. And it became something

18

to look forward to, long after the Persian had recovered from its eczema if not from its owners.

One wet Monday in March, he had called just before closing time, and she had asked him, 'What does your wife think of you calling here for coffee?'

Again, the steady gaze, no ducking of the question on or below the surface. 'There is no reason for me to talk to her about it.'

And so the coffees continued. And for a while it was just coffees.

2

Tuesday lunchtime during school holidays meant lunch with Neil.

He was waiting for her by the portcullis of the closed indoor market, fending off pigeons.

'There ought to be notices asking people not to feed them, like in London.'

'I thought you liked birds,' Helen countered.

'I do. I can even quote a poem in which the "iridescence on a pigeon's neck" is seen as one of the beauties of the world. That doesn't mean I like pigeons bombing me.'

They were both half-shouting to be heard over the noise of the nearby pneumatic drill.

'Too noisy. Let's go to Penclacwydd,' Neil mouthed.

The Wildfowl and Wetland Centre was only a five-minute drive and a peaceful alternative for lunch. Neil was a fully committed telescope-toting member and Helen enjoyed his enthusiasm for waders whose names she could never remember. Penclacwydd was also where they had first met three and a half years previously.

Helen had seen a leaflet advertising the Wildfowl Centre in the local library, and had thought it a sensible place to visit on a wet Sunday afternoon in November. She had followed the route indicated on the little map which came with her ticket and found herself in the British Steel Bird Hide ('First of its kind in Europe') looking out at the marshes and across to the Gower Peninsula – a gloomier estuary version of the view she had admired from Cefn Sidan. She had rented some binoculars from the reception desk but she wasn't totally conviced they were the right way up (did it matter?) or focused, as she peered out at what she considered to be ducks. The only other person in the hide was clearly a professional, with binoculars, telescope and a little notebook covered in dates and tiny writing. After five minutes she was fidgety and couldn't imagine how people could stay here all day with the concentration of the man at her side. She wondered if she should say, 'That's a hell of a big seagull,' but before she could commit this unforgivable solecism, the man turned to her, beaming, his excitement at his first sighting of a little egret overcoming his natural shyness.

'You can see it better through my telescope. Have a look.'

There was no mistaking what she was supposed to see. The telescope was focused on an elegant long-legged white bird – her seagull – motionless by the side of a tidal pool. However, she still didn't know what it was.

'It's a really good one, isn't it,' she said, adding for good measure, 'it's so clear through your telescope.'

As far as Neil was aware, this was the first little egret ever sighted in Wales, possibly in Britain, but he was too kind to puncture her pose directly. Instead, he shared his knowledge with her until she relaxed and showed real interest in the rare heron and the more ordinary visitors to

20

the marsh; the redshanks ('Yes, it does mean red legs), the two cormorants ('they can swallow whole eels you know') and seven grey herons.

'Why do they call a group of herons 'a priest'?' she mused. 'Colour, I suppose.'

'Possibly.' He was scanning the marsh with his field-glasses, looking for something else to show her. 'Not just that though. Look at the way they walk, deliberate, stalking, knowing what they're after. Perhaps it's their missionary-like single-mindedness – awesome when there's a few all intent on their fishing.'

'Fishers of men, you mean.'

'Something like that. Each has its patch and there's no contact between them.'

'No denominational warfare then,' she pursued the thought. 'They're too beautiful to be "like" anything.' He looked at her with approval.

As increasing numbers of bird-watchers joined them in the hide, Neil retreated to whispered comments, continuing to point out birds to Helen. She sympathised with the little boy who ran into the hide, looked through his dad's binoculars and shouted, ' I can see a white bird!' but she too glared at him to show her solidarity with the new comrades ranged along the window bench.

Still feeling the need to celebrate the little egret, and resenting the intrusion of the newcomers, Neil had asked Helen if she would like a coffee and a friendship was born. They looked an odd couple; her hair made a long, wild halo flying around a dress of panne velvet and he looked like one of his cherished herons, tall and angular with an awkward stabbing motion as he walked. When she had pointed out this likeness, he had been quite flattered and had taken to wearing grey, black or white until he tired of people offering their condolences.

21

They had arranged to meet again at Penclacwydd and Helen had continued her marsh-watching lessons. When she had found out that he was a teacher, Helen had been taken aback. There had always been four rows of desks between her and a teacher unless she had actually been summoned to cross the divide. When, at sixteen, Helen had said that she wanted to leave and get a job, and that she was engaged, the Careers Adviser had looked at her with pity and said 'You silly donkey.' If she had known about the pregnancy, Mrs Fisher might have said even more, but Helen had found it easier just to disappear from the school's attendance statistics.

It had, then, been very confusing to discover a human teacher, but it helped that Neil taught French. Helen had tried evening classes in Leeds with a slightly deaf tutor in her sixties and although the lessons had taught Helen to read and understand basic transactional French, her spoken French had no chance of being understood outside a limited audience in West Yorkshire. Helen was unaware of her shortcomings as she had always been told 'Bien, bien' by Madame Carter, whatever her pronunciation, and she had not had the chance to experiment on French nationals after learning to string a sentence together. Neil welcomed his friend's enthusiasm for his subject and had given her further lessons at his home when he could spare the time and (more difficult) the energy. Under his careful tuition Helen was speaking a language that was now definitely French, under the happy illusion that her previous efforts had been an excellent Gascon dialect which was unfortunately little understood in other parts of France. Neil saw no reason to tell her the truth.

Twice a year Neil went to a French Teachers' Conference in London and a year after they had met, he invited Helen to join him. Their friendship had seemed a little strained

22

over the previous couple of weeks and Helen wondered if this was the preliminary to him making a pass at her.

The train journey passed with few words, as each sat reading and wondering how the weekend would go. Neil had told her that they could stay with friends of his who had a flat in Earls Court and that they could go out on the Friday evening to a nightclub. She could not imagine Neil at a disco and she thought she was really too old for this sort of thing but she had played along with the plans.

The friends were very welcoming arty types, who kissed both her and Neil on the cheek as they walked into the flat. She found it strange that Neil, so reserved himself, didn't mind the free physical contact, but then she remembered that he was used to French manners and had even worked in France for a year. She was relieved to find that she and Neil had been given separate rooms; it was a pity to put Min out by making him share with Kevin, but as that was clearly what he was going to do, she wasn't going to stop him. She'd been given Thomas' room and he'd stashed a supply of clothes by the settee, which was obviously going to be his bed for the night.

Min ('short for some Jamaican name even he can't pronounce') cooked Chicken Creole ('He only cooks that to pretend he's in touch with his roots') for them all, then there was some cheerful clearing up. Neil clearly felt at home, drying dishes, catching up on news and answering the others' questions, so Helen dropped gratefully into an armchair and returned to her book.

'Come on then. I thought you girls needed hours to get beautiful,' was Neil's reminder that they were going out that evening. Obediently she freshened up, put some make-up on and changed into a burnt orange silk shift dress and drifted back through to the living room to wait for Neil. Kevin was sitting there, also dressed up for the evening in a

23

loose white shirt and designer jeans, with just a hint of bouffant height in his brushed-back hairdo and the one earring glittering.

'First time at Poison Pen?' he asked.

'Sorry?'

'The club we're off to tonight.'

'Oh, yes, first time. First time in any London disco though I used to go out now and again in Leeds. Cinderella's, that sort of place.' Helen registered the word 'we', and it became clear as the other men appeared that 'we' meant all of them. This was not what she had expected at all and she was feeling a bit of an intruder, despite their efforts. Neil's appearance was a revelation. He was still wearing shirt and trousers but instead of his usual ill-fitting tailored shirt in nondescript check, with polyester trousers, he wore the same style of loose fine-woven shirt and designer jeans as the others. Even his hair looked different, that same brushed-back style that the others favoured. Nothing would disguise his tall angularity but there was a new spring in his step and the impression he made had changed completely. Perhaps this *was* as Helen had thought, and he would make a play for her with his friends around to give him confidence.

Kevin gave the thumbs up that they were all ready to go and they headed off to Poison Pen via a tube journey, some walking and two pubs, which made the atmosphere even more relaxed. By this stage of the evening, Neil had linked arms with Helen, but then Kevin and Thomas had both linked arms with Min, so Helen didn't read anything into it.

Poison Pen, as indicated by the green neon sign and flashing arrow, was down a flight of stone steps in a basement. A couple of bouncers looked them over as they paid their entrance fee and actually checked through Helen's handbag. She was streetwise enough not to wind up

24

the granite-faced security with sarcastic comments, but she did turn to Neil as they passed the cloakroom.

'Do I look like the violent type?'

'It's a pain, but safer that way. They don't always check. Once I had this with me,' and he indicated his Italian style black bag on a wrist strap, 'and inside it was a flick knife I'd confiscated on a school trip and forgotten about. I saw it when I pulled out my wallet to pay the entrance and I was on pins in case they noticed. You can imagine the headlines! I don't think "I took it off a sixteen year old" would go down too well as a defence.'

'I kept looking at their socks,' said Helen. 'There was a story in the papers back home about a Swansea bouncer caught with grass in his socks. He said he was keeping it safe after taking it off a customer, so I don't see any problem with your flick knife.'

'Did he get off?'

'No,' said Helen and they both laughed at the absurdity of it. Then chat ceased as they went into the noise and lights.

Kevin and Min were ahead of them and already on the dance floor. The sheer fluidity of Min's dancing was complemented by the spiky energy with which Kevin attacked the music, and it took a few moments before Helen took in what she was watching. They were not just dancing at the same time, they were dancing together, as a couple. She had been so slow to work it out. She saw Thomas put his arm round a slim, good-looking man who smiled, kissed him on the cheek and started to dance with him. She registered the fact that there were no other women here. No, she was wrong; there were two, perhaps three. At least, they were people wearing skirts. She was starting to question everything.

'They're all gay,' she said stupidly, then had to repeat it

for Neil to lip-read through the noise. He was facing her, watching anxiously for her reactions.

'Yes,' he said, and waited for it to dawn on her. As they stood there someone whose white T-shirt flashed on and off in the ultra-violet light came over, kissed Neil and said, 'I wish you came more often.' There was a private smile between them, then Neil introduced Helen as a friend from home, to Jimmy 'a special London friend'. To Helen's surprise (and she didn't have much capacity for surprise left) Jimmy asked her to dance and was fun to dance with. She gave up thinking and just enjoyed the movement. After Jimmy, there was no shortage of partners, including Neil himself, although she could see him with Jimmy most of the time. She realised that she had never danced with as many good-looking men in one evening and that knowing they were gay had taken all the stress out of just dancing. Even the slow dancing had been easy, not the passionate smooching she could see around her, just friendly human warmth.

When she took time out for a quiet drink at the bar Neil joined her, still waiting for some kind of verdict on him and his friends.

'I like it,' she said. 'It's like the best of a normal disco, but without the threat, the feeling of being in the market-place, up for sale. How come so many people have asked me to dance?'

He winced inwardly at 'normal' but was too used to the wrong words to react. 'It's kind of understood we welcome outsiders. It's to help people come out, show we're good to be with. It's just part of the atmosphere; we're safe here and we want anyone here to feel part of that.'

'It could have a more welcoming name.'

'Cockney rhyming slang; Poison Pen – Boys 'n' Men – get it?'

26

'The conference . . .?' she queried.

'No such thing,' he confirmed. 'Just a way for me to spend two weekends a year hanging loose.'

'Why did you want me to know?'

'I didn't want you to expect man-woman stuff from me.' She smiled at the irony, while he continued, 'and I trust you. It'll be good to have someone else in Llanelli who knows. Sometimes I think I'm dreaming this side of my life.' So he knew she could keep a secret. If only he knew just how well she could keep a secret. She thrust her own problems firmly out of mind, gave him the warmest smile she could muster and said, 'Thank you. I'm flattered. Let's dance.'

'One more thing?' He hesitated, looking away. 'I'd like Jimmy to come back to the flat, but if you'd be upset . . .'

'Don't be daft. Do what you do. I don't ask your permission before I have sex, do I? And before you ask,' she responded to the query in his eyes, 'I do not want to be fixed up. I'll sleep quite peacefully for twenty-four hours after all this.'

Pleased at her own tolerance, she would have liked a verdict on the bodies in skirts, and her dreams that night were troubled with an onion. The extrovert vegetable cavorted round a dance floor, tearing off skins one at a time to reveal . . . another skin – blue, shocking pink, yellow polka dot in turn, but definitely onion skin.

After a late start, the next day saw some serious exploration of department stores. Neil had realised early on that his tolerance of haberdashery departments was limited and he had left Helen to her own devices. Armed with several carrier bags of sale yarns, she met him for coffee and asked some of the 'But why' questions which continued over the weekend and on the train journey back home.

27

'But why don't you come out in Llanelli?'

'I'm a private person. Your private life isn't public property – why should mine be?'

'But it's living a lie.'

'Why? Because people don't know my sexual habits? They're private, I've told you.'

'But it's not against the law. What if you wanted to hold hands with a man in Llanelli, or to cuddle him?'

'I couldn't. I'm a teacher, Helen. What people think counts for more than the law. I need the trust of kids and their parents.'

'But that's not fair.'

'That's how it is. I don't want to take on the world; I just want to do what's important to me and not stand out in a crowd. Everyone makes compromises. If you want to fight for gay rights, go ahead.'

'What about Jimmy?'

He smiled at her naivety. 'Jimmy's only one friend and I'm only one of his. It's not a possessive scene for us. Two weekends a year, that's all the escape valve I need.'

The both sat back and watched the towns rattling past the window, comfortable in each other's company.

The Wildfowl Centre's Coffee Shop had not changed in three years. Their table was right beside the floor-to-ceiling windows which opened onto a view of a reedy pond and the Gower in the distance. One coot ('white above a coot's beak, red above a moorhen's') was paddling on the pond, next to the 'Dim pysgota' (No fishing) sign. Helen was not sure whether the sign was a deliberate attempt at humour, given the number of wildfowl likely to fish beside it, or – more likely – an indication of the total lack of humour characteristic of the environmentalists who formed a hard

28

core at the Centre. Neil had earnest tendencies, but accepted her teasing with good grace, which he counteracted with gentle disapproval of what he considered to be her flippancy.

'So what do you think of it then?' he asked eagerly, as he passed her baked potato across the table and put the tray out of the way.

'Of what?' she asked, knowing perfectly well that 'it' could only be the new car to which she had paid no attention to whatsoever.

'My P reg Megane of course.'

'I like the colour,' she began, 'and it's a smooth ride.'

He gave her the look she usually earned by confusing a snipe with a redshank. 'I'm sure you don't want to fit a female stereotype and that you can do better if you try.'

'Ouch. You ... teacher, you! "Helen Tanner can do better" was the best comment on my reports. I think it's a lovely car but I'm not going to pretend I know about cars when I don't.' His smile said 'for a change'. 'What I don't understand is why you've given up a holiday abroad to buy a car you're afraid to take to school.'

'I thought the "s" word would come up,' he said gloomily.

'I know,' she said, quoting him, 'the so-called long holidays mean one week trying to become human again *if* you don't go down with the flu or a child-contact lurgy; two weeks of normal no-work holiday, and three weeks' nervous dread.'

'Usually the first week is wrecked by the flu or whatever child-contact lurgy you've been fighting off, and you haven't mentioned the preparation for going back.'

'You mean the bit where you spend two weeks saying, "I must prepare", two days grabbing files and writing notes, then collapse into a gibbering heap saying "I can't go back – I'm not prepared"?'

'You don't understand,' he muttered. 'Youngsters are

29

hardwired to follow detailed invisible instructions. Normal adults like you can't imagine what it's like sitting on that sort of time bomb. My car has letters on it six feet high saying "Make a deep scratch along the bodywork". Student teachers have the message written across their foreheads, "I fall for every trick. Try them all on me." Windows are labelled, "Smash me", doors, "Kick me in".'

'But you didn't worry about your last car.'

He gave her a withering glance. 'The only message on that was "I wish I'd retired before I died".'

'So why did you get something so . . . so new-looking?'

'Because it's beautiful. Because it's me. Because it called to me from the garage forecourt.'

'You're mad. You deserve to work with kids.' She still found it difficult to take his 'back to school' seriously, just as he thought 'running a little shop' was stress-free.

'What about him?' Neil asked. 'Still on?'

'Who?' she asked, unconvincingly.

'Dai,' he said patiently.

'I've told you – he's married, it's just sex.'

'Still on then. I know about "just sex" and this isn't it. He's taking risks for you, Helen. It could be a mess and I don't want to see you get hurt.'

She reached across and held his wrist, touched. 'I'll be careful. There's no future in it but I'm enjoying it now. Friends are for keeps, lovers are for fun.'

'That's me, not you.' He sighed. 'All right, have it your way. Why don't you marry me then, and we can both have more company.'

She grinned with pure mischief. 'I couldn't cope with you sleeping with my lovers.'

He looked hurt. 'Since when has being gay prevented a man getting married?' In a more serious tone, he added quietly, 'Not here.'

30

'Whoops – I forgot. I don't know how you can be so controlled in what you say and not let something slip.'

'Habit. Anyway I'm not such a big talker. My mother complains that she finds out about my job from her neighbours.'

'You talk to me.'

'Yes. Sometimes you nearly talk to me.'

She ignored the insinuation and smiled brightly. 'I can talk enough for two so you suit me fine. Anyway I need the French lessons.'

French lessons with Neil included poetry, which she read as practice for her fluency and because she loved the sound – and increasingly the meaning – of what she read. He lent her books, photographs and music, and kept alive the romance of France which Helen retained although she had long rejected the reality if not the pain which it had left in its wake. The tea ceremony would take place halfway through a lesson, and would be signalled by Neil's mother knocking on his study door. She would enter with the tea tray and set out cups, saucers and a plate of Welsh cakes, scones or the baking of that day. She would join them for a cup of tea, discuss knitting techniques with Helen and fish for gossip, then discreetly retire with the dirty dishes.

'Does your Mum think we're an item?' Helen had once asked, uncomfortable at the thought of being there on somehow false pretences.

'No.' He had searched for words to explain how it was with him and his mother. 'There are things we don't need to talk about, but she knows. Not in any conscious way perhaps, but she knows all the same. She knows I don't want a partner. When Dad died, she worried that she was stopping me from having a life of my own, but it's not like that. We get on well, we both love this house and we look after each other in different ways.'

31

Helen could understand him loving the three-storey Georgian town house, opposite Parc Howard, where he had a bay-windowed study furnished in old mahogany.

'I enjoy my binge in London but that's enough for me. I do think sex is overrated and you're not going to convince me that marriage makes everyone happy.'

'I wouldn't try,' she said drily.

'So Mum and I are all right, better than all right. She missed Dad – so do I, but not the same way – but she's strong, she carries on.' Helen felt smaller, trying to take in a vision of how different people could be. There was no way she could picture herself living with her mother without it being a state of war and admission of failure.

After lunch, Neil gave Helen a lift back home.

'You could leave off a layer of clothing in this heat,' he observed critically.

'It'll be cold again tomorrow.'

'We've had four weeks' continuous sunshine,' he laughed.

'You were born here. You're brainwashed to say, "There's lovely the weather is," if there's less cloud than usual. You sit on a deckchair on the beach in a gale force wind.'

'So how come you have to wear sun block to stop your skin burning?'

'I'm a redhead. I weather too easily.'

'You are gloomy beyond, and I'm off to the beach.' He waved a cheerful goodbye and tried for a racing start in his new car which was totally wasted on Helen if not on her neighbours, whose curtains had definitely twitched.

'Friends are for keeps. Lovers are for fun.' How had the friendship with Dai become more? After a friendly coffee session, it had seemed natural to invite Dai back to her house, using his four-wheel drive even though it was such a

32

short distance. The usual coffee and conversation seemed so comfortable that they let it continue until the night was settling in. The need for physical contact was strong but neither wanted to make the first move.

Helen had no moral qualms. After all, he was the married one, not her. But she liked to remain aloof, in control, and there was an unsettling quality to this man. Also, there was a natural curve to an affair which usually burned itself out and led to an embarrassed avoidance – 'How could I have?'- or to absolutely nothing at all, which was not what she wanted. She wanted to keep whatever it was that they had. Dai was equally concerned to keep this relationship, but he had no doubts that he wanted all she would give. He found her unreadable, withdrawing just when he finally felt a certain closeness. His feelings ran deep enough to keep him patient. But not, he thought, if he looked much longer at the elegant angle of throat to the creamy curve into her breasts. Not if he looked at her skin, even on her wrist, which fascinated him with its translucent pallor. He stood up to leave.

Surprised at his abruptness, she stood at the door watching him leave. He turned as he reached his car. She thought he'd changed his mind about going, but what he actually said was 'I've got a parking ticket.' At least her frustration now had an outlet and she stormed over to the windscreen and snatched the piece of paper from him. She worked out from the police jargon that he had been fined for parking on the pavement and she exploded.

'The bastards,' she yelled as she kicked the front tyre.

He felt this was a bit extreme as the police did have a job to do, but he was sensible enough to refrain from saying so.

'They were tipped off. Why do you think there are no other cars parked here today? My bastard neighbours were tipped off that the police would do a check and they've all parked somewhere else. No one warned me.' She continued

33

pacing to and fro and thumped the bonnet. Instinctively he caught her as she passed.

'Hey, that's my car,' he said and kissed her to quieten her down. Then he kissed her again because he couldn't help it. There was no question of him leaving after that, regardless of how many tickets the police might place on his car while they were in bed.

Gradually they adapted to the new pattern of their relationship, well matched and holding nothing back when together. Or at least he wasn't. Living for the moment without a thought for the future. Or at least she hadn't.

In the early days they played 'Any questions' games in which Helen was clearly more interested in finding out about Dai than in talking about herself. At first he found this a refreshing change, but her blocking tactics were so successful that all he really discovered could have been printed on a postcard. Her parents and sister lived in Leeds but they'd lost touch and didn't see each other. Why? Oh well, these things happen. After leaving school at sixteen, she'd worked in one of the big wool factories in Wakefield, testing out their patterns by knitting them up. Why did she leave school? Oh well, these things happen. She'd been married but was divorced now. Why? Oh well, these things happen. She was more forthcoming on her favourite colour – gold, food – pasta, and most of all place – France. When she spoke of France her face lit up; she described places she'd read about, as if she could see them. She could quote French poetry and French songs. A teacher friend who'd visited the Pyrenees on a school French exchange had brought her a boxed set of songs by Francis Cabrel and from her feelings about the songs he assumed this 'teacher friend' to be an ex-lover. She would play Cabrel for him, translating odd phrases, and then, as if a shutter came down, she would switch the music off, discuss some neutral topic, brush off emotion.

Once he'd asked her, 'Why don't we – or you – go to France, even for a weekend?'

It was as if he'd hit her. All she said was, 'I won't go to France again,' but her mouth twisted in bitterness. At first he'd thought she was reacting against his married status, against the lies she'd imagined he would tell. However, after a glorious May Bank Holiday escape for two days to the Cotswolds, he knew it was nothing to do with him. He tried opening the subject again, but this time she warned him off.

'Do you know the story of Melusina?' He shook his head, wondering if this was merely a srategy to distract him. She recounted the tale in a melodramatic voice, 'She was a lady of great beauty who attracted the heart and hand of Raymond, Count of Lusignon. Their marriage was joyous,' she ignored the faces he was pulling and continued with emphasis, 'their marriage was joyous but Raymond found it increasingly difficult to keep to the promise he had made his wife, that he would leave her unobserved every Saturday afternoon. His jealousy gave him no peace and when he spied on her he saw her dreadful secret; each week she became a serpent from the waist down, in the time she had asked to be left alone. 'Le cri Melusine' is the scream she gave at the end of her marriage. Perhaps her husband was right to reject his monstrous wife, but without the wrong sort of curiosity they would have been happy.'

'Perhaps she rejected him for breaking his promise and for not trusting her.' He was wise enough to lighten the mood. He reached towards her, running his hand over her thigh, teasing her. 'There would be certain interesting technical problems with serpent scales, that I think we could do without.' She allowed herself to be steered to safer ground.

She was far more successful in finding out his life story, although she showed no curiosity about his marriage and he volunteered nothing. He was Llanelli born and bred, ex-pupil of the Boys' Grammar School and if you wanted to talk rugby (which she didn't) there was no school like it, although Gowerton and Gwendraeth would stake their claims.

Clearly he had done well at school or his grades would not have gained him entry to Bristol University's Veterinary Science Course. Then back to Llanelli where, after a few years proving himself, his parents' thrifty hoarding of money from the farm bought him into a practice as junior partner. He was an only child and seemed to be close to his parents, who farmed on the bleak hilltop of Mynydd Sylen. Favourite colour? Operating coat green. Favourite music? Loud rock. Favourite film? Impossible to choose. The very question led to heated debate over the respective merits of various actors in their favourite film.

'Schwarzenegger's a comic genius. He's underrated because his muscles distract from his acting talent,' declared Dai.

'That's like saying Bette Midler's underrated as a romantic heroine because of her looks.'

'True enough,' was the smug response.

'Or that Black Beauty's delivery of lines was underrated because he couldn't speak!'

'He was fluent enough in the last version!' They both smirked, remembering the unconvincing voice-over on a recent re-make of the old story.

'The crucial element in comedy is timing and Schwarzenegger is spot on every time. The pause, the delivery . . .'

'No range,' objected Helen. 'Compare him with say, Tom Hanks. Now he becomes a different person in every film. He's got timing, characterisation – and he doesn't speak like a metronome.'

The disagreement continued amicably, ended by total accord as to the destructive effect of Disney films on the cultural heritage of the Western world. Dai produced a video and they curled up together on the sofa, competing to name the original of each scene parodied by the spoof comedy. Definitely a lover and indubitably fun, but was Dai 'for keeps'? Helen thought instead about the friends she had made in the last five years. She didn't see the others as regularly as Neil, but there were three 'girls' she met up with to go shopping, to the cinema or for an evening out in a pub. Laura worked in the local branch of Helen's bank, and through her Helen had met Jane and Charlotte, old school friends of Laura's. They were all in their mid-twenties, younger than Helen, but she enjoyed the girl-talk and the problem solving. Should Charlotte try for a baby now that she and Dan had been married for three years? Would she have to give up her work as care assistant in the hospital and would Dan do his bit to help look after the baby? If Jane employed a male hairdresser would she lose some of her shyer customers? How could Helen tactfully fend off the advances of a colleague? Somehow Helen found all of these questions entertaining to discuss; she even contributed dilemmas for their consideration. Should Jane employ a Saturday helper? If she did, what about the gender issue? When she was with her friends, Helen had no pangs about life before Llanelli and the raw memories stayed away. At other times, she would be ambushed by a hurt that she could not control.

She had good friends; she didn't need anyone else. Dai was an extra, however enjoyable, and she wasn't waiting for the phone to ring. She didn't rush to answer the phone when it did ring and she wasn't at all disappointed when he said he couldn't make it to see her that night. She was self-sufficient, . . . wasn't she?

37

3

Dai wanted to leave his wife. He had wanted this at regular intervals over the past six years but this time his dreams of what it could be like with Helen had made him think he could really do it. He hated the person he became with Karen and he hated the way she was so easy to blame for everything. There, he was doing it again. His long erratic hours had provided a cover for sexual flings in the past and made home irrelevant enough to survive there. His observation of the human condition had led him to believe that his marriage was typical rather than the exception so he had seen no point in leaving. No point to risking the whole sorry repeat pattern of attraction fading after a year or so to a war of attrition. Until he had met Helen. Being with her had made him wonder if there was such a thing as a good marriage. He felt it was his right to find out, which brought his thoughts once again to the person who was stopping him. He sighed, parked the car in his driveway and went into his home.

Karen jumped up when she heard him come in. 'I'll put the kettle on. Your meal will be ready in ten minutes. There's some lamb casserole.' She presented her cheek for its ritual kiss.

'I'm not really hungry. You should let me fend for myself when I'm late.'

She looked hurt. 'It's as easy to cook for two as one. I don't mind warming something up. I'm your wife.'

I know, he thought. *That's the problem.* 'I'll just get changed.'

When he came back downstairs, the dining table was carefully set for one, with a can of Double Dragon placed by his tankard. He shook his head irritably.

'I'll eat in front of the TV,' he called to her, pouring the beer and grabbing the cutlery. He couldn't face her keeping him company at the table, asking trivial questions.

'All right,' came the reply from the kitchen, which conveyed tight-lipped disapproval, even from a distance.

My wife has a whim of iron, he quoted bitterly to himself. Karen brought a tray through, deliberately cluttered with condiments. There was a separate plate for bread and butter and a serviette, making it clear to him that it was more work for her if he chose to eat like this, but far be it from her to comment. She carefully didn't look at the shoeless feet up on their coffee table, but the slight stiffness in her attitude made her opinions clear and it took all his willpower to leave his legs where they were.

'Jan came round today,' she said.

'Mmm,' he replied and turned up the sound on the television. Unfortunately the newsreader was describing farmers' outrage at the lack of government support and Dai had heard enough farmers' outrage for one day, so he idly channel-hopped.

Undeterred, Karen continued. Dai wondered if there were special elocution lessons to train a voice to pierce television sound while appearing gentle and womanly. 'They've just had a new three-piece suite and she was saying there's a good deal on in that new out-of-town store.'

'Mmm.' His mouth full of somewhat stringy lamb casserole, he remained safely out of the conversation.

'This one's seen better days.' She pulled at some protruding threads. Then she stepped up the pace. 'Don't you think it's time we had some new furniture?'

There was no way of ducking a direct question. If he tried, she would just repeat it more insistently; if he held out, she'd cry, it would be patently obvious he had behaved badly, he would have to apologise, and she would wear that smug, long-suffering air.

39

'This isn't old,' he replied, thinking nostalgically of his parents' faded easy chairs with dodgy legs and broken springs.

'Eight years is too old for a suite,' she said reproachfully. 'We bought it when we got married.'

Christ he thought *eight years is too old for this marriage, that's for sure.* He whistled softly and called the wolfhound, Meatloaf, who eased himself onto the sofa by his master and was offered the dinner plate to lick.

Karen, sitting elegantly on the edge of a chair, was provoked beyond endurance and two spots of angry colour appeared in her cheeks. However, she was still careful to speak with restraint. 'I wish you would not let the dogs on the furniture,' she said. 'I had to pick dog hairs off Jan's clothes and however much I hoover, I feel embarrassed when my friends come round.' Now he had the excuse he'd been waiting for and he lashed out. 'Then your friends needn't come here, need they, if they're so picky!' Disturbed by the tone of his master's voice, Meatloaf had abandoned his hopes of a tummy rub and slunk off to bed, despite Dai's attempts to keep him on the couch.

Now the tears came. 'If I talk to my friends it's because I can't talk to you. You just say things to hurt me. I try so hard, you know. I don't complain about you working all the time. I haven't held it against you that . . . you know . . .'

Not much you haven't. You only bring up 'you know' every time you don't get your own way. 'You know' was her supposedly tacit understanding that a man's needs might take him outside marriage, as she had put it to him three years earlier. He suspected that friend Jan had given much advice on the subject and this allowed him to grow angry again – so much easier than feeling guilty.

'Saint Karen, a martyr to marriage,' he sneered. 'Give me a break.' He crashed off to the kitchen, blundering against

40

the contentious furniture en route. While getting another can of beer out of the fridge, he could hear his wife's whimpering noises and the adrenalin stopped flowing. He felt sick. Two minutes earlier he had felt the urge to kick her; he wasn't even sure whether he had wanted to stop the noise or increase it. He had never hit her but he couldn't guarantee to himself that he never would, and that knowledge sickened him most of all. He walked slowly back to the sitting room and sat in a chair at the opposite side of the room, facing his wife. His right arm almost crooked up to slide round her in their reconciliation routine, but, he promised himself, not this time. He would not shut his eyes and remember the warmth of their young promises, He would do this with his eyes open.

'I don't want this any more, Karen.'

She cried harder, preparatory to accepting his apologies.

'I want a divorce.' There should have been a shocked silence, dawning realisation, then some practical decisions. Instead she said, 'No you don't. You're just saying that. It's just another of your ways to get at me.'

Exasperated, he said, 'If it's so awful living with me, you should be pleased.'

'You won't go. I married you and that's that. I've been faithful – not that I couldn't have . . . You won't find anyone else who'll put up with the hours you work and who'll clean your house and cook for you and not complain. You don't appreciate me.'

A good wife in a bad marriage. He wanted to laugh at the way she separated the job from the relationship. He wanted to tell her that was what was wrong. He wanted to show his pity for her, the best feelings he had towards her. What was the point.

'I'm going to Mam and Dad's. I'll take the dogs. I'll be in touch.'

41

'Don't forget your hankies or your reading glasses. You always forget something when you pack.'

Her refusal to take it seriously was weakening his capacity to act and he packed a suitcase automatically, throwing in clothes and toiletries. It was nine o'clock at night and his parents would not be entirely welcoming but he knew that if he didn't leave now he would sink into the well-oiled mechanism of habit, however unwanted. As it was, he didn't know how he would face the explanations, a day at work, the weeks ahead . . . He stopped himself. Just go. He left.

It was not the first time Dai had driven along country lanes in the dark, exhausted beyond caring. Usually he was on his way to or from a life-or-death emergency in the small hours of the morning, after a full day's work. This time the fatigue was mainly emotional. He responded instinctively to a rabbit caught in the glare of the headlights jamming on the brakes and swerving to a dangerous, uncontrolled halt. He sat still for a minute with the vehicle skewed across the road, watching the rabbit hop into the hedgerow. He knew that he had been lucky. If another car had been following him it would have had no chance of stopping. If the road had been wet he could have overturned. All for a rabbit. He looked after the rabbit, his nerves still on edge. 'A lucky escape for you and me both, boy. Let's make the most of it, eh?' He soothed the dogs, righted the car and drove slowly the rest of the way to his parents' farm.

There was a long, bumpy entrance drive with two cattle-grids and gates before he reached the farmhouse. The porch light was on, so clearly someone was expected. Dai shut the dogs into an unused stable where they settled down into the straw, recognising their holiday home, and then braced himself. He found his mother hovering anxiously by the kitchen door.

Dai had barely walked through the door when she started questioning him. 'What is going on, Dai? Karen phoned. She sounded so upset. I don't understand what's going on. She said you were in a crazy mood and we'd probably see you soon. She said to tell you to sleep it off. You're not drunk are you? Is it an argument? Dad's gone off to the barn with Cai. He said he's doing his rounds but he's worried, I can tell. Have you had something to eat? Look at you, you look awful. Cup of tea?'

'Mam, let me get a word in!' Dai eased himself onto a stool by the scrubbed table. 'There's no easy way to say this . . .' he started and broke off in response to her gesture at the teapot, 'yes please, I'd love a cup of tea.' It was easier to say the words while she was fussing with the kettle, tea-bags, milk and mugs. 'I've left Karen. For good. I want to make a fresh start. I want a divorce.'

If anything, her hands moved more quickly in their organisation of the tea things, and she put the biscuit jar on the table. 'Oh, son. Why?'

Why indeed? What could he say to convey eight years of a gradual wearing away of the emotions when he had said nothing before? He was weary to the bone and he couldn't find the words.

His mother couldn't bear the silence and prompted, 'Is there someone else?'

He gratefully accepted the easiest answer, knowing that the truth, whatever it was, could never be explained simply. 'Yes.'

'But you've come here. Is she married?'

'No, it's nothing like that.' His dad came into the kitchen followed by an ageing sheepdog. Man and dog greeted Dai with a nod, a sniff and a grunt. Will Evans helped himself to a cup of tea, leaned against the sink and listened to the rest of his son's explanation.

43

'I haven't told her about me leaving Karen. I haven't talked to her about the future at all. It's complicated. Can I stop here for a bit?'

'I'll say it's bloody complicated,' Will started, ignoring a look from his wife. 'I don't suppose you thought about us in all of this mess!'

Gwen couldn't restrain her impatience. 'Well of course he didn't, you daft man.'

'I might be daft but if he's so clever what's he doing here then? You've enough to do with Grandad without having this one back again.'

'One son you've got, Will Evans and if he needs help he gets it. Dai, you come and help me make up the spare bed.' Dai knew when to keep quiet and allow his mother to keep the peace between the men she loved. He followed her up the creaking stairs, taking his tea with him.

The spare bedroom smelt musty and unused, with a drift of camphor from the old oak wardrobe in the corner. Together they tucked in the floral sheets to go under the duvet and put the old counterpane back on top of the duvet in its new cover. 'Don't take any notice of him,' his mother began. 'He'll come round. It's going to take some getting used to for all of us. If you don't change your mind?' She looked at him.

'No,' he said. 'it would be the worst thing that could happen to me if I did. It would probably be the worst thing that could happen to Karen too. She doesn't know it yet, that's all.'

'She wanted children and you were always too busy.'

'She didn't want children. She just wanted more things around the house, things she was supposed to have. Mam, don't start me off. I don't want to talk like this.'

'I don't know what to think. To me and your Dad, marriage is for keeps. We've had our ups and downs you

44

know,' she smiled wryly, 'and I think you know there was a time I thought it was a wrong choice, your Dad, but there was you and I'm glad now. I wouldn't want it different. I could see the two of you were papering over the cracks, like it was once with us I thought, but now I think you were papering with arsenic.'

She'd lost him this time. 'Arsenic?' he queried.

'Yes, like Napoleon.'

'Mam, what are you on about?'

'There was this documentary which showed that Napoleon died of arsenic poisoning from his green wallpaper, on that island they put him on. Only green wallpaper had the poison in and they didn't know. I've never liked green wallpaper. And that's what's been going on. Not mending but marring.'

There was a lump in his throat from the unexpected understanding. 'I thought you'd be harder,' he said.

'Get some sleep.' She closed the door quietly.

Dai woke early, disoriented, with a heavy head after a fitful night's sleep. His mother was already up and he let her make him some toast and a quick cup of tea, while he saw to his dogs. They were allowed round the house during the day and had stayed here in the past for Dai and Karen to have holidays away, so they settled in easily enough. 'Don't worry about them – they'll be fine. You get off to work now.'

'I'm on evening surgery. I should be home about eight. Thanks Mam. Thanks for everything.'

He whistled to Demi, a black and white mongrel who went to work with him, and they both jumped into the car. His Dad was at the far end of a field and acknowledged Dai's car horn with a half-raised hand. Dai decided this was

45

a good sign. He was not looking forward to telling his senior partner about his separation from Karen but he intended to do so straight away, partly to get it over with and partly to hear himself say the words that would make it real.

He left it until he was back from his rounds and David (definitely not a Dai) had finished morning surgery and the pre-booked routine operations. His 'private word' had been heard with stiff discomfort and David had moved with relief from 'Sorry to hear that' to outlining a new surgical procedure he'd read about in *Focus*. Dai was equally relieved to change the subject as he had felt like a small boy confessing to an embarrassing misdemeanour. He was almost surprised that David hadn't said, 'Well I hope you won't let the firm down like that again.' He had felt a terrible urge to apologise and wondered why he suddenly felt inferior. He suspected – perhaps unfairly – that if he'd confessed an affair and temporary anger from his wife, there would have been sympathetic understanding of a man's problems.

He felt a sudden need to see Helen and remind himself that he had opened up a future. Things were under control at the practice so he headed into town for an hour. Town was quiet too and Dai found Helen knitting behind the counter, balls of wool tucked under her arms. She smiled at him.

'If I'd known you were coming I'd have taken on a more seductive pose. I resent the fact that knitting has such a staid image.'

'How about Madame Lafarge knitting at the guillotine as the heads rolled?'

'I expect she was too busy concentrating on an Aran pattern to realise where she was.'

He looked at her animated face, at the dextrous hands

46

completing the row, and he wanted to ask her there and then to marry him.

'You look like fate to me, designer of destinies.'

'I thought that was weaving? Or three blind old ladies passing their one eye between them. Thank you very much. For that, you can take me down to the beach for a lunch break and some fresh air.'

He pulled himself together. He couldn't ask her to marry him – he'd only left Karen the day before. He would tell Helen that he was in the process of becoming free. How clumsy that sounded. Wasn't he free now? If he told Helen he had left because of her, it would put pressure on her. She might feel forced to live with him; knowing Helen, she might react against the pressure and reject him against her own wishes. He would have to take this slowly. The only thing he was sure about was that he must tell her he had left Karen. But then, didn't that imply 'so we can be together'? All right then, he would play it by ear. He would know when the timing was right for him to tell her and the right words would come naturally. Satisfied with his non-decision, he relaxed a little. Perhaps the right moment would be on the beach, this lunchtime. It wasn't.

Driving back to the farm after work, Dai went back over the outing to the beach, thinking of all the missed opportunities. He could have told her when they were laughing at the old couples sitting in their parked cars looking at the sea through their windscreens. He could have said, 'Are we going to be like that one day? We could be if that's what you want. I have something to tell you . . .'. When they saw a teenage couple passionately and openly eating each other, he could have told her how open they could be now. When they looked at the mud flats and shimmering tidal pools he could just have said, 'I love you. There is something you should know . . .' Instead, he had

47

felt the moments were too precious for him to change the mood so drastically. He'd told Karen herself, his parents, David – he'd had enough 'little announcements' and he'd had enough emotional flak. Helen's reaction was the most important but it could wait and he would be better prepared for it.

Meatloaf greeted him when he arrived back at the farm and Janey came tearing out of an outbuilding, followed by Will Evans and Cai.

'Good ratter that,' said Will with approval. 'She'll earn her keep.' From which Dai gathered that the Jack Russell had earned him some grudging acceptance. Both men went into the kitchen where Gwen was already busy warming up Dai's evening meal.

'You'd best say hello to Grandad. I'll give you a shout when this is ready.'

Dai went through the dark passage to the living room with its two bright spots of television and fire, the latter a source of irritation to his grandfather although it was for his sake they needed the consistent, manageable heat. He maintained that the Calor Gas cylinder would explode and kill them all, not to mention looking like a Zeppelin. He would also vehemently assert that you couldn't see the pictures in a gas fire 'for all that real flame nonsense'. Sitting with Grandad was firstly a matter of adjusting to the tropical climate of the room, and then adapting to a cyclical style of conversation in which topics were revisited once his grandfather had digested the information. Sometimes the sharpness of the observations which resulted from this procedure left Dai feeling winded.

'How are you Grandad?'

'Nothing wrong with me that a pint or two wouldn't put right.' Lloyd Evans sat in what had always been his chair, but which seemed to have grown too big for him over the last ten years, filling with cushions to ease the old man's aching joints. He had always been wiry, but the spareness of his frame now was due to decreasing appetite rather than constant manual labour. 'Your mam says you've ratted on your wife.'

'We're going to get a divorce, yes.' Dai stumbled over the words, feeling he had spent all day repeating them.

'I'm still eating beef you know. This mad cow business. Typical scaremongering. It's all to cover up another Tory cockup.'

Dai followed gamely. 'We've written to our MP to give the vets' angle and we're doing all we can to help the farmers.'

'Can't you give it another go? Think of how the woman must feel. How is she going to get by? She's given you the best years of her life and you walk out on her.'

'It's not like that, Grandad. Things are different these days. Women manage on their own.'

'Not that sort of woman.'

Dai thought bitterly that Grandad had a point. It wouldn't take Karen that long to find another provider. He kept silent.

'Your Mam is working too hard. She's always in here moving things around and fussing. Do me a favour and tell her I'm all right. She'd be better off helping Will with the cows.'

'Are you worried about the farm?' Dai knew that Lloyd might have handed the farm down to his son but he kept a shrewd eye on its management. They'd just had new gates and Lloyd had checked that Gwen hadn't paid over the odds for them or forgotten to account for them in 'Business Expenditure'. He was also well aware of the threat now posed by BSE.

'You've got to give it to the French. The farmers there

have balls. They wouldn't whine and whinge to up the compensation. They'd be outside the Houses of Parliament with tractor-loads of dung, demanding their rights. Dung on the dunghill, that would shake those hoity-toity clean hands MPs.' He chuckled softly at the imagined scene. Just as suddenly, he changed tack. 'Damn French are stopping our exports. Telling more lies. As if our stock's contaminated. About time they looked to their own livestock. I tell you, any disease hits France kills everything. Can't beat Welsh farmers. Best breeding, best rearing, best meat. Not surprised the French don't want the competition. You'd think they'd feel the obligation though. After all we did for them.'

Luckily, before the war could rear its familiar head in the conversation, Gwen called Dai for his meal.

'See you later, Grandad.'

'I don't want to see Will lose it. He's too proud to ask for help. You've got to sometimes you know.' Dai put the tobacco tin closer to the old man, who was too proud himself to ask for help, and went to the kitchen to eat.

His mother busied herself, washing dishes and tidying while he ate.

'Mam, what's the latest with the farm?'

'You know the answer to that. You're the vet.' His mother's voice was unexpectedly curt.

'What do you mean?'

Gwen sighed. 'This disease has come at a bad time for us. There's plenty thought your Dad was a fool investing in those Charolais but he's bred the best beef herd in the county. You know what farmers are like – when things are going well they've only one thought – more land. Those extra acres cost all we had, and some. It's not the cows that's mad, it's the government. And it's our profits going up in flames.'

50

Dai realised guiltily that he had not thought too deeply about how the new regulations would hit his parents, and he'd been only too happy for his partner to make the routine visits to Brynlglas in recent years. It must be two, no, three years since he had paid a professional visit to the farm and his calls home had mostly been to leave his dogs while he holidayed. He had not enjoyed Karen's social airs with his parents, and he sparred too much with his father to be with him often or for long. Dai was well aware of all he owed Will but he had been told so too often. He had been careful to ensure that Will was given priority – and free – treatment from the practice, but if he wasn't the vet to provide it, so much the better. It shamed him now to realise how out of touch he was, how things had drifted. Living with Karen had only been possible with all senses dulled, trudging his way through the years and caring for no-one. She had a lot to answer for! Doing it again, he told himself. *He* had a lot to answer for.

'I'm sorry, Mam. Dad's right. I haven't given you a lot of thought. I've seen the returns, so I knew you'd sent a few for incineration and claimed the grant. If I'd thought, I'd have known the money would be tight.' According to government regulations, cattle over thirty months had to be slaughtered and incinerated unless the herd had been declared free from BSE. The Charolais, slow as it was to mature, could not put on enough weight under thirty months to go for meat and make any profit, so the farm's only income was the compensatory grant, and no one knew when this would actually arrive. In the meantime, the mortgage on the land was due and the family had to eat. Each time young cows went to market, there was some short-term relief and a hole in the farm's long-term prospects, with no profits to come.

'How bad is it?' Dai asked.

51

'Bad enough, but your Dad says we'll get by. He's started doing all the paperwork, so I don't know the details any more. Truth is, he won't talk about it and I can't seem to help him. I don't like him doing all the records and accounting after a long day but he snaps at me if I try to stop him.' She gave a weary smile. 'You know how determined he is.'

'Stubborn old bugger, you mean.'

'Dai!'

'Well, it's true.' Dai thought for a few minutes. 'You bought me into the practice. I haven't any money now, but I'll have to talk to Karen anyway about selling up. I reckon we'll make something on the house and I can pay a bit back to you.'

'Don't even hint at such a thing to Dad. He's so proud of you and of himself for making enough money to help you. It would bring him to his knees to have help from you and he's very low just now. Please Dai, don't let on you know how hard it is. We've had it hard before, we'll get by.'

Dai stood up and hugged her, wondering when this strong woman had become so small. He took her hand, aware of the dry cracks and callouses, and squeezed reassuringly. 'There are ways of getting help, bank loans, extensions on payments. This madness won't last much longer – of people or cows.' He smiled. 'Do you think he'll go out for a pint with me?'

'He might. But you won't let on, will you?'

'Don't worry. I need a roof over my head too much to misbehave.'

That drew a smile from Gwen. 'It never stopped you at seventeen – I can't see it stopping you now.'

Dai wrapped a tea towel round her as a blindfold. 'What you don't see can't hurt. This is men's talk now. Dad,' he yelled, 'Dad? Fancy a pint?'

52

An hour later the two men had their feet up at the bar in the Sylen Arms, which served local bitter impeccably hand-pumped and lethally strong. Nothing matches the first creamy mouthful – no electrically-pumped froth – when the hops bite, giving an edge to your thirst. The pub was old-world in style, with stone walls and horse brasses, an ancient trading post on the Llanelli-Carmarthen route. In the days when the Tywi River had carried prosperity to and from Carmarthen, land routes had been few and alcohol-stops rare. Many of the pubs in the area retained their freemason atmosphere in rooms as plain as chapels, where men drank beer, spoke Welsh and greeted strangers with frozen stares, but the Sylen's succession of English immigrant landlords had welcomed a mixture of locals and tourists to its village setting. As part of the ongoing war with the Pontdu opposite, the current landlord had knocked down walls and food prices, so that Dai had difficulty recognizing the place.

'There used to be a snooker room there,' he said in amazement, looking at a plastic gnome fishing in an aluminium foil pool surrounded by rocks and plastic flowers.

'Look at that.' His father pointed gloomily. Displayed with pride on the wall was an advert, cut out from a local newspaper, encouraging people to 'make that occasion really special – eat in the Swiss Room at the Sylen Arms'. Dai looked again at the artistic miniature landcape and noticed a big rock with a tiny plastic cable car running up a wire to its summit.

'Why don't you go to the Pontdu?' asked Dai.

'Two reasons. This,' Will held up his pint glass, 'and it's my local. I've been coming here forty years. This is where I come.' Dai had drunk enough for this to seem perfectly logical and the two men sat in silence, observing their surroundings in companionable contempt. He had forgotten what it was like to sit like this with his Dad. Gwen had once asked what the two of them talked about all night, when there was no sign of them talking in the house. At twenty-two he had tapped the side of his nose and said mysteriously, 'Men's talk.' He had no intention of letting his mother know their secret. They just sat. From time to time Will grunted and said, 'Nice pint,' or 'Cold out,' and Dai grunted back in agreement. Sometimes he wondered if it was much of a relationship. At other times, when Karen's chatter had made him feel he was being nibbled to death by goldfish, he knew that just sitting drinking a pint with his Dad was the purest form of love in the universe.

4

Dai was settling into a routine at Brynglas in which time passed in working, eating, sleeping and planning to talk to Helen. There had been two unpleasant phone conversations with Karen, followed by a letter from her solicitor initiating divorce proceedings. He had been both relieved that she was taking him seriously and faintly insulted that it was so quick. He noted that she was salving her pride by avoiding adultery as grounds for divorce, going for separation instead. One evening he had driven to his marital home, intending to discuss selling it, and having had no reply to phone calls. He found it empty, not just of Karen, but of all furniture and fittings – the phrase came to him from dim echoes of estate agents' handouts.

There was a strange nostalgia in seeing the house as it had been when they, about to wed, had thought it had potential. He and Karen had also had potential. Now there was dust on the mantelpiece, where it had never been allowed to settle, and bright patches on sun-faded carpets, where furniture had always stood. Always. Now that it was over, it seemed that his marriage had always been. He couldn't really remember time before and, faced with the empty rooms, he stopped believing in time after.

The realisation that Karen had even taken the toilet-roll holder broke into his defeated mood and he laughed. He wondered cynically who'd used the screwdriver and he felt free once more. He looked out across the overgrown vegetable patch that he'd never had time to tend and he left mere good intentions firmly behind him. He would see Helen the next day and start a new life with her.

When he reached Brynglas, he found that his father had waited to have his evening meal with him, a measure of acceptance he found touching. Gwen left them to it, in the homely warmth of the kitchen. Surprisingly, Will wanted to talk.

'I sold Ben Nevis in Carlisle, this August. There was a boy!'

'Did they appreciate him?' Ben Nevis was a prize young bull raised by his father in hopes of a sale to Scotland. Nowadays, the big annual cattle mart at Carlisle was a chance for both Welsh and Scottish farmers to improve their Charolais breeding lines. In the old days, Will had used foreign input sires via artificial insemination and gradually built up a beef suckler herd that had quieted criticisms of his way-out farming notions. It had not been easy as neither the farming community nor British veterinary science had been ready for the problems of the beautiful foreign breed. Charolais were ideal cattle for the thin, scrubby grazing land of a small Welsh hill farm, but the large size of the calves' heads made for difficult births. French vets were trained to give Caesarian operations as standard practice, but it was still a rarity in Wales when Will was establishing his herd in the early days. He had lost money and cows each spring, fuelling his neighbours' criticisms and his vet's disapproval. Dai had absorbed his father's dreams of the future and gained the surgical skills to ensure the survival of the creamy cows who had leaned against his childhood, their breath steaming with his.

'Market's down, people running scared or just taking the chance to strike a hard bargain, but I reckon the boy who bought him knew his luck was in.'

'Buy in?'

His father's face lost its enthusiasm. 'No money for buying in.'

Dai kicked himself for forgetting his mother's warning. He remembered the days when he had first qualified and taken great pride in attending all calls to Brynglas, bombarding his father with scientific jargon and stopping at the house for tea, cake and a chat with his mother. He remembered routine checks two years ago and nearly three years ago, just before Christmas, a long and painful birth from which he had brought mother and calf safe and suckling. In the last eighteen months he had lost touch and it was about time he put it right.

'Dad, you'll need an age check soon.'

'There's a few to go to market,' Will acknowledged. By government regulation, cows over thirty months were considered too risky to sell for meat and had to be slaughtered and incinerated. Cattle under thirty months could be marketed as usual but were not grown enough to make a profit for the farmer. Batches of cattle for incineration or sale had to be checked by a vet against the farmer's herd record book to confirm ages and then the farmer could proceed to market or to claim the compensation.

'I'll book it in and do it for you.'

'Don't put yourself out. That David's come before and he knows his way.' Dai thought his father too proud to welcome his son's offer.

'It's time I put myself out for you. Things are going to change.'

'As I say, it's easier if David carries on, but I won't argue. See how it goes.' With that, the conversation ended but Dai felt he had made some progress. He thought back to what clients had told him over the last couple of years since the BSE scare had really taken hold. One had said as a joke, 'Your Dad's all right then Dai, I bet he's got the only certified BSE-free herd on the hills,' and then he had winked knowingly. In case the point had not been clear he had added, 'I wish I had a vet for a son.' Perhaps that had been the start of Dai's withdrawal from the farm. Perhaps it had nothing to do with Karen after all. Who knows? There had been no decision, just distances that grew and absences that were easier than visits. It had indeed been easier for David to visit.

Dai had never doubted his father's honesty, but he knew the ways in which the more unscrupulous farmers milked the system – or tried to. Some had worked out that they could get more money in compensation than at the market so were declaring their young cows old enough to get the maximum amount, or as old as they thought a busy vet would pass as possible. Locum vets and new vets from out of the area were very popular with these sorts of farmers. Rumours told of gunshot in the night, a buried cow and a BSE free herd marketed as usual. After the first scare when Carmarthen Mart had been empty for the first time in living memory, names of 'helpful' auctioneers and butchers were passed on by those in the know. When beef was banned from the menu in all schools in the county, when the beefburger chain restaurants proudly claimed 'No British beef', it could have been assumed that the general public believed there was a health hazard. What then did you make of the crowds around the supermarket counters buying cut-price beef? Or butchers' customers angrily demanding that the price be cut so they could buy beef? Dai sympathised with the farmers' reaction but his professional duties were clear and he observed them rigidly. Still, that was no reason to avoid the family farm.

Dai felt the need of solitude and, feeling like a teenager, went to his bedroom. On the small set his mother had lent him, he played one of the two tapes that had been in his car, sparing a bitter thought to the disappearance of music Karen had hated, and yet had taken with her. He dismissed the thought and Karen with it, thinking instead of Helen. He had to act. Before he could change his mind again he rushed downstairs, phoned Helen and invited her out he next day. He would take her to Mynydd Llangedeyrne, where the limestone scarp swept up to the standing stones. He would tell her there.

'If there's a molehill, it's a mynydd in Welsh,' she pointed out when he took her to his favourite place.

'It's not like you to make a molehill out of a mynydd. Anyway, if it's a molehill you've climbed, I'm surprised you're so short of breath.' Helen had been pleased but surprised by Dai's phone call the night before. She had no hesitation in accepting the prospect of an afternoon out and Sunday had dawned clear and bright. She had been a little taken aback when she had jumped into the passenger seat to feel three sets of heavy breathing on her neck. She was used to Demi, the black and white mongrel with more than a hint of sheepdog, who accompanied Dai on his rounds – which meant he also came to Helen's. Usually she would remain 'on guard' in the car; in reality this meant sound asleep, as far as Helen could establish. Sometimes Dai would bring her into Helen's house where she would take up much the same inoffensive position. There had not been much contact with pets in Helen's life and although she had no objection to them, she was a bit stuck for conversation – either with them or their owners – after an initial 'What a good dog'. Dai's other two dogs had been mentioned, but she had not taken in just how big a wolfhound could be, nor how evil the look in a Jack Russell's eye. She had been introduced to Meatloaf and Janie Russell, who had been as equivocal in their reactions to her as she had been to them.

The Mynydd was a stretch of open heath on the top of a hill. Some ponies were grazing freely, straying across the rough access road which quickly became a farm track and private property. They had walked through gorse and scrub, up a limestone escarpment and then up another ridge to reach the triangulation point at the top.

'You can see five of the old Welsh counties from up here, across to Cornwall and to Ireland if it's really clear.' She looked in all directions, spinning round till the view became a blur of hills, fields and distant sea. He pointed again. 'See that double mast on that hill? That's Mynydd Sylen, the only point nearby higher than this. My parents' farm is lower down on the hill but bleak enough in winter. The wind tears across, and if there's snow anywhere, it'll be here and Sylen.'

Within a stone's throw of the trig point was a prehistoric stone circle.

'It's not exactly Stonehenge,' she said critically, sitting on a grassy mound. She would have walked past the boulders, not seeing any pattern, if he had not stopped her.

'But once it was, don't you see? Just like our triangulation point, raised for all to see and wonder at.'

'All this religious ritual jumbo is probably a load of rubbish. I bet this is where stone age women hung their washing, their deerskins or whatever, to get a good drying wind.'

'You could be right.' He smiled. 'No one really knows, so any speculation is valid. Anyway, make a wish by the washing posts.' He put his arms round her and kissed the back of her neck. She twisted round to kiss him fully, the summer breeze whipping her hair into her eyes and mouth.

They linked arms and walked along the ridge, further and further away from habitation. He showed her the burial chambers; a mass one at the foot of a smaller ridge and an individual one high up. She shook her head, still convinced that she was being conned about a load of old stones.

'How do you know all this anyway?' she asked suspiciously.

'It's one of *my* shameful secrets. The village historical society brought a tractor up here about twelve years ago and re-erected the big standing stone, the one you can see from the road. It was quite a little ceremony, with a guided walk led by a real historian. I like to come up here with the dogs so I went along out of curiosity. Now I'm telling you what I was told then.'

'How come there's no one else here?'

'Now you're asking. I sometimes think people go round blindfold, so they can't see the places closest to them. Or with special filters over their eyes which only come off sometimes, on holidays far away. Even then most people keep their eyes shut.'

'Or even *complain* that the new place is different!' she warmed to his theme and then felt self-conscious. 'Do you think I'm a bit like that? Do I take where I am for granted?'

He considered the question. 'You don't exactly enthuse about Leeds and you love faraway France. You even keep it far away. But no, you don't have your eyes shut. Too open-eyed sometimes. Especially about me.'

They walked in companionable silence, enjoying the dogs' exuberance as they tumbled down a slope or bounced

60

through the boggier patches where reeds grew as high as Meatloaf himself. His long legs gave him an advantage on the terrain and it was comical to watch the other two dogs jumping above the reeds, then disappearing again.

'Over there are old fieldworks but I think we've gone far enough. They say that the land there is so treacherous that cows have disappeared without trace, sinking right down through the peat bog.'

'Who owns the cows and horses?'

'This is common land, with ancient grazing rights for the commoners whose properties back onto it. There's not much common land in Wales any more. This is a part of the old Cawdor estate and every now and then someone tries to make a quick pound by privatising it. So far, the commoners have won and then the whole business returns to the *status quo* for another decade or two.'

They were heading back towards the standing stone and the path to the car when he said, 'Oh, I nearly forgot. This is a Ring Cairn.' She looked at a hollow circle lined with grass-covered rocks.

'What was it for?'

'No one really knows, but when they excavated similar ones on the Gower they found something strange.' He paused for effect. 'An ancient container placed in the same relationship to the ring cairn in each case. In the container was always a part skeleton, and strangest of all, the bones were those of a child. The experts think this might have been the setting for a particular religious ritual. People were nomadic then and often took some of their ancestors' bones with them to new settlements. As to why, well that's always speculation of course.' He broke off. 'What's wrong?'

She was shivering and her face was white. 'It's horrible. I'm cold. Let's go back.'

They hurried back to the car and neither broke the

61

silence on their drive back to Llanelli, where he dropped her off at home and did not go in.

She hardly heard the car drive off, for her thoughts were elsewhere. Although it was six o'clock and she'd only had a light lunch, she wasn't hungry. She took the stoppered half-bottle of wine from the fridge and drank her way steadily through it. There was no point looking for more alcohol as she only kept in enough for one evening's restrained drinking, to prevent evenings like this doing even more damage. She cradled the empty glass in her hand as the wine took effect on her empty stomach and she had no choice but let the memories come.

Tony, herself and Rebecca, heading for their first holiday, camping in France. The car journey to St-Geniez-d'Olt had not been as bad as she'd feared; Rebecca slept easily in the car, pulled toys out of the box and shook them to entertain herself. Helen sat with her in the back and when all else failed she read to Rebecca and sang 'Postman Pat' and nursery rhymes. By this stage Helen had grown used to the paraphernalia of motherhood and had efficiently packed the tippee cup and juice so that they were to hand, with plenty of less immediate necessities in the boot. She had found that Rebecca was happy and at home as long as she had her favourite items with her, so it was worth the trouble of transporting Rebecca's environment with her, including a cuddly toy dog which Helen called Heathcliff and Rebecca called 'Dog'. Helen knew the favourite books off by heart and could no longer remember a time before the weather in Greendale was a matter of deep significance. Postman Pat appealed more to Rebecca than to Helen but they shared appreciation of the tiger who came to tea when Daddy was out at work.

Helen had given up work at twenty-two to have Rebecca and their life at home during the day often felt like a shared secret, to which Daddy-Tony was an evening and weekend visitor. Tony would ask Helen what the 'procedure' was but however hard she had tried to let him take the lead and make everyday decisions over Rebecca's food and games, he saw this as her job and there was an end to it. The holiday had been the suggestion of Helen's parents, who had just visited this area of France and been enthusiastic in describing it to their daughter and son-in-law. Privately, Joan and William Tanner felt that Tony could give a little more time and attention to Helen, however much money he was making in the garage he ran with his father. Tony had, surprisingly, agreed that they could do with a holiday, and had liked the idea of testing out camping gear which they had added to extra stock lines at the garage. It would help him advise customers and choose sales lines if he had actually tried them out himself.

It was only when she was tearing along a French motorway, looking at road signs with magical foreign names, that Helen realised how much she needed this holiday. However much she loved Rebecca, the daily diet of talk with or about a child was wearing her down. She hated meeting up with other women just because they had babies in common (and nothing else) and yet she had no friends of her own left. She had married at sixteen, pregnant, then miscarried. Despite the physical shock, there had been some relief because she had not really accepted the fact that she was going to be a mother. She had worried that Tony would feel tricked but as he pointed out, getting married had been his idea and would have happened in a year or two anyway, so not to worry. At nineteen he had seemed the fount of all wisdom and she had accepted his reassurances. Now, looking back, she felt she was the one who had been tricked – out of her growing-up years. She and Tony were all right though, and the decision to have Rebecca had made her feel excited about life again.

They spent two weeks on the camp site. On their first day there, Tony established that this was the heart of French fishing and he spent most of each day positioned on the Lot, swapping tips from time to time with fellow anglers. It took four days' fishing before Tony's silences relaxed into smiles over a meal. If only they could have campsite meals every day, then they would be a real family all the time. Helen bit her lip. Of course they were a real family. Tony worked hard to support them and the times he played with Rebecca were precious to her, partly because they were rare. Like his father and his friends, Tony enjoyed an hour or two in the pub on a night, and his fishing. He always came home to her and made it clear that she was the only woman for him. It was just that the place occupied by a woman in his life did not seem very fulfilling to her. Perhaps she did want too much, as he had once accused her. Perhaps she was different from the other wives, an observation he had intended as a compliment but which had lingered awkwardly in the air. She watched her husband uncorking a bottle.

'How do you say this one then?' Tony asked her as he poured the wine for the evening into two plastic beakers.

'Estaing,' she told him, with a combination of vowels that would have been a credit to Liza Doolittle's cockney but bore little resemblance to French. Luckily Tony knew no better, though his contact with other fishermen had given him a good ear for the sound of local place-names, without any notion of how they were spelt. 'It's further down the river.' She would have liked to have shared the history with him, told him how Olt was the Celtic word for Lot, laughed at its dyslexic nature, but he didn't like what he called 'know-all comments' from her. She had learnt to keep him happy by keeping quiet.

64

'Wonderful river,' he said, and with that she could agree wholeheartedly. 'Five pounds is nothing here.'

'Spend it in a minute,' she teased.

'Fish, you cloth-head,' he corrected her, taking her ignorance seriously. He was always happiest when she allowed him to feel indulgent and knowledgeable, so his lengthy explanation of bait and flies made him very happy indeed. Helen nodded appropriately, thinking, *I have kissed this man after he has warmed maggots in his mouth.* This had been his most cherished angler's tip as a teenager and she could still summon the frisson of disgust mixed with fascination that the revelation had first aroused in her.

'How big was it again?' she asked, miming the angler's proverbial biggest catch, with a provocative edge to her voice.

A little more wine and laughter ended pleasurably with first Rebecca being put to bed then Helen. Tony's relaxed mood led to greater tenderness in making love and he was rewarded by unexpected warmth from Helen. He would have been less flattered if he had realised that she was making love to the summer breeze over the river, the old stone blocks of a twelfth-century church, the eagle she had heard and then glimpsed as the mist cleared over the river early in the morning. He would have found the airbed rather too crowded for comfort if he had known all that he shared it with.

As long as Tony was 'contented with his Lot' (as Helen put it to herself) she was free to take Rebecca and explore the village of St-Geniez. The village was a five-minute toddle along the river bank, with Rebecca shouting 'blackbird' and pointing at every swift skimming for insects on the water. Old terraces leaned over narrow streets and Helen stopped the pushchair to inspect every famous birthplace indicated by the campsite guide book. She had heard of none of these 'famous' men, but she breathed in the centuries of human history and made up stories for Rebecca about the rabbits that lived in the cellars. They actually saw a rabbit bobbing down an alley on one of their village visits and Rebecca clapped her hands as the story came to life.

On each visit they explored a little more, sitting at the Café du Pont to watch the little tourist train and pony rides. Helen's favourite place was the Talabot Monument up on the hillside overlooking St-Geniez. It had been hard work to get Rebecca up all the steps but worth it. The monument itself was a mausoleum in white stone, its plinth supporting a forbidding statue of a Victorian lady. (Although if she were French, Helen supposed 'Victorian' was the wrong adjective, however well it suited her). While Rebecca sat on the grass, swatting harmlessly at two butterflies, Helen read the statue's story.

Marie Savy had been a pretty working girl who had left her home in St-Geniez 'in her clogs' to seek her fortune in Paris. Working as cook in the household of the famous railway engineer Paul Talabot, she had attracted her employer's interest and he had married her. Accepted in the highest Parisian society, sought after as a model by the renowned sculptor Barrias, she returned in grand style to her home village, where the bourgeoisie threw stones at her to remind her of her humble beginnings. She is supposed to have said, 'You may look down on me now but after my death I will look down on you for eternity.' She then bought the ruined chateau on a hilltop overlooking St-Geniez, and it was on this land that her mausoleum was erected.

Like the statue of Marie Savy, Helen looked down on St-Geniez. Roofs gleamed metallic black with fish-scale tiles; spires and turrets were crested with cast-iron weather-vanes; the river bubbled white over hidden rocks. That was when she knew she was in love, not just with St-Geniez on a sunny day but with France itself.

At three, Rebecca was growing ever more alert to her surroundings and more interested in the stories Helen told her about places. It still helped if there were furry animals in the story somewhere, but that was easy with the legend of the marmot.

On one of their little tours of the village, Helen pointed at a row of soft toys in the shop window.

'Look at the marmots. That's what they call the people who live here.'

'What's a marmot?'

'Look at them. They're like . . .' Helen thought back to the Disney cartoons they watched at home, 'like beavers and they live by rivers.'

'Is he a marmot?' she pointed a stubby finger at the shop assistant hovering in the doorway.

'No, dear.' Helen smiled apologetically and moved Rebecca along. 'They're just called marmots. Like Daddy calls you Moppet. It's a sort of nickname.'

'What's a moppet?'

'I think it's just a made-up word that sounds friendly.'

'I want a marmot.'

Usually this expression resulted in the time-honoured 'I want doesn't get' but Helen felt in a holiday spirit and went into the next tourist shop they passed. The range of cuddly marmots reminded her of the three bears – there was a choice of big, medium or small marmot.

'That one,' dictated Rebecca, and when prompted, 'please.' She was still at the age when consonants tended to hiss or trip over each other, but she had no problem communicating what she wanted.

'Once upon a time,' began Helen as they wandered the streets back to the campsite, 'there were two little boys who lived near St-Geniez with their Daddy.'

'Squashy nose.' Rebecca squeezed the hand-sized

67

marmot experimentally. She pulled on Helen's hand for the story to carry on. 'And one boy was called Jean and the other was Fredo.'

Helen accepted the two foreign names which Rebecca thought appropriate and continued. 'Jean and Fredo used to go fishing a lot.'

'Like Daddy. A lot in the Lot.' Rebecca had cottoned on to this phrase and would repeat it at any opportunity, singing it softly to herself like a strange mantra, stressing the word 'lot' each time.

'When they were out fishing one day they found a marmot and they kept him for a pet.'

'What did he eat?'

'Marmot food. They kept each other company for years until one day a terrible thing happened.' Helen paused for effect and to let Rebecca join in the story.

'Their Daddy brought home another baby.'

Helen shook her head, wondering where Rebecca had been when Auntie Sarah was talking about Sadie's reaction to the new arrival.

'I know, I know. Nobody gave the marmot his dinner and he cried and the boys was spanked and their Mummy spanked them hard and called them bully and pulled their hair.'

'Those are very good ideas but what really happened was that the marmot ran away.'

'Because he was very hungry.'

'The boys chased the marmot all day through the woods to try to find their friend.'

'They got spanked again for going off. Mustn't go off without Mummy or Daddy. Not allowed.'

'Their Daddy allowed them because they were big boys.'

'Where was their Mummy then?'

'They didn't have a Mummy.'

'Everyone has a Mummy. She was visiting Grandma.'

'They found the marmot but they were all lost and so they took shelter in a little hut till the morning.'

'Now they're for it.'

'In the morning they looked out of the window and they could not believe their eyes. A big storm had come in the night and there were rain puddles everywhere.'

'And they got no wellies.'

'I think they went out in their wellies to walk through the woods.'

'No, they forgot their wellies. They're in big trouble,' said Rebecca with satisfaction.

'So they had to go very carefully.'

'Because they had no wellies.'

'Because they had no wellies, and when they got back home they found their house had disappeared, washed away by the big floods of the river.' Helen thought of the house they had passed which had a chalk mark showing the high water level during the last flood, well above the level of the first storey.

'Because they were naughty.'

'So their pet marmot had saved their lives by taking them away from the house so they would not be destroyed by the flood.' Luckily Rebecca was not interested in what had happened to the Daddy and Helen had no intention of telling her that according to legend he had died.

'They remember to feed him after that. I don't like big boys.'

'And from that day on the people who live in St-Geniez are known as Marmots.'

'And the marmot went to live with a girl and her Mummy because it was nicer there.' Rebecca waited for acceptance of this ending.

'The marmot went to live with a little girl and her

69

Mummy and they lived happily ever after,' Helen confirmed.

'Big girl,' came the correction, but Rebecca was losing interest with their tent in sight. 'I want to go swimming.'

On their last night in St-Geniez there was a firework display. Helen and Rebecca had seen the preparations for it on one of their outings. Four men had been placing long metal cannisters onto trestle tables in the middle of the river where it flowed fast and shallow after the second bridge. Helen only realised they were fireworks when she read the posters advertising the Fête de Rive Droit – the Festival of the Right Bank – and the Grand Firework Finale.

Tony was in a mellow mood when he returned for his evening meal and she felt it was worth making the suggestion.

'There's a firework display tonight. Why don't we go? It would be such a lovely end to the holiday.' She heard the pleading note in her voice and wondered why it was impossible to treat Tony as a friend and equal. How come the decision was his anyway? She sighed inwardly but still waited for his verdict.

'If that's what you want, that's what we'll do.' He smiled magnanimously. 'Isn't it a bit late for Rebecca?'

'One special occasion won't do her any harm. She can sleep in the car on the journey tomorrow.' Helen spoke with more confidence about her own domain, childcare.

Later that evening they woke Rebecca, gave her a few minutes to come round from the bemused, unfocused glaze of deep sleep and took torches to light the path to the village. The camp site was alive with fireflies of torch beams and excited children's voices, as other campers headed the same way.

70

Pulling on their hands and swinging between them from time to time, Rebecca clung to her parents. Tony lit the way, warning them of potholes. Once they had crossed the main road they could see lights over the old bridge in the village, with the silhouettes of groups of people growing denser as they walked towards the bridge along the river bank. The village itself was eerily blacked out, the houses lining the river banks shuttered for the night. It certainly seemed that the whole 'Marmot' population was out to join in the festivities. The family went right up onto the bridge where the crowd was thickest, as Tony thought this would give them a grandstand view. In between the shoulders, heads and berets, Helen could see straight down the river to the faint shape of the next bridge, past which she knew was a curve round to the pitch occupied by their tent.

Tony had used the physical presence which Helen had often envied at pub bars to create a space for himself which was somehow inviolate and when he heard the inevitable 'Can't see, Daddy,' he hoisted Rebecca onto his shoulders with a splendid indifference to the people behind him. He even spared an arm to draw Helen beside him, so he could protect her view too. The arm stayed around her shoulders and she felt his warmth and strength.

Fireworks meant damp squibs on Bonfire Night, Catherine Wheels which fell off the garage wall, numbed feet and hot cheeks if the night was dry and the bonfire caught, brief bangs and whizzes, the tame sulphur of sparklers. *Feux d'artifice* at St-Geniez, by contrast, were sky paintings of power and passion. After the first gasps as rockets burst overhead into sprays of light, Helen could distinguish the different types; some sprayed rods of light, some burst high into flowers made of multi-coloured tear drops and others made urns of colour which shot sparking fountains upwards. Her favourite went high, 'til her neck

71

must break following it up, then broke with a soft plop into repeating umbrellas of gold tear drops, each umbrella starting from the fading one above. At first the background was deep black with only a few of the night's first stars; gradually black changed to billowing clouds of yellow-grey which hung so high that Helen mistook moonshine for smoke. The river filled with swirls of smoke so that they could no longer see the men lighting the cannisters on the trestle tables and it was as if strange dragons belched harpoons that broke into fire on the unseen stars.

'It beats Roundhay Park on Bonfire Night,' said Tony.

'Oh yes,' she said softly, 'yes.'

'A bit parky now though. Let's be getting back?'

'Carry,' was Rebecca's contribution and Tony carried back to her sleeping compartment where she sighed once and was gone.

'All right, love?'

'Yes,' she smiled, and perhaps she would have been if they had stayed at St-Geniez a little longer or if . . . a million ifs.

'We've a longish drive tomorrow. We'd better turn in.' Tony zipped up the tent door and they lay together with no foreknowledge of the nightmare that was so close.

As she sat in the armchair, holding an empty wine glass and staring at a wall, Helen could hear Rebecca's delighted voice as she added more and more words to her vocabulary. 'Butterpillar' had pleased her so much that no amount of explanation could sort out the confusion. 'Butterpillar, Mummy'. Helen used all the self-control she possessed to stop the memories there. The only helpful advice she had been given by the psychiatrist was that she should allow her memories a certain amount of time – as if she had a choice, she thought bitterly – and then cut them short, to let herself carry on with life. She added two painkillers to the evening's intake and went to bed.

72

5

Dai could not believe that three weeks had gone by and he had still not told Helen that he had left his wife. It never seemed to be the right moment, and the longer he left it, the more difficult it seemed. If only he could be sure that she wanted the commitment he longed to give. And what if she didn't? She had been so cold and distant on their return from Llangedeyrne and he still had no idea why it had happened, so he didn't know how to prevent it happening again. On the other hand, he really must tell her, if only to end the suspense. When he phoned her to suggest a day out (surely she wondered how he could spend so much time with her) he found her in a particularly buoyant mood.

'Why don't I take you somewhere special?' she said.

'Does that mean walking miles round Llanelli?' he asked without much enthusiasm, thinking of her non-driver status.

'You've heard of public transport,' she replied sarcastically and then paused. More cautiously she asked, 'Would it cause problems, going on a local train?'

'No.' It would cause no problems at all because he was free, he wanted to shout down the phone, but there was no point having waited for the right moment and then blurting it out down the phone. 'No, I look forward to it.'

'OK. Tomorrow morning at nine if you can make it then. Morning anyway. Oh – sorry but no dogs.'

'I'd guessed that. I'll see you soon.'

'Soon. 'Bye.'

How had such an ordinary conversation left him feeling this way? He raced up to his bedroom two stairs at a time, like a teenager, and put on trainers and a sweatshirt so he could walk off some of his adrenalin. He avoided his mother by shooting straight out through the front door, stopping only to grab a torch, then he whistled the dogs and headed out across the fields.

It was a clear August night with a full moon and the constellations clearly visible, begging to be named. He wished he'd listened more in school, or joined the boy scouts, but he could identify the Sospan easily enough. When he'd found out the Americans called it the Big Dipper he'd imagined it as a roller coaster ride through the sky, an image reinforced by the thought of the Milky Way. He wondered if Helen knew the Welsh term and he looked forward to sharing it with her. He looked forward to sharing so much. He had never before felt the need to share his life, and the feeling was all the stronger for hitting him so late on. The ache of absence and the fullness of shared time shaped the way he saw his life. There could be no going back now.

'Romantic idiot,' he told himself as his foot caught a pot-hole and he suddenly became aware of how far into the night he had walked. He retraced his steps and realised how cold it had grown when he was blasted by the warmth of the farm sitting-room. Will, Lloyd and Gwen were sitting watching a medical soap and Dai joined them quietly, grateful that it was not one of the jolly programmes he hated, about vets in the Yorkshire Dales. One aspect of his family which he appreciated now was their comfortable silence. His mother was knitting, his father nodding off surreptitiously and his grandfather fully engaged in the drama unfolding on screen. Their company did not interfere with Dai's thoughts at all, and he made a mental note to tell Grandad that you could see pictures in a gas fire after all.

Helen had used a great deal of imagination in planning the day out, in the knowledge that she could not afford to spend a great deal of money, but she wanted it to be her treat. She was pleased that he had made the effort to arrive exactly at nine o' clock.

'I'm in your hands.' He shrugged as he walked into the house.

'Not 'til later.' She escaped his kiss, grabbed her shoulderbag and pulled him with her back out of the door. She walked circumspectly beside him along the road, automatically considerate for him of what other people would see. She had disciplined herself to enjoy what was possible and didn't think twice about what was not.

'I know we're going to the station. Can't I drive you there?' he grumbled.

'It's only round the corner. You are so lazy! Anyway today is on me, so we do things my way.'

'But if the treat's for me, don't I have a say?'

'It doesn't work like that,' she laughed.

'At least tell me where we're going.'

'Wait and see.'

'There aren't that many options. It could be Swansea . . .' he eyed her sidewise but she gave nothing away. '. . . or Tenby.'

'What a place to get married,' she said, in an attempt to distract him. They were walking opposite a chapel, on a corner by the busiest set of traffic lights in town, just as a bride and groom came through its doors.

He flushed then saw what she was looking at. 'Difficult to park, you mean.'

'It's ugly and it's in an ugly setting.'

'They go to Parc Howard for photos.'

'Yes I know, Neil told me.' She carried on, unaware of his instinctive glower at the mention of Neil. 'But presumably they want the ceremonial feel of a religious wedding. What can be ceremonial about getting married in a warehouse?'

Their spirited discussion of the beauties or otherwise of Welsh Nonconformist chapels lasted until they reached the station.

75

'If I'd been a boy, I'd have been a trainspotter,' Helen said with regret. 'My Dad wouldn't take a girl with him. If he was late home, it wasn't a girlfriend that kept him, it was Leeds Station. His idea of heaven was the steam engine to Haworth, but he was happy enough wherever there were trains.'

'I can't say I understand it, although I did like Thomas the Tank.'

'I bet you've got the Fat Controller on your pyjamas – that'd suit you.'

'I can do it, I can do it,' he puffed rhythmically, shunting her through the waiting room.

'Act your age.' The frowns of two tweedy ladies stopped their fooling around and Helen directed Dai across the footbridge.

'Now I know!' he exclaimed triumphantly. 'It's got to be Tenby.'

She was particularly clear in enunciating 'Two day returns to Kidwelly' to the ticket collector and she enjoyed watching Dai's puzzled face.

'Not more walking,' he complained as she headed for the centre of town where she took him into a large hall.

'The Kidwelly Show!'

Helen had explored the local shows over her years in the area and still savoured the village atmosphere and variety of stalls. Every label told a story to her and she could imagine 'Mrs B. Jones' anxiously comparing the texture of her wholemeal loaf to that of Mrs D. Jones, so that next year it would be Mrs B. who claimed the red rosette.

'Where do you want to start?' she asked.

'You choose,' he smiled, amused by her enjoyment.

'Vegetables,' she said. 'No, save them for last. Home-made wines.' They headed for two bottle-topped tables, one for 'fruit/vegetable' and one for 'flower'.

76

'I once asked why they subdivided them that way and do you know what they told me? It wouldn't be right,' she emphasised a Welsh lilt, 'to ask a fruit to face a flower. It's so . . . what's the word? . . . tribal.'

'Well at least those snooty wine terms would suit the wines for once – I bet that "fruity little wine" has more than a "hint of blackcurrant".'

'I suspect the dandelion has a "floral bouquet" and the '95 beetroot might have a "vinegary tang".'

They moved on, each table offering new delights for gentle mockery or genuine admiration. Helen lingered by the Textiles entries, appreciating the intricacy of traditional stitches in a crocheted christening shawl. The hall was full of exhibitors and local visitors, chatting – as far as Helen could hear – about how this year's tomatoes compared with last year's, when Elen's baby was due, and whether council tax had been a good idea after all.

Finally they reached the vegetable stalls where, faced with outsize carrots and onions, Helen felt that she had suddenly shrunk Alice-like. She marvelled and read the labels aloud.

'Don't women grow vegetables?'

His expression was serious and informative. 'The important thing about prize-winning show vegetables is their size. They have to be bigger than big, they have to be gigantic. And every woman knows . . .'

She had caught the sparkle in his eye and finished the sentence with him, 'that size isn't everything'. They avoided commenting on the marrows and cucumbers, but some of the Siamese triplets of potatoes made shapes too grotesque for Helen's sense of humour and she started to splutter.

'Remind you of anything?' he asked coolly.

The next stop was the tearoom at Kidwelly Castle. Helen could afford to buy them lunch there, until Dai suggested a

77

bottle of wine. She agreed and was happy to let him choose. He told her the number of the wine and she was calling for service when she registered the price – £85. She cancelled the wine request, sat down quickly, glared at Dai and ordered a glass each of house red.

After the meal, Dai looked at her intently, reached for her hand and held it, stroking her palm. 'I would have bought the wine, to celebrate us.'

Helen took refuge in humour. 'You'd do better spending some money on new trainers. You'll have holes in those after all the walking we've done.'

'I suppose the castle's next,' he said wearily.

'Unless you're too tired?'

'Me, turn down a challenge from a good-looking woman? No way. Race you to the pay booth.' He lost the race but complained bitterly of foul play. Helen had hung onto his belt, then just before the pay booth she had stopped, doubling up and complaining of a stitch. He turned back to her and before he could put an arm around her she had sprinted past him and declared herself the winner.

'You cheat,' he said sourly.

'I won,' she crowed.

They wandered the castle's passages, finding each others' hands and mouths in the darkness of the dungeon. They climbed the towers that were still safe, and looked across the Gwendraeth River where black and white cows grazed on the flood plains.

'Welsh castles were used by the English to shut themselves away from contact with the barbarians,' remarked Dai.

'It's too late,' she said, 'I upped my drawbridge a while back. The barbarian is in the castle.'

'Let's go back now.'

They were quieter on the return journey to Llanelli. The

78

walk to her house passed in a haze and their sudden physical need overtook them before they reached her bed. Helen lost track of whether it was hand, tongue or man inside her and all thought ceased for a while. Afterwards, still feeling light-headed, she curled up in his arms, leaning against the sofa.

'I've left my wife.'

She though at first she'd misheard the softly spoken words but he repeated them. She grabbed some clothes and moved further away to look at him while he spoke.

'I love you.'

Her brains gave completely scrambled messages to her mouth and the best she could manage was 'When?'

'Three weeks ago.'

'What? How dare you, how dare you pretend to me that you're married when you're not!' She finished her hurried dressing and stood still in front of him, accusing. 'Three weeks!'

'You're the first woman who's shouted at me for pretending I'm married!' His smile looked presumptuous to her.

'Just go. Get your things. Go.' She left the room. Helen waited in the kitchen until she had heard shuffling noises followed by the quiet closing of the front door, then she went back into the sitting room. She didn't want this. All the times he could have stayed with her overnight and he had kept to the pretence that he must return to his wife! He might not have said so but it was understood between them and he hadn't told Helen otherwise. Everyone else knew he was free but her. She had been sneaking around like a fool for no reason when he was free. He loved her. What sort of love was it that kept her in the dark, dropped a bombshell then assumed she'd fit in with his plans? She'd seen those plans in his eyes. He wanted to change her life, to re-

79

arrange her life around him. No thank you. She liked her life. He had spoilt their day out. It had been fun though, and his body against hers had been all she wanted. Imagine having more days out, arranging time with him instead of wondering when she would next see him. It wouldn't be such a terrible change. Her life was arranged around him already, in the worst possible way. It was all very well pretending her life alone was rich and he was an extra, but the truth was she was either with him or waiting. Whatever she was doing, whoever else she was with, an important part of her was on hold. If they were together all the time, she would be more independent. She would know they were seeing each other soon. The security would free her. She shook herself. What sort of muddled thinking was this? She didn't want it. And yet, they were so well matched and they could be together. But he wouldn't love her if he knew the truth. Then there was no reason to tell him, was there. Perhaps she could risk seeing him more often, perhaps he could stay overnight with her once or twice . . .

A giant marrow with Dai's face closed in on her, saying, 'You will join the vegetables. There is no life for you outside the table. I will protect you from the others,' and she woke, still protesting that she didn't want to be a vegetable. The absurdity of the dream made her smile. She had over-reacted the night before, although she was still annoyed at how long he had taken to tell her. If only she could understand that, and she was willing to listen to him, then there might be a future for them together. Meanwhile, it was Sunday, sunny and she was going out for the day, alone. She was not waiting, she was living her life. Defiantly Helen packed a picnic and headed off for Cefn Sidan.

When she returned home at five o'clock, she couldn't resist dialling 1471 to see if anyone had phoned. She took in the strange number with a local code. He cared then. Satisfied, she sat down with her Sunday paper and started reading. Almost immediately the phone rang. She deliberately left it for seven double rings before answering.

'Neil here.'

She hid her disappointment. 'Hi. How are you?'

'Fine.' His tone was not fine. His voice sounded tense and she suspected he could not talk freely, which was strange. 'A friend has come to see you. You remember Jimmy? Well he didn't know your address but he had mine because of the conference, so he came here. Is it OK for me to bring him over?'

'Sure. I haven't got much food in.'

'I'll pick up a takeaway.' Relief but still strain. What was going on?

'See you soon.'

''Bye.' What different feelings could hide in the same formula. If it had been Dai saying 'See you soon', her nerves would have come alive, responding to the love and need in his voice. However it was not Dai and her friend clearly needed something from her. Jimmy and Neil's mother did not strike her as a happy combination and she could understand Neil wanting to put distance between the two. All this rubbish about Jimmy wanting to see Helen must be a smokescreen, but what did Neil expect from her?

Twenty minutes later came the expected knock at the door and in came a brown Tandoori carrier bag, supported by Neil and followed by Jimmy.

'Thank God you're home,' said Neil.

Jimmy's 'Hello' was as subdued as his expression. He was wearing cream baggy pants, braces and a T-shirt with a symbol Helen didn't recognize but assumed was left-wing. His artificially black hair looked in need of a wash and his whole appearance was grubby and unkempt. He was shivering and stood rubbing his arms, watching as Neil and Helen organized plates, cutlery and cans of beer.

Helen popped upstairs for a spare sweatshirt, which Jimmy accepted but without any change to the frozen look on his face. Eating gave each of them a breathing space before the explanations started and it was clearly difficult for Neil when he spoke.

'I was hoping Jimmy could stay here tonight.' Jimmy said nothing. 'He needed to get out of London, to talk. I can't . . . He can't stay with me. I hoped we could talk here.'

'That's no problem,' Helen spoke briskly.

Silence again. Neil's slightly shabby cords and the inevitable checked shirt denied any connection with the young man huddled in a chair, his earring defying the world and his expression crushed.

'I don't really know you,' Jimmy began, 'but then it looks like I don't really know him either.' The quiet bitterness of his voice was an accusation which drew Neil to him, but Jimmy rejected the hand that was offered. 'I needed a friend.' He spoke to Helen, slowly, as if re-learning speech. 'One of our friends died last night. I sat with him. Held his hand. You go part of the way with someone. Part of the way to death. I just wanted to find a way back and I thought Neil . . .' The word 'death' was spoken as if to say it was an act of courage. 'But I was wrong.'

'You weren't wrong. I'm glad you came. I'm sorry it's no good at my house. It's my fault. I can't be like you want me to be. If I were open, it would just heap problems on me and my mother. She'd be forced into lying or outfacing other people and what for? It would be no easier for me to see you. In fact, much harder. This way it's possible for people to think you're gay and I'm your hetero friend – that protects us from some of the worst rubbish.'

'Some friend. You were on pins to get me away.'

'You're right. I couldn't wait to get you away.' Neil looked at Helen, who would have made a tactful exit if presented with the smallest opportunity. 'Helen understands. We can be ourselves here. I mean our private selves.' This time Jimmy allowed the arm to stay round his shoulders. 'I can go home about midnight . . .'

'I don't suppose you've brought night things? A bag?' Helen asked.

Jimmy shook his head, his face white with stress and fatigue.

'Give me two minutes to sort the bed out and you can crash. You look like you need it,' she smiled and left them. Her spare room was functional, and never used, but neither man was in a state to notice. She called them upstairs, showed them bedroom and bathroom, then left them alone. She was weary herself by the time she sat down in font of the TV which she turned on deliberately loud. The knocking must have gone on for some time before she realised that there was someone at the door. She switched off the TV and went to answer the door. Only when she saw Dai standing there did her brain shift into gear.

'I was hoping you'd had time to think again. I've been phoning all day but you were out so I thought the personal touch?' Dai looked at her hopefully and moved towards the hall passage but she blocked him going further.

'I do want to talk but this isn't the best time. Could you call round tomorrow afternoon?' What timing! She couldn't risk the confidence Neil had placed in her and there had been too much emotion flying around for one evening anyway. Dai would still be there tomorrow and then she could show him how she felt.

She reached up to give him a quick goodbye kiss but he was staring past her and upwards to where Neil was standing at the top of the stairs, slightly dishevelled, clothes half undone.

'Helen?' Neil looked down. 'The knocking at the door . . .'

'I can see this isn't the best time,' Dai said curtly. 'Neil, I assume.' Neil nodded confused assent.

Helen made one last attempt to rescue the situation. 'It would be good to see you tomorrow. Really.'

'I'm the Monday slot am I?'

His sarcastic tone was too much for Helen's already stretched sense of what was fair. 'Look, yesterday you were married, today you own me. Neil don't say a word, there's no need – go back to bed.' It was impossible to determine whether Dai left before the door was slammed on him but the exit was certainly emphatic.

Neil did not go back to bed. He came downstairs and made coffee for Helen and himself, joining her in the sitting-room.

'Helen, what have I done?'

'You should be with Jimmy.'

'He's asleep.'

'You heard what I said. He's no right.'

'But you love him.'

'I'm old enough to know that's not everything. Forget him. What about you?'

'He talked. We made love. He cried. He needed to cry, I think. That's what let him sleep. I don't think he's slept much for the last week. He's been in the hospital most of the time.'

'The man who died, your friend . . .?'

'I didn't know him so well. Jimmy had slept with him a few times.' Neil acknowledged the raised eyebrow. 'That's how it is,' an ironic smile, 'you'd approve – no ownership.'

'AIDS?' Helen had to ask.

'Yes,' Neil intercepted her next question, 'no, no chance.

84

Not Jimmy, not me. After tonight if it is Jimmy, it's me too.'
He gave a wry smile.

'Surely you were safe. Please tell me that.'

'Sometimes,' he hesitated, 'you have to show your trust, show you care, by taking a risk you don't need to take. That's what happened tonight.'

'But you know better.'

'No one knows better.'

'If Jimmy has taken a risk . . .with someone else?'

Neil opened his arms in a wide gesture. 'Qué sera sera. What about you and Dai?'

'That's different.'

'Is it?' The words hung in the air.

'After tonight I guess there will be minimal risk, unless from killing looks. What's going to happen now, with you and Jimmy?'

'I'll call tomorrow after school, take him to the train. He'll sleep till lunchtime then watch afternoon TV till I come – if that's OK with you?'

'I didn't mean tomorrow. I meant long-term. It was you he came to.'

'He's young. He'll heal. He's already starting to talk about it, that's the first stage. He has friends in London – it's his scene. I'll go down there again soon, we'll enjoy the day, and that's all.'

Helen couldn't reconcile her knowledge of his kindness with what seemed callous indifference to the boy whose bed he'd just left. Her face must have shown some of her feelings.

'Hey come on! Imagine Jimmy trapped in Llanelli! Imagine him picking me up from school – the day before I lose my job – and eating Welsh cakes in the parlour.' She smiled despite herself. 'I do care. He'll be all right. You'll see. What about you?'

'I guess it just wasn't meant to be.' She felt a little numb in admitting the end of a half-formed dream.

'If you told him the truth about me, he'd understand how wrong he'd been . . .'

'You trust me, he doesn't. I've no reason to explain my every move to a man who thought it fine to go home to his wife when it suited him. Besides, you know it's safer not to tell anyone else that you're gay, or you're going to be forced into more and more openness. You know that's not what you want.'

'I don't want you to lose him because of me.'

'It's not because of you, it's because of him. No, it's generous of you, but no. Forget it.' She hugged him. 'You'd better go.'

'Thank you . . . for Jimmy and all. I'll phone you tomorrow after I've seen him off. It's going to be a hell of a long day in school tomorrow.'

'And a short night's sleep. Go on!' She shooed him out through the door.

When Helen at last dropped into bed and shut her eyes she knew the night wasn't over. For months after it had happened there had been visits, nothing as definite as a ghost. Helen would be almost asleep so that the boundary between dream and reality was too blurred for her to explain what she saw to someone else. She could see her daughter tiptoe to the bed as if to sneak up on her mother and shout 'Boo' as she had done so often in the mornings. She never spoke, just reached out both arms towards the bed, towards Heathcliff who lay beside Helen. She would try and try to pick up the battered dog and always failed. Then she would seem to see Helen for the first time and her expressionless face would crumple in horror and she would creep backwards, cowed, into darkness. Those searching arms had brushed Helen without touching her and

86

sometimes to avoid the cold non-contact Helen had jumped out of bed and stood watching. Wherever she was, the face turned to her in horror. It made no difference whether Helen's eyes were open or shut – she saw the same scene. Tony had seen nothing and heard nothing but he had pitied her at first. Then pity had turned to frustration and she had slept alone. Wherever she had slept, the visitor had called. Gradually the time between visits increased, leaving Helen torn between hope of healing and terrible emptiness at losing this little Cathy searching for her Heathcliff. Helen had told the psychiatrist, who had explained the way in which trauma could be externalised by the mind, and she had listened, seeing again the beribboned white clothes – why so Victorian? – and pale face of death. As the visits grew rare the nightmares came.

Time the healer had done nothing that could withstand the various versions of the past with which her subconscious tortured her. Sometimes there had been an obvious trigger during her waking hours, sometimes it seemed she had been without torture longer than was allowed. A straightforward re-living of events alternated with cruel variations on what had happened, both worse and better, until she wondered if she knew what had happened. Dream changes always faded from her mind however; the reality was hers for life.

Afraid of sleep, Helen could fight it no longer and so the nightmare came. If Jimmy had not been so deeply unconscious, he would have heard the troubled sounds from the neighbouring bedroom and even distinguished fragments of speech.

A short night's sleep it was, and Helen found her concentration drifting in the shop next morning. She gave up working on her designs, having made several stupid errors, and aware that the calculations would all need to be checked to prevent her knitting a jumper with a neckband bigger than a waist. At lunchtime she gave up, broke all her own rules and left a message in the shop saying 'Back at 4 o'clock.' Then she went home to keep Jimmy company, feeling that his battered state would distract her from her own and – who knows? – perhaps she could even be of use.

'Hey Jimmy,' she called through the door, 'it's me, Helen.'

'Hi.' A somewhat tousled Jimmy emerged from the kitchen with a plateful of unidentifiable splodge.

'I'm glad you found something to eat.'

'No problem. I put together some bits and pieces I found. This is cornflakes, tomatoes and tuna with melted cheese.' He cheerfully loaded the spoon and spoke between mouthfuls.

'I haven't eaten for days, I'm starving.' He pointed at the plate. 'This is great. You want some?'

'No thanks, I've eaten,' she lied. 'You're looking a bit better. How do you feel?'

'Strange. Like I've woken up on a new planet. I can't explain the feeling of, I don't know, not being dead, like it's a positive thing.'

'It must have been hard for you, being with your friend.'

'He was so thin and breathing . . . I didn't know how hard it could be just to breathe.'

His face brightened. 'But he had such friends. They brought in wild posters, anything and anyone that was beautiful, and put them on the wall. One guy was thrown out by a nurse for playing gay love songs on his guitar. She said gay was fine, loud and off key wasn't.' The smile saddened again. 'He asked for his parents. They wouldn't come. How could they do that?'

Helen just bit her lip and shook her head.

'At the end there was just me. And I really was dead tired. All I could think was Neil was alive, I could talk to

88

him, and I got straight on the train. Hadn't figured on his Mum though. Haven't seen my Mum in five years – you forget people have them, mums.'

'Don't be hard on Neil. His life here is important to him.'

'I know. I can't take in how different he is to when we were in London, but on our own last night I could see. He's still Neil.'

'He's still Neil,' she echoed, thinking that Jimmy's discovery had been the reverse of hers and yet led him to the same conclusion.

Jimmy talked easily until Neil arrived, telling stories of his friends, their jobs and love affairs. Helen couldn't believe the transformation from the night before. She said as much in a quiet aside to Neil when Jimmy was out the room.

'You were right – he seems quite recovered.'

Neil shook his head. 'Seems. The euphoria won't last. He'll grieve soon, but more peacefully. I think yesterday's desperation has gone.'

'How come you know this stuff?'

'I did a course on bereavement counselling once. The real understanding came when my dad died. I know it hits everyone differently but if you really suffer it even once, you know what grief is like.'

Helen stepped back. 'Jimmy's lucky you were here.'

'And you,' said Jimmy, walking in. 'See you in London. I can't cope with the pace in this Llanelli.' Helen and Dai both winced at his attempt to say the name of their home town, pronouncing 'll' as 'th' each time.

'I'll have to train this Sais,' said Neil.

'Is that better or worse than being called a poofter?' Jimmy adopted an extremely camp pose.

'Worse,' Helen laughed. 'You'll miss your train.' She gave Jimmy a hug and smiled at Neil as they left. The conversations had left her uncomfortable. She didn't want to talk about death and she was the last person to help someone cope with grief. Cope! That was a laugh. But Jimmy was at peace. *In pacem requiescat*. His conscience was clear and he'd had time with his friend to say how he felt. They'd both been adults, knowing the score. Jimmy wouldn't have to face the nocturnal visits, in and out of nightmares, poisoned whispers in the dark. It was probably for the best that it had all fallen through with Dai. The more she thought about it the more impossible it seemed that she should share her nights.

6

'They're all bitches,' slurred the voice in Dai's ear, as an arm round his shoulder jerked a snooker cue.

'Shit. That was a winning shot,' complained Dai as the white ball cannoned loosely round the snooker table. Leighton unwrapped himself from Dai but clearly needed something else to lean against, so joined Gareth and Robert propped up against the Pontdu bar next to a row of straight-sided pint glasses. Full of self-pity and looking for distraction, Dai had headed out for the evening, avoided his father's local, and settled in for some serious solitary drinking in the Pontdu. He had already sunk three pints when conversation had spilled onto him from the four men who were the pub's only customers that night. Dai had accepted their assumption that his 'face like a smacked arse' was caused by a woman, and the evils of women had alternated as a topic of conversation with more serious matters such as whether Llanelli could sort out a full-time coach who could bring back the glory days of Welsh rugby.

The men were generous in their purchase of rounds and the insistent 'I'll get one in' had led to a queue of pints in front of Dai. On his fifth pint he had observed that it was a bit like talking to his grandfather and he felt that he had had enough to drink. Emptying his bladder became increasingly dangerous as the Gents was a small stone shed out through the back of the pub down an uneven flagged path, following the stale smell of past customers who couldn't be bothered walking or wouldn't risk venturing as far as the basic facilities provided. Dai returned from one such visit practising the words 'Thanks boys but that's enough for me.' He might as well have said 'Same again,' for all the effect it had. He let himself be talked into another. 'If ever I saw a man in need of a drink, it's you . . . Where's the harm in it? . . . Don't worry, this is on me . . . What are friends for? . . .' As he carried on drinking, the slight queasiness left Dai, as did the pain in his ribs that had been with him since he had seen Neil half-undressed with Helen, the night before. His capacity to speak clearly and pot a snooker ball had also left him, but neither he nor anyone else was in a state to notice.

'His Maggie went off you know,' said Robert – or was it Gareth?- in a stage whisper. 'He sorted her out, no mistake.'

'What'd 'e do?' asked Dai, looking away from the fairy lights along the counter.

Glyn came away from the snooker table where he had been doggedly chasing a last ball with little success.

'He posted her underwear to her mother with a note saying 'Pity to waste it. Wear it to work like your daughter did.'

Dai was a bit puzzled by this as an act of revenge.

'Bit embarrassed was she?'

'Strong chapel the mother-in-law was. Catalogue stuff his Maggie wore, peephole bras and wet-look black thongs.' Robert licked his lips over the image.

91

'How would you know?' asked Gareth suggestively – or was it Robert?

'He told me himself of course, what do you think!' They all looked with great respect at Leighton, a man capable of such ruthless action. Dai tried not to think of Helen's underwear or that he knew no one he could send it to, so external to her life he had been. An optional extra. Monday's man. Leighton stood impassively downing his pint, pretending not to hear his friends' tribute.

Gwyn sniggered, 'Mam always said home-made tarts were best.'

'Have you heard the one about the man with two dicks?' The jokes continued for a pint or two, with Dai contributing from time to time when he could dredge up something suitably smutty from his student days. He found his company incredibly witty and he felt they were bringing out the best in him as a raconteur, so he was disappointed when the barman, yawning, stopped him in mid-flow. 'Sorry boys, it's time now.'

'Aw, come on Doug, just the one for the road. The night is young,' Dai heard himself pleading.

Doug looked at him with pity. 'One a.m. is young in the morning not in the night, and it's illegal enough for me. Everybody out.' There were no further complaints and the men shambled to the door through the darkened passage, where the landlord unlocked the door and hurried them out, shushing them as he had a quick look up and down the lane. The custom of a lockout which prevents customers coming into the pub after closing time is a dubious compromise between the law and the alcohol business, frequently tolerated by the police in the interests of common sense. On the other hand, you never knew when you might get someone new on the beat or just someone in the mood for a raid.

The men shouted loud goodbyes which set a dog off barking in a nearby house, then Dai was alone to walk the lane home. He felt tired and very hot so he took his sweatshirt off and tied it round his waist. Five minutes later he took off his Tshirt, noticing vaguely that the sweatshirt had disappeared and thinking how convenient that was because now it was easier to tie the Tshirt in the same position. It had started to drizzle and he enjoyed the feel of the rain on his back. Trickles ran down his face from his hair and he stuck his tongue out, surprised at the pleasant taste. He raised his arms and rubbed the rain around his arm-pits, thinking that he should do this more often.

When he reached the farmhouse he went as quietly as possible through the open back door, aware how late it was. His stomach was churning but he thought he would be all right if he could lie down. He took his shoes off and tiptoed slowly up the creaking steps, tripping on the fifth and swearing loudly, which started the dogs off barking. He continued upstairs but his overburdened stomach suddenly gave up the doomed attempt to retain its contents and he threw up uncontrollably over himself and the stairs. This made him feel better so he continued upstairs to his bedroom. Satisfied at having achieved his goal, he fell onto the bed, watched the ceiling whirl unpleasantly and passed out.

'I'll have a Cinzano and lemonade.'

'Dry white wine.'

'You'll be lucky if there's a choice of colour, never mind the finer details. Helen?'

'Cinzano for me too, with lemonade.' Monday was Laura's birthday, which the friends had agreed to celebrate with a basket meal and a drink or two in the Coach and Horses. While Dai was propping up the bar in the Pontdu,

Helen was sitting at a burnished table flipping a beer mat. She was not really in the mood for a night on the town but a couple of hours sleep after Neil and Jimmy had left meant that at least she would stay awake.

'You've changed your make-up – I like it.' Charlotte inspected Laura's face.

Laura pulled a face. 'It took ages. The eyeshadow's one you use wet, then smudge. First I looked like a panda, then I smudged too much off and had to start again. Then I sneezed and the mascara made those little black marks on my cheek and above my eyes so I was dabbing with cotton wool.' The others nodded understandingly. 'And as if that wasn't enough I flicked toothpaste in my eye. Is it still red?' They all reassured her that both eyes matched perfectly. 'They put a banner up in work and stuck a candle in a Welsh cake at coffee break.'

'What's happened about that perv?'

Laura blushed. 'He's not so bad actually.'

Three voices spoke at once. 'How can you say that?'

'You have rights.'

'You don't have to take that sort of crap.'

Laura hesitated. 'He's a bit shy really, and he wanted to ask me out and because he was building up to it so much he just went a bit you know, over the top.' Cynical looks all round the table.

'Laura, you told us this guy tried to run his hand up your skirt.'

'Yes but . . .'

'You said he never spoke to you but he followed you around and stared.'

'Yes but . . .'

'You said he gave you the creeps and you were scared to go to work.'

'Yes but . . .'

94

'Yes but what?'

'He has a nice bum.' Disbelieving silence as the others exchanged looks.

'You're beyond. It's women like you make it difficult to win sexual harrassment cases.'

'It's not just his bum. Now he's explained everything I can see it was his shyness, his inexperience. Anyway, his name's Ryan and we're going to the pictures tomorrow.'

'How did this relationship get to the talking stage, as a matter of interest?' enquired Charlotte sarcastically.

'My keyboard's been playing up, jamming on "shift" and I was into part of the programme I didn't know existed and couldn't exit. Ryan got me out of the loop, cleaned the buttons and by then we were talking. And he's recommended to our boss that I have a new pentium with increased megabytes.'

'Glad I asked.'

'I prefer it when she talks about mascara brushes,' muttered Jane.

'Men,' said Helen brightly, 'Can't live with . . .'

'Can't live without! Your round.'

'Why don't we go out somewhere different?' Helen threw herself into discussion of their next evening out, painfully aware that her diary was open and man-less. Rounds of drinks accelerated without a decision having been made and the conversation disappeared pleasantly down blind alleys. Charlotte was particularly keen on dance and was trying to talk them into an evening at Swansea Theatre with the Ballet Rampart.

'Dan'll go with me one evening but I'd like to see both programmes they're putting on. You loved it last year.'

'Was that the one where the music built up from a headache to the pains of natural childbirth while women in rags reached out to men in thermals who stood two feet away and they missed each other?' asked Helen drily.

'I remember.' An evil light dawned in Jane's eyes. 'And there were some dubious sexual practices in a big garden.'

'I don't remember that.'

'You were asleep.'

'I only closed my eyes for a minute to absorb the emotions.'

Charlotte stubbornly interpreted their comments as favourable. 'See, you all felt the poetry of it. *The Garden of Earthly Delights* was a masterpiece.'

'I don't remember any words. Were there words?' Confused, Jane tried to remember. 'How is it poetry if there's no words?'

Helen relented and helped out Charlotte. 'I know what you mean. Dance is physical poetry, like sex made art but without the messy bits.'

'I knew there was sex in it,' declared Jane triumphantly. 'Why don't we go and watch the Chippendales? They're good dancers.'

'Jane!' they all glared at her with contempt. The rounds of drinks were slowing down but still coming in steadily, and the conversation meandered cheerfully.

'My turn, my turn,' insisted Helen loudly. 'There were two little children on the beach and the little boy says to the little girl, 'I've got one of these.' So the little girl says, 'So what. I've got one of these and I can get one of those any time I like!''

Still giggling, Jane said, 'I don't get it. I mean he must have showed his willy but she'd look silly with one, wouldn't she.'

'Freud, Freud eat your heart out,' Helen told a wine glass.

'Time please ladies.' The little bell tinkled exactly at half past ten, the town centre pubs being of necessity cautious about licensing hours. Reduced drinking times were taken into consideration by the clientele who always drank at a faster pace to ensure the n+1 formula still applied (the universal law which decrees that the average pub customer will always drink n+1 – one more unit than is good for the body – before closing time). Helen and her friends were happily n+1 as they exited, singing.

Helen hummed along with 'Sospan fach' wondering anew about the cultural significance of the saucepan in Llanelli. She felt a sudden twinge of nostalgia and patriotic duty which led to a spirited rendering of 'Ilkley moor b'at'at'. Helen provided the verses and trained her friends as a passable chorus. It took several runs through because Laura pedantically insisted on understanding the meaning of what she was singing.

'Where hast tha bin since Ah saw thee
On Ilkley moor b'at'at.'

'Where's "bartat"?' she interrupted to ask.

'It means without your hat.'

'Do they wear hats in Yorkshire?'

'I suppose they must have. It's an old song.'

'Ah've bin a courtin Mary Jane
on Ilkley moor b'at'at.'

'Thal't ha' bin an caught thy death o' cold.'

Can you really catch cold from not wearing your hat?'

'Perhaps if you always wear one and then you forget. It's cold on the moors.'

'So he'd still be alive if he hadn't worn a hat in the first place.'

'Shut up Laura and just sing.'

'Then worms'll come and eat up thee, eat up thee
On Ilkley moor b'at'at.'

'Oh yuk. Don't they know any tidy songs up there?' The singing collapsed into laughter and despite, or perhaps because of the alcohol, Helen's brain seemed supernaturally sharp and she thought just how 'tidy' the old song was, the natural cycle of birth, love and death condensed into a pragmatic vision. You really should remember to wear your hat, she thought, once you'd started.

''Bye then. 'Bye. Lovely evening. Happy birthday.' Helen walked off waving, as Charlotte jumped into the car where her husband was waiting, and Jane and Laura headed for the taxi rank. The drizzle tickled her face and a little rivulet down the back of her neck, between her shoulder blades, made her shiver so she put her collar up. Tomorrow she would think about Dai and feel lonely. Tomorrow she would check that Neil was all right and that Jimmy was safely back in London. 'Safely' was certainly how Neil would see it. The warmth of the alcohol inside her was pleasantly numbing, and although she had drunk more than she had intended, she still felt in control. The evening's last gift to her was a deep, dreamless sleep.

Waking in the trenches must have felt like this. First, the feverish cold, cramped muscles and parched throat. Then the realisation that it was going to get worse. Dai felt sick again as he saw the dried vomit surrounding him, but even the smallest movement sent stabs of lightning through what was left of his brain. 'Water. Alka seltzer,' he mouthed, like the gunslinger collapsing in the desert, reaping the rewards of violence. Dai didn't think he had been violent but he had a feeling he was reaping just rewards.

He stumbled to the bathroom, his delicate stomach heaving at the overpowering smell of disinfectanct on the landing. He ransacked the bathroom cabinet but found only aspirin, muscle rub and cough medicine. He made do with two aspirin and four glasses of water, while waiting impatiently for the bath to fill. If only his old-fashioned parents had installed a shower; he really did not fancy lying in his own dirt on this particular occasion. The Japanese did have a point. Like an injured bird, he kept his head at the angle of a broken wing, as for some reason this eased the shooting pains in his head, and lowered himself into the bath, ducking totally underwater and sluicing himself down. Standing up, he poured one clean rinse after another over his hair and body, disgusted by the unidentified particles draining down the plughole. The soapy smell contrasted with the stale reek from his clothes and he wrapped a towel round him to return to his bedroom for fresh clothing. His mother was heading down the stairs as he passed and he risked a greeting.

'I'm sorry about the mess. Give me a minute and I'll clean up.'

Her response was frosty. 'I've done the stairs.' The full horror came back to Dai. No wonder there was a smell of disinfectanct.

'Oh God. I'm sorry, truly. I was drunk.'

She looked at him as if he'd knifed his grandfather and claimed he'd missed the bread. 'Oh well, that's all right then.'

'No, it's not all right, but I didn't exactly plan it and I couldn't control it. I certainly regret it if that's what you're wondering.'

'Well I'm sure that's your business.' She wouldn't give an inch.

Dai phoned the practice, collecting details of the day's rounds and re-organizing the day to make up for missing morning surgery. He struggled with his soiled bedding, loaded the old twin tub and ensured that all washing was hung out and carpets scrubbed before he and his aching head left for work. It was a relief to get away from the pervasive smell of chlorine and his own guilt.

Intermittent paracetemol, headaches and farm rounds prevented Dai thinking too much but he prodded the emotional ulcer from time to time. *Not so much an ulcer as surgery. Someone's cut me open and removed a healthy organ, leaving a swab or a wristwatch in my body. At first the foreign body causes mild irritation, barely breaking through the anaesthetic of last night's beer, but then pain radiates out until it kills. His teeth brushed her nipples and she smiled. To smile and smile and be a villain. Monday's man is full of woe. Kick me you cow, kick me where it hurts. What's one more cow kicking me?*

Unable to face food or frosty silences at the end of a long day, Dai turned down his mother's offer of evening meal and went to his room, nauseated by the lingering chlorine smell and by hangover fatigue. Meaning to rest for an hour, he closed his eyes. He woke, shivering, at four in the morning and crawled under the bedclothes, giving up.

'Talk to him, Helen.' Neil had phoned on Tuesday, concerned about her and unconvinced by her lively account of an evening out with friends.

'You spend too much time with your mother. You'll be a right nagging old woman.' The silence at the other end registered his hurt. 'I'm sorry. It's not a good time, Neil. Leave me alone for a bit.'

'Something Jimmy said. It's easier to love someone who's dying or leaving than someone you live with.'

'He doesn't live with me.' Despite herself, the bitterness and longing came through. 'Thanks for calling. I know you mean well. I'll be in touch.' She hung up before she could snap at him again. It was the unfairness of it which crushed her. She would work up to a tirade of abuse aimed at hypocritical oversexed bastards with the sensitivity of a rhinoceros then collapse, drained. She probably ought to see the doctor about this apathy, in case she was anaemic, but she couldn't be bothered. There was no one to share her grating laughter. 'How long had she felt like this?' the doctor would ask. 'Forever,' she would say, 'two days.' *Been here before. Go through the motions until the motions go through themselves. Feeling comes back. You're never the same but feeling does come back. How did I let it happen? How did he become so necessary? His ears aren't level and they stick out.*

Weather conditions are so localised in the valleys of southwest Wales that Dai could stand in a shaft of sunlight on Mynydd Sylen and look south at the stormclouds which had drenched him five minutes earlier unloading their burden onto Llanelli. By Thursday his imagination had provided so many detailed and unwanted visions of Neil entwined with a naked Helen, that he could not have given a clear account of what exactly he had witnessed if he had tried. His sense of betrayal focused on those details which hurt him the most and stimulated the creation of yet more details until his brain was screaming. Unable to talk to anyone, and not yet hardened to the stage where he would feel foolish for having destroyed his marriage over someone who thought so little of him, he could only face factual conversation. This made his father the easiest company and Dai determined to win back his parents' tolerance, which had clearly been strained by his alcoholic exploits. His grandfather was not helping, with suggestions that they 'market Buckley's bitter as paint stripper, for it's done a great job on the bannisters', and other such witticisms.

Thursday morning therefore found Dai out in his father's fields, aware that clouds which had been over him were speeding to Helen. *Promiscuous sputum* he told the rain in the distance, and returned to the business of looking into cows' mouths. On the field boundaries, the blackberries were tiny bullet-hard clusters amongst the hawthorn

101

hedging, which had recovered from its spring shave and waved new growth above the compact bolster of a hundred years' pruning. Will preferred the straight cut of the lopper which he attached to his JCB to the intensive labour of pleaching which some of the 'back to the land' immigrants practised on their smallholdings.

A typical hill farm, the land wasted around hedges, and, by entrances to the small fields, clusters of evening primroses and foxgloves, butterflies and hedgehogs. Conservation was a mere accident of farming and Will would have showered acid rain on his land if it came recommended by the packaging for short-term gain. However, farms on the hillside had hedges and cows, so Will's farm had hedges and cows. His innovations were all to do with the cows themselves, the breed and the breeding. Will had seen the great, flat cornfields of East Anglia where his entire farm would have fitted into one field, and he had shaken his head. Why, there were field boundaries round here dating back to the Stone Age. A man needed to see the tidy shape of his fields and where his land stopped. There could be no worse task in hell for Will than to plough an infinite field, not being able to set limits on the tasks to be undertaken that day. Today's task was to present eleven cows to his son for inspection, so that Dai could check their ear tags, their denture and their dates of birth, to verify that they tallied. The sooner it was over, the better.

This was a bread-and-butter job for Dai, and he gave more attention to the unnatural blueness of a patch of sky emerging from behind the storm clouds, and to the puddles steaming in the sun, than to how many of a cow's flat ruminant teeth were through the gum. He routinely confirmed the two teeth only, which indicated that the cows were below the thirty months and could go to market, rather than the three teeth which indicated thirty-six months and condemned by the BSE laws to slaughter and government compensation. It was equally important that a vet verified the latter case, to prevent farmers claiming animals were older than was true, to maximise the compensation.

Dai rubbed the beast in front of him along the bony bump on her forehead and she gave him a steady brown-eyed stare. Her creamy coat had a beige circle round one eye that had faded as she had grown but which he remembered giving her a circus dog appearance as a young calf. 'Patch,' he said, half to himself, and Will said nothing.

It had been a difficult birth, with Dai attending the midnight summons to his father's farm. Dai knew that his father had been unlucky with this cow, having tried several times to inseminate her and succeeding at an unseasonable time, so that it was an autumn birth. The mother had thrashed herself to exhaustion and was lying in the straw, dilated but unable to expel the monster racking her body and rippling under the skin as it struggled to find a way out. An emergency Caesarian was the only answer, to save at least one of them. Dai and his father had waited for the anaesthetic to take effect, sharing a glance as the frenzied movements inside the mother ceased completely. Resigned to what he would find, Dai scrubbed up and made the incision. No amount of clearing mucus from passages or pumping the limp body could rub life into the perfect calf which Dai pulled into the light of the gas lamp. Disciplined, Dai had returned to the mother only to shout to Will to look. Another calf was visible and Dai pulled her onto the straw, wiped all remnants of the sac from her, clearing her mouth and nostrils to breathe life into her himself. The pulse fluttered faintly and then the legs gave a little reflex kick. Will's soft 'Thank you' and his over-bright eyes had made Dai busy himself with cleaning up the wound. By the time Dai had finished with the suture, Gwen had brought a measure of brandy to warm the men and was nursing the little calf, whose mother would be too weak to be much help for a while. Sitting in the straw, Dai contemplated the nativity scene, and absurdly wished his parents and the newborn calf a Happy Christmas.

New life against the odds would always bring that thrill to Dai which he supposed was what vocation meant. It didn't worry him to see Patch here for market; he was a farmer's son and accepted the pact that people made with livestock. The same man who would risk his life to find a sheep in seven feet of snow, who'd raise its lambs in his own kitchen, would sell them three months later with pride in a good price. It did, however, worry Dai considerably that he was certifying a cow as under thirty months old, which he knew to have been born in mid-October, making it thirty-four months old. Dai checked the logbook again for the date against Patch's ear-tag number. There it was, the twenty-eightth of February, a lie in black and white. Will's hands had tightened on the stick he carried, and he waited.

'Patch was born in October, Dad. We both know that.' Dai continued stroking the cow's broad muzzle, without looking at his father.

'Let me look at that Record Book.' Will's previous experience of lying was confined to agreeing that his wife looked good in a new dress and he was very bad at it. His surprised tone rang false as he pretended to look at the Record Book. 'I wonder how that happened. That date of birth must have been entered wrongly. You know how over-worked I was – mistakes are easy made.'

'It couldn't have been entered in October and be in the correct place in the February entries.' Dai spoke quietly, without emotion, postponing the moment when he would have to decide what to do.

'That must be what happened,' Will persevered. 'I was so

busy I didn't enter her 'til February. I'll put that right, don't you worry.'

'When did Mam stop writing up the Record Book?' Will was silent. 'This is all in your writing. It's too neat. It's written all in one go. You've re-written the book, haven't you?'

Will's reluctant nod confirmed what Dai already knew. 'This one's false. The true Record Book is hidden away somewhere. You've been subtracting four months from the cows' ages to get closer to market profit, haven't you? Dad, look at me.'

Patch chose that moment to loose a liquid brown stream that made both men sidestep quickly and glance at each other. Will couldn't meet Dai's eyes and looked away again.

'The regulations are squeezing me dry and for what? That cow is as safe to eat now as she was four months ago, but the difference to me will feed your mother and keep a roof over our heads.' The indirect admission inevitably led to the question Dai dreaded. 'What are you going to do about it, son? '

The word 'son' hit Dai with an unfairness that winded him. David, not knowing the cows, would not have noticed the malpractice. If Dai had not been determined to help his father more, Will could have kept his farm going on the money saved by his ingenuity, for as long as the BSE laws were in force. There were already signs that BSE would be eliminated in five years and the panicky demands for mass culls were dying down, so his father would have been able to weather the storm. It was not any clearer to Dai than to Will why some of the current measures had been imposed, and both of them were aware of the ways in which other farmers beat the system. However, Dai had the letters MRCVS after his name, and he accepted the professional responsibility he carried. He had no option, and to think that it made any difference that it was his father left him open to the wink-wink charge of nepotism he had always found insulting.

'I have to report it to the Ministry.' Will's face showed nothing. He just turned and headed back across the fields, leaving Dai with the Record Book and a cow whose birth had joined the two men in celebration.

It was easier to come back late from the surgery, too late to face his father at an evening meal, but Dai still had his mother's queries to parry.

'All go well this morning?' Gwen asked brightly.

'Yes.' Dai made his mouthfuls of food an excuse for a brief response.

'I was so glad to see the two of you going out together. Like the old days.'

'Yes.'

'I've grown used to you being back. I shall miss you when you sort out a place with . . . what is her name?'

'You're going too quick, Mam.'

'Well you must have been sure, to give up your marriage for her . . . I just thought . . .'

If he were not careful, Dai knew he would cause hurt where he was trying to spare it, and he was barely forgiven for his wild night out. Was there no topic of conversation which did not tighten barbed wire in his chest! 'Helen has choices Mam.' *And she likes to take up all of them.* ' I mustn't put pressure on her too soon or I'll lose her.' *Lose her implies having her to start with. Everyone has her.*

'Helen's a pretty name. A school friend of mine was called Helen and she always wished she hadn't been. She was a little plump and very self-conscious. Well, we all were at that age, and someone told her she had the name of the most beautiful woman in history. I wondered what happened to her.' His mother chatted in the background and

106

Dai's thoughts drifted, finding no safe resting places. He tried his grandfather's company for distraction. He should have known better.

'What did you say to your Dad today? He's like a scalded rabbit. Came in here and left straight away. I told him if he won't sit still and talk to you then he won't get to know you. Only got himself to blame if you can't be bothered with him. A man likes a bit of conversation.'

'Scalded cat's the usual expression Grandad.' Dai gathered that Will had walked from one humiliation involving his son straight into another.

'It's badger in Welsh.' Lloyd's foolproof response to any criticism of his English was to declare that it was a translation. Dai's Welsh was too colloquial for him to be sure that his grandfather's statements were pure invention and Lloyd would answer any challenge from Dai's parents with the assertion that they knew nothing of traditional country Welsh. Dai was too polite on this occasion to point out that 'badger' had translated as 'rabbit' two minutes earlier.

'We haven't seen that woman yet. Your Mam would like to meet her you know.'

'It's early days, Grandad.'

'Where are you going to live?'

'Why? Are you tired of me already?' Dai's attempt to deflect Lloyd with humour merely encouraged badinage he could do without.

'We'd miss your power cleaning. Spraying paint stripper.' Lloyd chuckled to himself and said, 'What a night you must have had, eh? I wish I'd been there.'

'I don't remember.' *I wish I didn't remember.*

'Don't be so boring. I remember me and Gordon Walls had a night on the town once. There was bright red lipstick on my cheek when I got home and your Gran was tamping. So I told her, 'It's not what you think,' and she says, 'You

107

don't know what I think,' and I says, 'Well I bet you're not thinking what a boy Gordon is.' Gordon took my meaning straight and put his lips to fit the marks and I says, 'Like Cinderella see, it fits.' So Gordon gave me a smacker on the lips and we all laughed so much your Gran couldn't remember what had started her off.'

Dai had heard the story before, but it was preferable to sharp questions. 'So where did you get the lipstick marks, Grandad?'

Lloyd tapped the side of his nose. 'All I'm saying is, you take after me, you do. I've always said you should have studied at the bar.' He laughed at his own joke, repeating the words softly, then aimed at Dai again. 'Time you had money from that woman.'

Nonplussed, Dai looked at him blankly. Suddenly it dawned on him that Lloyd was talking about his ex-wife. 'Karen. The house is up for sale and I'll get my share of the profits – if there are any.'

'Like your share of the furniture.' Village gossip had informed Dai's family of Karen's house clearance and the dubious nature of a strange Englishman who had helped her (who had used the screwdriver, thought Dai, when Lloyd berated him for his unmanly indifference). Karen had ceased to be 'poor Karen' from that time.

'It's only things.'

'This farm's only things. Have you talked money with your Dad?'

Dai thought ruefully that his father was only too aware of the financial implications of being reported to the Ministry. 'He's too proud to take help. I'm slipping rent to Mam but she's wary of what he thinks.'

'Why don't you farm yourself?' Lloyd was keen to see the family farm passed down to the next generation and Dai was equally keen to avoid the commitment.

'Vet's a full-time job, Grandad. Isn't your programme on TV now?'

Lloyd acknowledged no tangents but his own. 'Your house profits would buy a few cows.'

'I need somewhere to live.' The words rolled emptily from Dai's tongue and he knew they were true. He'd been living day to day, wishing for a future with Helen but never considering where. Now he had no one to live with but he couldn't stay here. Especially after what he was about to do to his father.

'You're all right here 'til you fix up a place with that woman.' (Helen this time). 'Or there again, she could live here too. The money'd come in useful.' Dai smiled at the image of Helen as dutiful daughter-in-law, living with him in his boyhood bedroom. His instinctive physical response made him shift uncomfortably and lingered cruelly long after he had reminded himself that Helen was over; soon he would be over Helen.

'I'll keep it in mind. I'm a bit tired now. Goodnight Grandad.'

'You're always tired. Your Dad's the same. I don't see anyone these days,' grumbled Lloyd.

Dai sat on the bedside chair, sucking the end of a pen, with a pad of blank paper resting on the confiscated Herd Record Book on his lap. Three screwed-up balls of paper lay by his feet and he was starting his fourth rough draft of his letter to the Ministry. He thought of the surname at the foot of the letter. They would realise he was reporting his own father. No they wouldn't; there would be the bland address of the surgery and there were millions of Evanses in Wales. The surname his father had passed on would protect his son's anonymity in this act of betrayal. He must stop this emotional self-torture; keeping quiet would be the real act of betrayal. He started the letter in his mind.

Dear Enemy whose only concern is political gain,
My Dad cheated to evade a stupid law. I'm a vet so I have
to tell you. You've already screwed him out of all he's
worked himself to the bone for all his life. When you get this
letter you'll place his herd under movement restriction.
There will be no sales, no compensation, no farm.

Dai stared bleakly at the blank page and told himself that
a farmer had transgressed the law. His pen traced black on
white, the cold truth – or the official way of seeing it – as
indelible in effect as the ink in the Record Book. His father
had met government regulations in this respect at least.

Dear Sir/Madam,
I regret to inform you of an infringement of the laws
regarding the Keeping of Livestock Records. Mr William
Evans of Brynglas Farm, Mynydd Sylen, attempted to
mislead the above veterinary practice by presenting a
forged Herd Record Book in which ages were four months
younger than in the duplicate true Record which he
maintained secretly. This could have led to

Dai broke off and sucked his pen again. This could have
led to the farm surviving a crisis, to renewed closeness
between father and son (if he hadn't found out), to virtually
anything except an increased risk of BSE. He refused to
support the law his father had broken, but he still had a duty to
report the breach. The fifth sheet of paper ended up in shreds
on the floor and at this stage there was a gentle knock on the
bedroom door. Dai answered his mother's discreet call.

'Come on in. I'm decent.' He gathered up the paper balls
and tucked them under his pillow with the Herd Record Book.
He lounged on the bed and let his mother sit on the chair
beside him, her back stiff and upright, her faded skirt clashing
with her home-knitted cardigan. She held an envelope which
she twisted as she spoke, without seeming aware of it.

'I'm glad you and your Dad are getting to know each other again. He doesn't show it – you know him – but he's missed you the last couple of years. It lifted my heart seeing the two of you today.'

'I'm sorry.'

'No, there's nothing to be sorry for. Children grow.' Dai thought of just how much there was to be sorry for, but he couldn't speak.

'It's just that, now you've seen how things are, and with your Dad asleep – he's not so well tonight, I thought I could talk to you. I need to talk to someone, but I don't want anyone getting the wrong idea.'

Dai would have feigned sleep, drunkenness or insanity to avoid what was coming but it was too late. When his mother found out what he had done, she would regret every word she was sharing with him, but he could think of no way to stop her so he just listened.

'I told you he's not let me do the books for a while. I've been worried, Dai. We've spent a lot on the farm and I listen to the talk. I know there's farmers marching in protest. I know ends won't meet and I know your Dad would do anything for me and the farm. Not in that order,' she acknowledged wryly, 'but we've been together too long to pull apart now. I want to help him but he shuts me out. I don't know what he might think of. And then this came two weeks ago. ' She held out the envelope to Dai. 'I still do the household money, bills and so on.'

Dai looked at the itemised phone bill without taking it in.

'16th June,' she prompted.

He read, '3.15 a.m. 16th June – Samaritans'. 'Dad?' he asked, unnecessarily. She nodded.

'He won't talk to me. He must have talked to them.' Dai tried without success to imagine his taciturn father confiding in a total stranger why he wanted to kill himself,

111

for there was no doubt that nothing less could have led to that phone call.

'Things are always worst at three in the morning, and it was only one call.' He attempted to sound reassuring.

'If I wake in the night and he's not there, I wonder where and when I'll find him.' Her eyes filled. 'I daren't get up and check. It would shame him so, if he's all right. I'm afraid, Dai. If you could talk to him. You're a vet. You understand the pressures. And you're his son too. Stop him doing something he'll regret. With the farm or with himself. I just feel so helpless.'

Dai reached out to hold his mother's hand and could hardly bring the words out. 'I'll do what I can.'

Her tearful thanks were lost against his chest as he hugged her, thinking his back and more would break as he bent over her.

'A trouble shared . . .' She smiled bravely at him as she left the room. He waited until the door had closed before he whispered to himself, 'is a trouble doubled,' and he fished out the various papers from under the pillow. The discarded letters were put into his coat pocket and the Herd Record Book went into the bottom of his overflowing vet's bag. He left no evidence for his mother to add to her store of painful revelations.

Considering the previous week, Friday could be counted a success, Dai thought bitterly. He had avoided decisions on all counts, merely following his feet and his work, eating when it was necessary and sending reassuring signals to his mother. The surgery was processing a batch of bovine certificates the following week, so he had given himself another four days to write the final version of his letter to the Ministry. That meant he need give it no further thought yet. The only point on which he was totally clear was that further thought on any aspect of his private life was to be

112

avoided. Perhaps he should publish a paper on 'Avoidance therapy: survival by waiting.' Some people might use the word procrastination but that was merely a derogatory term invented by the impatient. By counting such philosophical sheep, he eventually managed to fall asleep.

Saturday morning surgery contained its usual mixture; pups for vaccinating, a cat with an ear infection and a rabbit with eczema. Dai waited while the nurse scrubbed the table and called in the next client.

Rather flustered, Sarah held the door to the consulting room half open, as if she were trying to prevent entry rather than encourage it.

'I'm sorry, Mr Evans. This man,' her voice dripped disapproval, 'insisted on seeing you out of turn. He said you would think it important.'

Pushing into the room, past Sarah, came the lanky form of Neil.

7

Jimmy's visit had left Neil feeling more disturbed than he was willing to show. His inability to reach Helen made it worse and the phone call hadn't helped. However strong their friendship, she must be thinking that he had cost her the man she loved. Her friendship was the only constant in his life other than his mother. Neil thought back to Helen's acceptance, almost relief, at discovering he was gay. If only everyone were as open-minded . . .

Neil's mind raced round several mental mazes in search of a solution to what he saw as Helen's problem, but they all required her to speak to Dai and he knew there was no chance of that, partly because she would never betray Neil's secret. However he considered the matter, it was his fault, but it never crossed his mind to explain the truth to Dai himself. His life depended on habitual secrecy regarding his sexuality and, when in Llanelli, he barely acknowledged his homosexuality even to himself. Jimmy's visit had confused the boundaries of his life which Neil preferred to be clearly maintained. He had even become sensitive to the daily homophobia of staffroom and school corridor, which he had shut out for years as not applying to him.

'Hey gay boy,' a fifteen year old had yelled and he had almost turned to answer, observing instead as the lad who was evidently the intended butt of the remark retorted cheerfully, 'Up yours,' which was followed by some wit's muttered 'Beside the sunshine.' The humour was clearly part and parcel of an accepted pattern of behaviour. 'Are you gay or what?' could be a response to a liking for classical music or an unfashionable shirt collar, but the peer reprimand was unmistakeable. Politically correct, Neil promoted tolerance among youngsters, treating them with meticulous politeness, protecting the victim and seeking the soft spot in the bully, never revealing any personal investment in the morality he taught. His detachment was his defence, and had prevented any of the whispered suspicions that he dreaded. Had protected him so far. Neil felt that there were cracks in his identity since Jimmy had brought London to Llanelli, and he was scared. He was having to think rather than respond instinctively and he found the days at work a strain.

Home remained a haven, for all that Jimmy had actually been there. The domestic rituals that ordered his life with his mother had the effect of reducing the small ripple of the visit to one comment. 'I'm glad you helped that young man find Helen,' was his mother's way of saying she accepted whatever versions of events he chose to give her; she accepted him with no need to analyse what that meant.

114

The running of the household depended upon small acts of mutual affection, disguised as fuss. Neil always laid the table for dinner, savouring the laundered smell and texture of the old family linen with the tiny embroidered monogram added by his mother, in the early days of her marriage, to the corners of the napkins. His napkin ring was blue Welsh plaid while hers was pink; each was placed centrally on a rose-rimmed side plate from the dinner service which lived on the dresser. The cruet set was a silverplated wedding gift and matched the butter dish in which Neil's mother carefully placed a slab of the low fat margarine that he considered healthy. Frequently there would be a small posy of flowers at the centre of the dining table and Neil would compliment his mother on the arrangement. She would ask after his day in work and he would ask about the neighbours, the shopping and the cooking. Neil would put his feet up in his study, where his mother would bring him a coffee and leave him to listen to some Mahler or Paganini or whatever matched his mood. Then he would start on his school work, with the low sound of TV soap operas drifting in from the sitting room. Before going to bed, he would spend half an hour with his mother, reading or making notes, either in comfortable silence or chatting occasionally. She would check his plans and shopping needs; he would check on 'little jobs' around the house and say what he would do and when. He had started her on the habit of a glass of Bailey's last thing and their 'Iechyd da' clink of Fifties liqueur glasses, all lurid colours and sharp edges, would be the closing ceremony of the day.

He loved the peace of the old world he shared with his mother, their mellow oak furniture and faded linen. She freed him from household chores so completely that he had no idea whether they had a vacuum cleaner nor where dusters were kept. He was the man of her house and the ceremonies they wove round each other shaped their days. Sitting in the buttoned, leather swivel chair at his desk, he worked on his poetry and listened to Gregorian Chant, thankful that for him at least sanctuary existed. Not even Jimmy's visit could shake his faith in home and he would do nothing to risk his place there.

What changed his mind was a chance remark by a fourteen-year-old boy with dyed blonde hair deeply undercut, who was brought to Neil's classroom by a highly irate History teacher.

'Mr Phillips, I have had enough of John Wrentmore!' Jennie Thomas glared at the youth in question, who slouched against the wall, his head retreating between his shoulders. If a vulture could look hard done by and defiant at the same time, such was the impression made by John, who knew better than to make eye contact and stared fixedly at the floor. His school uniform had been customised by cutting the tie so that a thin jagged edge was level with the buttoned breast pockets of a non-regulation school shirt, which had at least been white once. His appearance was not enhanced by a trickle of blood from his nose and a swollen eye which was already beginning to close. Neil didn't have to ask what had happened; Mrs Thomas was in full flight.

'Instead of waiting sensibly outside my classroom, this thug,' she dripped dramatic contempt, 'was beating up a classmate, presumably for something to do while he waited, going on past history. When I intervened, he told me to mind my own business. I am teaching now, but I'm sure Mr Philips,' she glared balefully at John again, 'will know what to do with you! Take your hands out of your pockets, stand up straight and look at me when I'm talking to you!' She exited with a flounce that created a feeling of unity between Neil and John that he knew he had to resist. In one speech,

116

Jennie had made clear her superiority to both of them. Neil began the painstaking work of finding out the truth and passing a judgement which would support his colleague but also allow John to see a way out of his 'thug' reputation and to believe that the school's 'caring' policy might even apply to him.

Neil remained stern and distant as he asked John into the classroom. 'What happened then, John?' Neil motioned the boy to sit down.

'It's personal, Sir.'

Neil sighed inwardly. The younger ones would grass before you leaned on them, but you had to have the interrogation skills of a top TV detective to crack the older ones. Neil increased the pressure.

'You have been exceptionally rude to a member of staff – don't interrupt – after fighting in the school corridor. If I have to take this to the Head it might very well be the final straw that leads to you being suspended. That would cause more trouble at home, which is not what you want and not what I want. Neither do I want you behaving like a thug.' John winced at Neil's deliberate choice of Mrs Thomas' description. 'You are not a thug,' Neil continued smoothly. 'You are capable of thuggish behaviour and you are capable of great maturity, as you showed in helping Keith overcome his problem with bullying.'

'I didn't think you knew about that, Sir,' muttered John, his cheeks pink.

'I find out about most things,' Neil bluffed, 'which is why I get very annoyed at people wasting my time instead of telling me the truth straight away. I will find out in the end and any punishment is far worse because you've wasted my time.' Neil let the silence grow uncomfortable but although John chewed his lip, he showed no signs of giving the required explanation.

117

Neil sighed obviously. So much of this job was acting. 'Let's make it easy, John. Who were you fighting with? As half your class saw you, I think that should be something you can tell me.'

John recognised the first defeat and knew how quickly it could lead to others. 'Michael Sands, Sir,' he said reluctantly.

'Right. Wait outside the door.' Leaving him to stew for a bit might weaken his resolve and now there was someone else to shed light on the fight. Neil felt there was more to this than met the eye and he was irritated at Mrs Thomas' automatic assumption that John was to blame.

As Neil passed John, the boy said anxiously, 'It was my fault, Sir. Can't we just get on with it?' Neil continued on his way to collect Michael Sands for questioning.

'John has told me all about it, Michael, but I'd like to hear your version,' Neil lied, looking down at a blank sheet of paper and pretending to read back over his notes. 'I like to get the small details correct and to hear both points of view.' Michael looked nervously towards the door but caved in.

'He's been hanging round my girlfriend and the others have told me I need to sort him out. I didn't expect him to go wild when I tapped him.'

'And your girlfriend is . . .?' Neil again looked at the fake notes.

'Ann, Ann Jones 9B.' Neil talked about possessive behaviour, strong feelings taking over and others' right to choose, then sent Michael back to class 'for now.' Something still felt wrong. John might have kept silent at first over a girlfriend matter, but not when he knew that he was one referral away from being suspended. There must be more to it. Either way, Ann Jones could complete the picture and was duly sent for.

Neil contemplated the school profile of Ann Jones, which was unremarkable. He contemplated the thin figure in front of him, displaying two rows of cheap beads above her blouse and thought what an unlikely femme fatale this was. But then, who was he to judge what could light the sexual spark? Forty was no saner than fourteen as far as he could observe, so he treated fourteen-year-old passion with sympathy and understanding.

'Michael and John are in trouble for fighting. It seems that this had something to do with you and I want to make sure it stops now. I might be able to help so tell me about it.' At the open invitation, Ann's eyes filled and she started crying openly. Neil passed over a tissue, from his desk and waited patiently.

'It's my fault but it won't happen again. I'm going out with Michael, see, and he sees John talking private to me, then John won't tell Michael what he's saying, and I'm not saying, so Michael hits him even though we both keep saying we're not going out.'

Neil thought he had understood most of that and couldn't face going through it bit by bit, so he just asked one last question. 'Perhaps you can tell me what you were talking about, that you couldn't just say to Michael.'

The tears came again but she spoke through them, smearing her face with her sleeve. 'John told me he'd seen me taking cigarettes in their shop, and that he wouldn't tell, but if I did it again he'd have to. I knows there's others done it, but it's different when you get caught and the way John said it was like I was stealing from someone I know, you know like someone who needed the money.' A sudden thought struck her and she asked anxiously, 'He didn't say, did he? I don't want no one to know.'

Neil accepted the implicit tribute of trust in him and made a mental note to raise discussions in class about shop-

119

lifting. 'No, he didn't say.' Neil sent the girl off to clean up and return to her class, and called John back into the room.

'Ann told me, about the cigarettes and the shop.'

'You won't say, will you, Sir? She won't do it again.'

'No, I won't say. You know you could have told Michael and kept yourself out of trouble.' The boy remained silent. 'You know you could have explained it to me and put the blame on Michael. You could have been suspended.'

John shrugged and looked Neil straight in the eye for the first time. He shrugged that all-purpose adolescent shrug . . . 'Friends, innit? Take what comes. You'd do the same, Sir.' Dismissed 'for now', the young hero loped out into the corridor, his head retreating morosely into his shoulders and his hair covering all expression. Neil felt exhausted, having spent an hour untangling the situation. All that remained now was to mete out some standard punishment, such as detention, to the two boys, even-handedly, and to pacify Mrs Thomas. He also had four hours teaching plus any other crises of the day, before he could sit in his study and think. He knew that 'You'd do the same, Sir,' had determined a course of action his subconscious had already considered and rejected. Like a gutsy fourteen year old but with more communication skills, he would visit Dai and explain how he had misread Neil's relationship with Helen. *Friends innit*, he shrugged to himself. *I'll take what comes.* He'd re-route a love affair that was meant to be and hope the cost was no more than a black eye.

Neil had phoned in advance to check that Mr Evans would be taking Saturday morning surgery, and had timed his visit for the end of the hour, when he assumed it would be quiet. He had not bargained on the packed waiting room, which looked as if it would take another hour to process. At first he sat patiently, after giving his name, and let the conversation flow round him. One large lady in a floral print, who was clutching a cardboard box with air holes in it, took responsibility for gathering as much information as possible about those around her.

'Poisoned,' was the terse reply when she asked an unshaven man in overalls what was wrong with the Doberman lying beside him. 'One of the neighbours it must be. All these stories on telly making them think he's not safe. Nearly better now, aren't you King?' The roughened hands stroked the silky black ears and the dog's tail gave a half-hearted wag in response. The man's eyes darkened. 'It'll happen again.' Mrs Floral cooed embarrassed sympathy and was about to satisfy her curiosity with regard to a labrador pup, when a man standing at the counter turned towards them and spoke.

'Ground sheep,' he pronounced. 'That's what started the cows off. There's no telling what's in animal fodder – or pet fodder.' He pointed significantly at the Doberman, which gave the sort of rumble that on a healthier day could be construed as serious disagreement. 'It's God's justice, that's what it is. Punishment for sinners and the animals will suffer for the sins of the masters. The world will be cleansed of wickedness and the day is upon us. Only the pure in heart will escape AIDS and the righteous will be saved.'

'That'll be three pounds for the tablets, Mr Graham.' As Mr Graham paid his three pounds to the nurse, who seemed unaffected by his tirade, there was a collective shuffle of embarrassment among the others in the waiting room. Mrs Floral turned to Neil, who decided he'd had enough and headed towards the consulting room door, which was opening for the next client. Nerves on edge from rehearsing his speech and from waiting, Neil brushed past the nurse who was trying to call the name of the next patient.

Once in the consulting room, Neil pushed the door shut

121

behind him, despite some resistance from the nurse, and faced Dai. He saw that the expression on Dai's face was exactly as it had been when he had last seen it picked out by Helen's porch light.

'I'm sorry I had to come here but we must talk you've got it wrong about Helen and I wouldn't have come here if I didn't think I could put you right. Damn, I sound like the kids.' Neil smiled ruefully and wondered where the prepared speech had gone. At least the aggressive set of the jaw opposite him had softened marginally.

'Hey, it was my turn and this one jumped the queue.' Neil was pushed from behind by a brown mongrel coming through the door with an indignant owner in tow.

Dai took charge. 'Sorry Mrs Weston, but I need to see Mr . . .?'

'Philips,' Neil murmured.

'Mr Philips. This won't take long, so if you'd just sit down again . . .? Sarah, give us a minute will you?' Sarah sniffed and left.

'I'm listening.' But not for long and not with an open mind, was what Dai's tone said.

Neil steadied himself. 'I'm sorry you misread the situation on Monday. I had asked Helen if I could see someone at her house. It wasn't Helen I was with, it was someone else. You have misjudged Helen. Her feelings for you are very deep and there is no competition.' There. He'd managed enough of his speech to get the point across. He could feel the colour blazing around his neck and he fretted at the already loose collar. The dark, stocky vet whose eyes were level with the blotchy neck stood, considering.

At last he spoke, making the sort of eye contact that Neil thought would have been more appropriate for the Doberman in the waiting room. 'So why didn't she tell me that? *If* it's true.'

122

Because she wouldn't betray my secret. Neil stammered, 'I suppose she was annoyed at you jumping to conclusions.'

'I don't know what you're up to but it doesn't make sense. Of course I jumped to conclusions. She made it clear she was entitled to screw whoever she wanted to.' Dai spat out the words. 'If you've had enough of her, you've come to the wrong man. I don't want your leftovers Mr Philips. You really expect me to believe that a man your age and intelligence would take a girl to another girl's house to sleep with her! Get out.' His voice had dropped but the movement towards Neil suggested a barely contained urge to hit out.

Neil backed a step, looked at the floor and thought of John Wrentmore. He could barely get the words out for the tightness of his throat. 'It wasn't a girl. It was a man.' At least it had stopped Dai's advance, Neil thought bitterly, watching the instinctive flicker of disgust that accompanied the recoil.

'A man?' As if he were saying, 'a worm, a toad, a slimy thing'.

Neil's nerves vanished as uncontrollably as they had affected him. There was no going back now. He would not have chosen this stereotype of Llanelli man as a confidante and he wondered what Helen saw in her lover, but he would never be diminished by ignorance and prejudice.

'A man.' He met Dai's eyes. 'Clearly, being gay has disadvantages in Llanelli society, so I prefer not to make it an issue. That's why Helen wouldn't tell you the truth. To protect me.'

Dai said nothing.

'I would appreciate it if you could be as discreet as Helen.' That was the understatement of the year. Neil tried not to consider the consequences of Dai lacking 'discretion'. 'You might find this helpful.' Neil spoke very

123

quietly but with authority and Dai took the piece of paper handed to him. He couldn't read the French words and looked up, puzzled.

Neil pronounced them. 'J'ai besoin de toi pour vivre – To be alive, I need you.'

'Cabrel,' both men said together.

Dai dropped the paper on the table. 'I've listened to the songs often enough so I should know the words. But this is something from you, not from me. I have my own words thank you.'

'She's angry. She'll know I've seen you and that will make her listen to you.' He spoke with no emphasis, in the same quiet tones. 'She respects me and will assume that you do.' With nothing more to say, Neil left. As he walked through the unnaturally quiet waiting room, he was aware that the collection of pets and owners would have sensed the atmosphere if not picked up parts of Dai's comments. He smiled, said softly 'J'ai gardé toujours mon panache,' and briefly considered introducing Cyrano de Bergererac to John Wrentmore. Sunlight hit him as he stepped into the street and it was with a sense of doors opening that he closed the shabby one to the waiting room firmly behind him.

'Next please, Sarah.'

'Mrs Weston couldn't wait. It's Mrs Jones.'

'I've been waiting three quarters of an hour out there . . .'

'Yes, I'm sorry, Mrs Jones but emergencies do arise and I'm sure you'd want us to consider Timmy first in the same situation. Now, what can we do for Timmy?'

'I don't know quite how to say this but I think he must have some kind of rash on his privates. He keeps rubbing himself against the furniture,' her voice lowered, 'and against me.'

Dai kept a straight face, enlightened Mrs Jones and survived the morning's surgery.

124

Some routine calls during the afternoon gave Dai plenty of time to think about the visit from Neil and its implications. He believed what he'd heard, although there were details of the story which seemed implausible. Why was Neil taking a boyfriend (again the instinctive revulsion over which it seemed he had no control) to Helen's house? Dai's imagination balked at the thought of Helen providing a venue for casual homosexual relationships. This was foreign territory and Dai found it equally difficult to imagine the quiet, sensitive teacher abusing his friendship with Helen to vent his unnatural passions. Dai considered himself to be tolerant but he preferred to keep the idea of homosexuality at a distance. His instincts had been obvious and – let's be honest – downright rude, never mind prejudiced. Dai felt that his own behaviour in the last week had shown more in common with Mrs Jones's Timmy than with civilised man.

Where were all his careful opinions? His beliefs on equality and tolerance? When it came to real people, his lover and her friend, his instincts were not just basic, they were base. He bitterly regretted his lack of control and his lack of reason, acknowledging the Timmy in him which even now gave the physical response of shame as a sour, iron taste – like geraniums, he thought. Finally, he thought of Helen, and the shame was replaced with salutary speed by the hope that he might still have a place in her life. He unfolded the little piece of paper Neil had given him, thought a while, then drove to a shop where he could buy a greetings card.

At seven o'clock, Helen responded wearily and with irritation to the doorbell, expecting some local salesman. Her fears were confirmed by the envelope shoved through the letter box, but at least, she thought with relief, whoever it was had gone. She didn't even glance at the envelope as she threw it in the wastepaper bin and sat down once more with a novel. An hour later, a four-wheel drive moved off its parking space outside Helen's house, unnoticed by her amid the noise of the television soap opera she had turned on to pass the long empty hours of the evening. After the news at ten, Helen crunched her way through an apple and aimed it idly at the bin, missing. She drifted over to pick it up and noticed the writing on the envelope already sinking under bits of the evening's debris. The one word 'Helen' had her grabbing tissues and bits of fruit peel to rescue the envelope and extract the slightly stained card, with a still life on the front and an additional arrow and label saying 'Kidwelly Show', attached to the French arrangement of cheese, preserves and wine on a chequered cloth. She smiled but her hands were shaking as she opened the card to read the handwritten message. 'Neil told me *j'ai besoin de toi*, but I already knew that. Please let me say sorry in person. I'll wait outside. If you change your mind, ever,' and then there was the phone number Helen had called once before. She rushed to the window but the street outside her house was empty. It was a bit late to phone. She sat chewing her fingernails, picked up the phone twice and put it down again, decided to go to bed and then watched her index finger dialling the number on the card.

An unknown woman's voice with a strong Welsh accent gave the number.

'I'm sorry to phone so late but is Dai there?'

'You'll be Helen, then,' the voice had more than a hint of complicity. Helen heard the call, 'Dai, it's Helen for you.' She heard scurrying noises, a thump (furniture falling?), Dai's voice in the distance 'Oh bugger – sorry Mam. Tell her I'm on my way' and then a door slam. Footsteps returned.

'He said to tell you he's on his way.' The message was repeated as primly as a little girl repeating her parents'

126

instructions but was followed by an independent verdict. 'And he's acting like there's ten cows all bearing down. I hope you'll tell him to take more care on the roads.'

'I will,' seemed the safest response.

'And it would be lovely to meet you some time.' The voice was wistful. 'Tell Dai I said to bring you over.'

'I will.'

'You mind and tell him now. 'Bye then.'

'Thank you. Er, goodbye.'

Helen was confused when Dai did not reach out to her and kiss her the moment he appeared in her hallway. She didn't know of his soul-searching and self-condemnation for lack of control. Indeed, she found it surprisingly cool as the first moment of a reunion.

'Come on in,' she invited him, awkwardly.

'Thank you.' Each of them sat down, taking sneaky side glances at the other and then looking away. They both spoke at the same time, laughed nervously and then Dai tried again.

'I love you, but I haven't thought enough about what you want. All I could imagine was someone else touching you and I couldn't bear that.' Helen tried to interrupt but he carried on, 'I know what you're going to say. I know what it must have been like for you, me being married. If you feel the same way that is . . .?' Then he paused and waited.

'It's not as simple as that.'

'It never is with you.'

'I knew you were married. It was accepted. The feelings came despite that, and I could accept anything except knowing you were free and hadn't told me. Like it didn't matter. Like I didn't matter. And then the unfairness of what you thought about Neil and I was only helping him. I can't believe he told you. He must have seen he could trust you. It would kill him if people knew. His job, his life here . . . he did explain all that to you, didn't he?'

127

'Yes,' Dai lied, realising the extent of the risk Neil had taken, for friendship. 'He's a remarkable man.'

'The two of you would like each other. You will be careful in what you say, so no one thinks differently about him . . .'

'Gossiping about another man's sex life is not my style.'

'No, but, inadvertently . . . a flippant comment?'

'I promise. Neil will have no reason to regret telling me.' Dai felt the weight of Neil's enforced trust uncomfortable to carry. His promise at least made some attempt to repay the debt.

'He's a special friend.'

'I know that now, but that's not how it looked.'

As he tried to explain how his feelings had taken over, how he understood what she must think of him, Helen crossed the room and knelt at his feet, circling him in her arms and reaching up until she could interrupt him with kisses. His response left her in no doubt of the spark between them but he still let her lead. She started to enjoy the challenge of teasing him up a more active response and she let her hands slip under his shirt, loosening his belt, easing him out of his clothes, taking her time. Whatever moves she made, he partnered her, held her, responded to her, but always letting her take control. She revelled in the new game, riding the waves of his compressed energy, releasing them both gradually to a warm, sleepy closeness that dropped them quickly into actual sleep.

Dai was the first to stir, woken by pins and needles in his right arm, and his movements disturbed Helen. She grabbed his sweatshirt which was lying among the clothes strewn on the floor.

'Hey – what about me?' he tugged on the sweatshirt but she had already slipped it over her shoulders.

'What happened to all that New Man sensitivity?' she teased.

'If you want to appreciate it again, you'd better keep me warm.' He reached out to her, feeling up the sleeve of his own sweatshirt to find and hold her hands.

'Coffee?' she asked

'There are more imaginative ways of keeping warm,' he grumbled, 'like wearing clothes.'

She escaped, returning in her own jumper. 'Here.' she threw him the sweatshirt and they collected items of clothing from where they had landed. Her pop socks looked like used black condoms, wrinkled and abandoned, and their underwear had become impossibly tangled. They tidied, laughed and drank coffee.

'We need somewhere to live.'

'I have somewhere to live.'

'We'll talk about it in the morning.'

'Did I invite you to stay 'til the morning?'

'Yes, I think you did.'

'What side of the bed do you sleep on?'

'The left.'

'What side of the bed do you sleep on?'

'The left.'

'Toss you for it.'

'Mmm.' And so he stayed the night.

8

There was no room for the increasing numbers of Dai's socks appearing in Helen's drawers, or on Helen's bedside chair or indeed on the floor. She considered herself to be reasonably tidy, with emphasis on the 'reason'. She thought it a sign of anal fixation to have 'a place for everything and everything in its place', but she liked clutter to be limited in

129

amount and setting. What it came down to was that she liked her clutter to be in her places; a little pile of knitting patterns on a low table, her hand-washed woollens in a basket in the kitchen, a selection of herbs on the kitchen worktop. Alien objects jarred upon her senses; apart from the ubiquitous socks, there would be an electric razor plugged into a kitchen socket, newspapers covering her knitting designs, peanut butter (which she hated) oozing its rancid smell into the living room, where it had been abandoned without a lid. On one occasion, Helen had retrieved a dubious item from a vase of flowers. She had speechlessly offered it to Dai, who had grinned and said, 'My castrating tool. I wondered where that had got to.'

She had rashly pursued the issue. 'How did it end up pretending to be a carnation?'

'Oh, I was rinsing the blood off. Must have got distracted. Good job you found it, the rust is starting,' and he had cheerfully disappeared to grease both the instrument and part of the kitchen, where he could be heard singing very loud love songs.

Technically, they were not living together. In reality, Dai had spent most non-working hours of the last fortnight at Helen's house, only putting in a token appearance at the farm to pat the dogs, collect some clothes and make brief contact with his mother. Everyday chores had all become either honeymoon fun or impossibly difficult, requiring lengthy discussions as to who did what and how. Dai was happy to wash their clothes but to do so, he had to ask Helen where the washing powder was, what setting on the washing machine each item needed, whether something ought to be washed separately or by hand . . . Dai was happy to cook a basic meal but then surgery overran by an hour and it turned out that he had forgotten to get the planned packet meal out of the freezer to thaw. Without everyday routine, life was unpredictable, exciting and exhausting. Helen had been woken by emergency calls in the middle of the night and drifted back to sleep, only to be roused again by Dai on his return. Pleasurable as it was to respond to the urgent pressure of his body, still cool from the night air, the disruption to Helen's habitual sleeping patterns was affecting her concentration during the day. Her body ached from indulging sexual greed, her brain ached from sharing decisions, and she prayed it would never end.

Their first trip together to a supermarket was undertaken in a spirit of discovery. After the discussion of which supermarket came the writing of the list. This they forgot and left behind, along with the three plastic carrier bags which Helen considered indispensable to the future of the planet. The car, which Dai took for granted, enabled them to use a trolley for a bigger shopping load than Helen had risked for years, being limited to what she could carry, and used to catering for one. Having selected the medium-sized trolley with a long basket at waist height and a shelf underneath, they made slow progress along each aisle, pausing to discuss the merits of different varieties of apple, considering the effect of EEC legislation and trade restrictions on the range of fresh produce; pausing again to calculate the comparative value for money of different length toilet rolls, taking softness into consideration; pausing yet again to disagree over the virtues of butter (Dai's choice) as opposed to low-fat spread (Helen's choice). Disagreement was resolved with brief kisses, to the irritation of more businesslike shoppers whose path was blocked.

Such minor, optional decisions seemed speedy compared with the protracted debate over meals for the forthcoming week as they selected the ingredients. It was miraculous that they preferred the same brand of toothpaste; it was

131

disappointing that he was so keen on peanut butter. Every shared taste seemed a signal from the gods; every difference a source of wonder.

Weary from their shopping mileage, they treated themselves to coffee and a stodgy bun in the supermarket café.

'What's the time?'

'Eight o'clock.'

Helen looked at him, horrified. 'We've been in here for three hours!'

'Why, how long do you usually take?'

'Half an hour at most! What about you?'

Dai looked a bit sheepish. 'I haven't been shopping that often.'

'Exactly how often is not that often?' She looked at him sharply, suspicions growing.

'Well, Karen used to do all that sort of thing. It's been a long time . . .'

'I don't believe it. You're just playing, aren't you? And the hoovering? The dusting? Cleaning the bathroom?'

'I've seen it done. Nothing to it.' He grinned at her. 'I don't know what Karen and my mother always complained about. It's good fun once you get a rhythm going. And this shopping stuff is great.'

She groaned. 'You're not even house-trained. What am I going to do?'

'Marry me.' He reached for her hand across the stained plastic table.

She stroked the back of his hand lightly but turned the conversation. 'I'm not sure I can cope with someone who thinks Mr Muscle Oven Cleaner is a contractor who carries out the job in person.'

Desperately trying to cram all the items which had seemed a good idea at the time into her three kitchen

132

cupboards, Helen considered the downside of Dai moving into her house. Which brought her back to the socks.

Curled up beside him on the settee, she raised the issue as delicately as she could.

'Do you think we could do with . . . perhaps we could . . . you know, we need some more cupboard space, for you to put your things in . . . your own space.'

'I knew you'd agree with me.' She had learnt to worry about that particular expression. 'We need somewhere we've chosen together. We'll go out looking for a house. Somewhere that suits us,' the addition was just loud enough for her to hear, 'and the dogs.'

She panicked. 'But this is my place – I like it here.'

His hands worked on the back of her neck. 'Those muscles are tense. Our luck's in. I think there's a buyer for the old place.' A thought struck him. 'I take it you don't want to buy Karen out and live there?'

'It's too fast, I can't think about it, I don't know . . .'

The dexterity of his hands did not help her think.

'I want to make it work. This is crazy – I make good money as a partner and I want us to have a place that's ours.'

She turned to face the intensity of hazel eyes which dissolved into rings of brown, green and grey the longer she looked. How could you look in your lover's eyes and think? She shook her head to clear it. '*Ours* means you, me, Meatloaf, Janey and Demi?'

'Of course.'

It was the boyish openness of his face which destroyed her defences. He really couldn't imagine not getting what he wanted and she couldn't imagine clouding his happiness. 'We can look.' Nestling in his arms, she heard 'forever' promised and she shivered. 'Nothing,' she told him, 'it's nothing.'

133

'I want to share everything with you. Why don't you come to the surgery, spend an afternoon there, see my work?'

She demurred. 'I've got work of my own, and anyway I'd be in the way.'

'No, you wouldn't. We have students on work placements and David's teenage children haunt the place – visitors are OK. Besides which, you're with me.' The fierce pride in his voice made her smile.

'All right, perhaps once. How about Tuesday afternoon, when I've shut shop?'

'There we are then.'

She laughed at the local idiom, he took mock umbrage and serious discussion was once again postponed, indefinitely.

So it was that on a Tuesday afternoon, with the shop closed, Helen forced open the heavy surgery door through which Neil had exited so recently with his panache intact. She was curious to see Dai's workplace but she also felt like a little girl starting school, not sure where to go or what to say. She had been told to ask for Dai at the counter but she disobeyed instructions and read the notice board first. 'Flufy kittens' wanted 'good homes', 'Ragamuffin Tilbury' was 'available for stud' and there must be 'payment on the occasion of treatment'. This was the world which used Dai's expertise and bag of tools, and although she told herself that he would be equally lost in discussion of knitting designs, she felt diminished.

The girl behind the desk, severe in standard overall and square-cut fringe, queried her business.

Helen smiled too much and said, 'I'm expected. Mr Evans, the vet . . .?'

'I see.' The lips were compressed firmly. The nurse walked through to invisible quarters where she could be heard saying, 'There's a lady to see you, Mr Evans,' in a carefully neutral tone. The relief of hearing Dai's welcoming 'Hi' with accompanying hug, prevented Helen turning on her heel, but only just.

'What's wrong?'

'I feel out of place.'

'It's just new, that's all. Come on through.' He led her through a consulting room to a maze of what had been Georgian downstairs rooms and were now a surgery, a room with clippers and hairdryer, a scruffy utility room smelling of wet dog and disinfectant, and finally, a room with caged animals.

'This is Lucky.' Dai opened a large cage to stroke a dog. 'He's had a leg amputated after a car accident.' The dog shivered as Dai stroked him, its rib cage clearly visible.

Helen reached out a tentative hand and stroked the brown fur along the little rolls of fat where Lucky's neck was curved towards her. Doleful brown eyes gazed up. 'Is he cold? He's terribly thin.'

Dai smiled. 'He's a whippet. They do feel the cold but they tend to shiver with nerves or excitement – he's just reacting to the strange place and the aftereffects of the operation. The reason they're fast is because of that big rib cage and lithe body – like a small greyhound – it's normal for the breed.'

'How will he manage without his leg? Wouldn't it be kinder to put him to sleep?' Helen hated even saying the words.

'You'd be surprised how well he'll manage on three legs. I'm not saying he'll win races, but he'll be up and about in no time. After all, that's one more leg than I have!' Dai continued with the history of each animal, and although Helen couldn't share his enthusiasm for a rare case of wet eczema – there was no temptation to stroke the pink, oozing skin – she was gaining a clearer understanding of what his work involved.

'You seem more concerned with the neatness of the surgery than the recovery of the patient,' she observed drily after listening to a lengthy account of a tricky search through a dog's intestines for a swallowed needle.

'If the surgery's good enough, the patient will recover,' was the dismissive reply. 'We've time to go out on a call before surgery. Do you fancy piglets?' He took her bemused silence for assent, yelled 'I'm off to see Gardener's pigs,' and paced off towards a back door, with Helen and Demi trailing behind him. Well trained, Demi jumped through the opened driver's door into the back; Helen waited bemused by the unlocked passenger door until Dai pushed it open from inside. 'Come on – what are you waiting for?' This professional whirlwind was a new side to him and she had little option but to do as she was told.

Even Helen had to admit that green was what the Welsh countryside did best, and the greens of late summer unrolled through hedgerows, fields and the old Strade woods as they drove the high road west, parallel with the coastline and looking down on glimpses of sea to the left. The Gardeners' farm was sheltered from northeast winds, tucked at the foot of a hill, with a view across the sea to the Gower. Dai strode off to the barn, with its patched, corrugated iron roof, but Helen couldn't resist pausing to look before chasing off after him.

In a corner strewn with straw lay a sow, suckling her young. Helen counted. Ten, no, eleven piglets. Instinct made her reach out to pick one up but she didn't have to be told not to disturb an animal with its young and her hands dropped back to her sides.

'I thought they were dirty and ugly!'

'You ask a farmer and he'll tell you they've the brains of

136

a dog and the brawn of a bull. Isn't that right, Mr Gardener?'

The darkness of the barn in contrast to the bright sunshine outside had prevented Helen from seeing the dark shape of the man crouched beside the pig.

'They know what's what. They know what side their bacon's fried.' The farmer wheezed with throaty laughter.

Helen winced at the tasteless remark and was grateful when Dai got to the point.

'What's the problem then?'

'They're suckling all the time but they never seem to get enough. They're not gaining weight like they should and the mother's getting tired and bad-tempered.' Helen wondered how you could tell when a sow became bad-tempered, but she didn't risk asking. Dai picked up a piglet and squeezed its tummy, then placed it back on a teat. He carried out some more squeezing, then delivered his verdict.

'Mum's run down and the milk's thinning. The piglets are hungry, so they're suckling more, she gets more tired and it's a vicious circle. I can't see any signs of milk fever or blocked teats – nothing nasty at all. I'll give Mum a vitamin supplement – mash this in her food once a day.' Dai pulled odd packets out of his bag while he spoke. 'And here's some milk supplement to break the cycle – give it to the piglets four times a day for the next couple of days, then reduce it to twice a day as Mum picks up a bit. That should keep everyone going until they start solids.'

'I was hoping that would be all, but you always wonder. I expect you'll be charging an arm and a leg again?' The farmer looked sharply at Dai, who just smiled good-humouredly.

'A lot less than the price of a piglet, Mr Gardener. I won't be retiring to the Bahamas for a while yet.'

137

'I don't suppose you know someone who'd take a donkey?'

'You can put an ad in the surgery – we don't charge for that. Why, got one for sale?'

'Not for sale, for giving. The boy's left home now and he's making a living in these damn computer things. Talks a foreign language when he does come home. Anyway, there's no chance of him taking on the farm and we've enough to do without looking after his pet. Morgan's ten year old, soft with kids and only digs his heels in with someone who don't know better.'

'I'll ask around for you. He's with horses now?'

'Yeah, bit of company like.'

Helen couldn't not ask. 'What will you do if you can't find a home?'

'Dog food,' was the laconic reply.

Dai covered the silence quickly with a cheery goodbye that got them into the car before Helen turned on him.

'Do something! He means it – he'll have that poor animal killed, or he'll do it himself.' Her eyes widened. 'he'll probably shoot it, or club it to death, or … or poison it!'

'Wouldn't be any use for pet food then.' Helen looked furiously at him. 'OK, OK, although a legal point which might interest you is that you shouldn't even bury an animal with medication in it, never mind pass it on for food, to avoid polluting the food chain.' He added hastily, 'Or which might not interest you. Seriously, that's a farmer, Helen. His livelihood is growing a crop – a live crop. He'll look after them, he'll even love them, but at the end of the day they're producers that have to earn their keep, and some of them are dinner. Lamb chops don't grow in Tesco's, you know.'

Helen cooled down. 'I do know. It's just . . .'

'I know. Everyone who works at the surgery has succumbed at least once to the 'Save it' urge. Sarah – the nurse you met – talks hard enough, but she has a dalmation with one ear who was brought in to be put down and went home with her.'

'What about you?'

'Sentimentality about animals is no good when you're working with them,' Dai pontificated and then relented. 'How do you think I got Meatloaf?'

'Go on. How?'

'He was a Christmas puppy, all paws. Posh family too – he's a pedigree. They did it right, had him vaccinated, wormed. He chewed a bit of furniture, they didn't have time to train him or look after him, the twelve year old had no interest in him, and he just kept growing. Designer dogs are still animals. So they brought him in and said he was too difficult to handle and it would be kinder to everyone to put him to sleep. They left him with me, said it would upset them to watch. Not half as much as it would have upset me to do it. So there we are. You can't adopt them all, though.'

Helen felt a little more cheerful, but the evening surgery presented even more ethical dilemmas, until she thought her head would burst. She stood silently, listening to the consultations while Sarah shot her grim sideways glances. Inbetween clients, Dai would feed her extra snippets of information, often turning her assumptions inside out. The man in dirty, torn denims and shabby jumper, who brought in a malnourished Jack Russell with scabby patches on its face, had rescued the dog and was pouring money into getting it back to health. A lady in pearls and tweed jacket argued with Dai when he advised her not to breed her Scottish terrier a fourth time. Dai explained that the size of heads in the breed would inevitably mean another, probably fatal, Caesarian section. The breeder merely told Dai what the puppies were worth and told him she could always change vet.

As she flounced out, Helen muttered, 'Good riddance if she does change vet.'

139

Dai shook his head. 'Whatever she decides, someone has to look after her poor bitch.'

'How come Scotties have such big heads then? Surely, if it's so difficult to produce them, evolution will sort it out.'

'Humans counter evolution and if the Breed Standard gives prizes for big heads, then the breeders will go for the rosettes, however many dogs suffer.'

'That's sick.'

'Next please.' And so the evening continued. Two yobbos in chains and leathers carried in a swan they'd found at the Water Park, distressed and tangled up in a fishing line. They promised they'd come back the next day to check how it was; a golden retriever puppy in for vaccination made everyone smile by widdling with excitement all over the table, wagging its entire hind quarters with its feathery little tail, clearly expecting – and getting – plenty of attention. Helen was finding it increasingly difficult to control the urge to intervene, to offer money to someone unsure whether she could afford the necessary operation, or to provide a home for the seven mongrel pups found by the railway line and sent on to the Dogs' Home. Her head was aching by the time the last client came in to the consulting room, and when she shut her eyes for relief, she could see a small figure in a long white dress, outlined in the too-bright light of migraine, mutely accusing her of standing by, watching, doing nothing. She opened her eyes with an effort, blinking into the middle of the consultation.

'I can't do it, I tried.' A middle-aged woman with badly permed, highlighted greying hair, was crying as she spoke, unconsciously stroking the wrinkled roly-poly bodies of five furry rats. No, wrong shape. Imagine fur growing and covering the little whipping tails, smug mouths, round faces and whiskers – kittens.

'It's a terrible strain.' Dai was sympathetic. 'As you

140

know, it's two-hourly feeds, day and night, at this age, and no guarantee they'll come through it. Perhaps it's better if . . .?'

'I was hoping you'd know of a foster mother?'

Dai shook his head. 'I'm really sorry but I can't help.'

'It's all that's left of Tibby, but I just can't keep it up. There's only me and I've got the baby to think of, plus the two little ones. I've got to put them first. It'll have to be. I knew that when I came here. But I don't want them to suffer.'

'They won't.' Sarah started bustling around getting a syringe and little glass jars, as the woman turned to go, with one last stroke.

'No.' Helen's voice seemed loud, even to herself, and she tried to control it. 'Would you let me try? I can feed them, I'll try to keep them going. Would you have them back then, if I manage it?'

There was not enough control to say more than, 'Please. Oh yes, please.'

Dai smoothly took control. 'We'll give it a try, Mrs Rees, and I'll let you know how they're doing. I can't make promises, you know.'

'Thank you.' The weary face shone and as she went into the waiting room Helen caught a glimpse of two children swinging their feet and looking miserable, minding a pram. Even as she watched, their faces changed and they waved goodbye to the 'nice lady' who was going to try to save Tibby's kittens.

'Have you any idea what you've taken on?'

'She will soon,' said Sarah with a grimace. 'When I started here, I was forever feeding babies until I was like the walking dead. Still, it's worth it.' Her hand rested encouragingly on Helen's arm and suggested that for all her brusque manner, Sarah would be an ally.

141

Helen looked at the precious basket of warm bodies, noting the hot-water bottle peeking out from the fleece, and wondered just what she had got herself into.

'How did Tibby die?'

'Run over. Unusual looking cat, one green eye and one brown, with a purr like a Rolls Royce.'

'Right then. Give me the full instructions and the hardware. I'll take them into work with me during the day, so I'm going to need a closed basket in case they reach the crawling stage too quickly.'

'But you've never looked after animals. How are you going to manage?'

'Babies are babies.' She spoke without thinking, reaching out to touch the soft prickles of young fur, intent on her new responsibility.

He let the remark pass without comment.

For the next two weeks, Helen's nights and days were punctuated by mewing, two hours stretching to three-hour intervals as the kittens' bellies slowly filled out. Exhaustion quickly reached the stage beyond sleep, and there was more than one occasion on which Dai quietly nursed the kittens as he went to or from a call-out, saving Helen an interruption to the snatches of sleep she managed. He watched the stubborn determination with which she learnt to use her little finger to start a kitten suckling, then make it latch on to the pipette. He watched her despair as the kitten's too-big head rolled towards the movement and warmth of her hand, away from the life-giving milk; her patience as she ensured the kitten had taken in enough milk, and as she repeated the same long process five times and then again two hours later. He watched the mixture of pain, longing and love which flickered across her tired face, and her vulnerability touched him.

'Look – their eyes have opened.' She was just home from

142

work, carrying the inevitable cat basket, her eyes shining with excitement. 'They're all going to have blue eyes.'

He shook his head. 'No, sorry, but you won't know till they're about twelve weeks and the colour changes – or of course stays blue, though that's not likely. We still need to be careful to keep them out of bright light for a while.'

'Oh.' She shook off the minor disappointment. 'Still, you can really see them coming on now. Cashmere has such a pretty coat – there are so many colours and it's so soft.' Dai did not point out that the kitten Helen had named Cashmere was a run-of-the-mill bog-standard tabby; perhaps Helen was right and if you saw what was ordinary with fresh eyes, you realised how beautiful it was.

The relief for Helen (and by association, Dai) was intense when the kittens started mixed feeding. The need for night feeding diminished and the preceding month faded into a vague memory of crying, feeding, waking, worrying and feeling responsible for life itself – in a word, parenthood. To celebrate her return to near-normality, Helen phoned Neil and arranged a French lesson-cum-social evening. She had discontinued these of necessity while nursing kittens. Her assumption that Dai would be delighted at the opportunity to renew his acquaintance with Neil was accepted with good grace and hidden, well-founded apprehension. The arrangement was that Dai would arrive at Neil's to collect Helen, but she cheerfully warned him that Neil and his mother were bound to invite him in for a long gossip.

'Fine,' he said, stoically.

Neil's front door was impeccably polished and gleamed with good Welsh housewifery, the brass doorknocker reflecting Dai's gloomy face as he rang the door-bell.

A welcoming smile and a flutter of hands accompanied a warm 'Dewch mewn' from a little woman neat in appearance, from her subtly-tinted grey hair to her low-heeled court shoes, a trace of magenta lipstick suggesting either that she was dressed for a visitor or that she was always ready for one. Either explanation struck him as possible, from the way she carefully hung up his shabby jacket, and told him how pleased she was to meet Helen's 'young man'. His automatic 'Diolch' as he accepted her invitation and entered the house had started them speaking in Welsh and so they continued, with Mrs Philips making the automatic switch to English for Helen's benefit, as she showed Dai into Neil's study.

Dai sank into a deep leather armchair, somewhat awed by the luxury of a room shelved with books, some of them clearly valuable, bound in leather with marbled edges to the paper, and dominated by the grand desk and leather swivel chair, facing the bay window and view across the main road to the park where sunlight threw long shadows from the railings and glinted through the trees. Neil relaxed in another armchair, his long frame fitting the angles of his furniture. Dai squirmed a little more, sitting forward to avoid his legs dangling. He sneaked a look at Helen, but she was no help in suggesting a comfortable posture. She was curled up on the huge leather sofa, shoes off and both legs tucked under her, a small pile of books and half-written notes abandoned on the carpet.

'This'll be the third time you two have met,' Helen said helpfully, prompting.

Dai prayed for the return of Mrs Philips. Mothers, he could chat to. A man who was not Helen's lover because he was homosexual, he could not. In fact, he was expressly forbidden to mention Neil's homosexuality, so that was closed as a topic of conversation – as if, he thought ruefully, it would have helped. Neil not being Helen's lover struck Dai as equally limited in conversational potential. He

144

inspected the carpet, which was not one colour the more you looked at it but made up of tiny flecks of brown, grey and green. He cleared his throat, then both he and Neil spoke at the same time.

'No, after you.'

'It's nothing.' Dai swam in the carpet. 'I was just going to ask how the French lesson went.'

'Very well. Helen has a real feel for the language – and the country.' Neil continued hopefully. 'Are you a Francophile too?'

Dai felt as if he was drowning. 'I'd like to go there,' he tried gamely, 'but I haven't. Been there, I mean.'

Helen's pose was stiffening, and Dai felt he was letting her down without having any idea how to put it right.

'What were you going to say, Neil? Before I interrupted you?' He winced at the unnecessary use of the man's name, like one of those appalling chat shows. *Well, Raymond, you did say, Raymond* . . .

Neil smiled apologetically. 'I was only going to ask how work had gone. Yours, today. Or whenever you were in work.' Dai remembered Neil's only experience of the surgery.

'Busy. Farmers have a lot to complain about at the moment and God knows they moan enough at the best of times. Sometimes it's a relief to work with the pets. You had anything to do with animals?'

'Not first hand.' A pause. 'I enjoy watching the nature programmes on television sometimes.'

If this conversation were an animal, Dai would give it a lethal overdose. Anything that lame was so close to death, killing would be kindness. He half rose from his chair just as the door opened and a tea-tray entered, supported by and half-obscuring Neil's mother. He instinctively moved to help her and responded in Welsh to her ''Paned o de?'

145

Neil too switched to Welsh, surprised. 'I didn't know you spoke Welsh!'

The two men exchanged their first smile of genuine sympathy.

'Boys, you're forgetting Helen,' Mrs Philips gently reminded them as she handed out paper doilies, plates, fruit cake and scones.

'It's all right.' Helen cheerfully tucked into some cake. 'I like to hear the sound of Welsh, and I can tell people's mood from the tone of voice. I can even pick up the gist of it sometimes

Mrs Philips leaned over and patted Helen's knee. 'Now then, I wanted to ask Helen about this cardigan I'm knitting.'

'Asking about' clearly involved Helen unravelling some rows of knitting and correcting an error in the pattern. While she was engaged in this, her long hair hiding her face, Dai relaxed enough to ask Neil about his job and to establish mutual aquaintances and Llanelli background. Helen's suggestion that it was time to go caught Dai by surprise, not least because he was enjoying himself, and the calls of 'See you again' as they left, held genuine warmth.

'I knew you'd like each other,' Helen said with a self-satisfied smile, as they drove the short distance home.

'And you were right, my love. As always.'

'Not so bad then?' asked Neil's mother perceptively.

'You know how I am with someone new. And he means so much to Helen. I wanted it to go comfortably for her sake.'

'You were fine. A good host.'

'They have that slight awkwardness of a new couple.'

'I don't think they know each other yet. Ten minutes 'til dinner.'

'OK. Give me a shout when it's ready.'

146

9

Surfacing from sleep, Dai reached automatically for the warmth of Helen's body and registered her absence. As his eyes adjusted to the darkness, he made out the shapes of wardrobe and chair which reminded him he was in his parents' house for the night as a tactical move before Helen's first visit to the farm. It was time they satisfied his mother's curiosity and he wanted to make his commitment to her open and public. The sooner he could lie every night in the bed he'd made, the better. Preferably in a country cottage with a view of the stars . . . Just as he was drifting back to sleep, a bang and muffled human yelp came from downstairs. Now he was aware that someone was up and about, he could hear the small regular noises of stealthy movements. His mother's words came back to mind and he suddenly pictured himself diving across the kitchen to put a chair beneath the hanging body of his father.

Fully awake now, he listened as if holding a stethoscope to the heart of the house. 'Suicidal' was a word blunted for him by association with stereotypes; crying women on television dramas. His father was different. Men like him didn't speak, they acted. Yet he had spoken to a complete stranger on a Samaritans' Helpline. Did that make it more or less likely that he would act? What had the stranger said? Dai tried to imagine the unimaginable.

There would have been a silence of course, his father not being able to say why he'd called, the stranger using one of the ice-breaker phrases he – or she – had learned in training. His Dad would have said, 'It's the cows, see . . . and Mam, Gwen . . .' From this full, detailed explanation of his problems, the stranger would have had to adopt an appropriate line of counselling. Dai's imagination failed at this point but of one thing he was certain; his father would have offered no more than those few words. And if Dai went down to the kitchen, where he could hear the reassuring sound of a kettle boiling? What wisdom could he offer to solve the problems of the cows . . . and Gwen? His mother was probably lying awake, like him listening to the sounds of a man unable to sleep, thinking, like him, that a man would not make a cup of tea then kill himself, worrying, like him, that she had no idea what a man would do. Even if the Ministry file did not exist, lying postponed in his desk-drawer, Dai had little comfort for a cattle farmer, and the habit of silence with his father ran too deep for him to break. Protect his Dad's pride, his Mam had said, so Dai turned over and went back to sleep.

A wiry lock of red hair was kinking outwards with great determination, resisting all Helen's attempts to brush or wet it into shape. She was discontented with what the mirror showed her; the wildness of her hair was the least of it. She still had time to phone Dai and say she had woken with stomach pains or flu or yellow fever. Whatever she said she had, the truth would be obvious and she would only have to go through all this again some other time – or give up on Dai. She sighed, wishing it was another easy evening at Neil's that was in store. How she envied Dai's social ease; he relaxed so quickly with total strangers. Putting clients at ease was part and parcel of a vet's job, she supposed. She sighed again and wiped off the lipstick, which she had just carefully applied in the hope of adding poise to her appearance. The result was a blurred smear of red around her mouth that worsened as she rubbed, giving the effect of a four year old after a lollipop.

The beep of Dai's car brought her back to herself. With a regretful stroke of a kitten, whose company she would have

148

far preferred today, she shut the kitchen door on the furry family and faced the ordeal that awaited her.

'Do I look all right?'

'You look fine.' Dai kissed her briskly as she jumped in the car beside him.

'You're just saying that.'

'My mother's looking forward to meeting you – I don't know why you're worried.'

'I hate being on approval. If they don't, we're finished, you know that. I shouldn't be here. I'm not the type for mothers and tea parties.'

'Sunday dinner. There isn't a type, and how I feel about you has nothing to do with my parents' opinion. You know that. What is all this about anyway?'

Helen knew differently. Once she was introduced to his family she would have to find her place in it. She didn't want to be part of a family ever again and she didn't want to explain why not. It had been such a risk to get involved with this man, enough of a risk in itself, without careering out of control. His very openness was a threat, reminding her of all that separated them, that should have separated them but for her stupidity. It was too late now, and she was doomed to Sunday lunch with his Family – the capital letter loomed large in her mind.

She half ducked the question. 'I don't like to talk about myself.'

'Then don't.'

'They'll think I'm rude.'

'I don't care what they think.'

Helen was grateful that she had not tried too hard to 'dress tidy' as her Welsh friends would put it, since Meatloaf, Janie and Demi tripped over each other in their enthusiasm to greet her, pawing her for attention as if they knew any long-term reunion with their master depended on

149

her goodwill. Fussing over the dogs gave her a welcome breathing space in which to glance sideways at Dai's mother, who had followed the dogs into the yard and whose words of welcome were lost under the barking. The trampled earth of the farmyard had baked dry over the summer and Helen's heels wobbled over the uneven surface as she walked to the back door.

Mrs Evans' features were a rounder version of her son's and there was a smile in her eyes as she filled the air with well-meant commonplaces which varied in audibility as she walked and turned, carrying out her pre-dinner tasks. Helen looked around at the scrubbed table and chairs, the traditional dresser displaying old crockery, wellies on a sheet of newspaper by a range cooker which hummed and gave off an aroma of gravy and baking. A biscuit tin on a high but accessible shelf might as well have been labelled 'Petty Cash', its function was so obvious, and a shopping list on the window sill gave another glimpse of the household style. A fat black cat lay curled up in an armchair on two clashing floral cushions. Any upholstery had a fine down of animal hair drifting across it and onto Helen's black jumper. It was difficult not to contrast Dai's childhood home with her parents' immaculate Leeds semi, where thrift and hire purchase had furnished it wall-to-wall in middle-class, middle-of-the-road taste. Helen became aware that Mrs Evans had paused and was looking expectantly at Helen. Clearly this question required an answer.

'I forgot to ask Dai – are you a vegetarian?' Mrs Evans patiently repeated the question.

'Sorry, no.'

'I hate having to ask this – sign of the times,' Mrs Evans continued with some embarrassment and Helen crossed her fingers behind her back, praying for a polite parry to a query about marriage. 'Do you eat beef?'

150

'Oh yes . . . yes, no problem.' Helen was nonplussed at the intensity of the relief but touched by the politeness of being asked at all. She was vaguely aware from the TV news that schools had taken beef off the menu and that farmers were generally upset but she had not considered the matter further. 'The media are always making a fuss about food – one year it's soft cheese, then it's eggs, now it's beef. The way I see it, we're lucky we have enough food to worry so much about exactly what we eat.' She stopped abruptly, worried at having expressed such a decided opinion, but she was reassured by Mrs Evans' nods of agreement.

'I couldn't agree more. Now you go and sit with Grandad while I finish making dinner.'

'Can I help?' Helen asked, not just out of politeness. Sitting with Grandad sounded hazardous.

'Indeed not. Now Dai, take your Helen through and introduce her.'

Dai mimed a good little boy's 'Yes, Mam' and earned a flick of a tea towel from his mother as he took Helen by the hand and drew her after him.

Helen allowed herself to be towed along the hall passage which was musty and dark after the kitchen's glow. Dai paused before opening a door, half turned and kissed her with a tenderness that brought tears. He smoothed her unruly hair and she felt the smile that she could not see. Then the door opened onto a sitting room cluttered with chairs, all draped with various antimacassars and small throws in Welsh tapestry patterns and odd remnants, roll-hemmed by hand. A blast of hot air brought out a line of perspiration along her forehead and she noted the flickering gas fire, switched on even though it was August. Small clouds of smoke hovered over a chair by the fire and the unmistakeable sweet earth smell of pipe tobacco caught at her throat and reminded her of grandparents she'd hardly

151

known. Formal visits as a little girl had left no trace of people or personalities, just essence of pipe smoke for 'grandfather' and parma violet for 'grandmother'.

'You're letting in the cold, Dai. Hurry up and come in.' The voice rasped a little, less in its owner's control than the words strove to suggest.

'This is Helen, Grandad.'

'I know that. Who else would it be, and about time too.' Helen hurried towards Mr Evans, taking his hand in order both to greet him and to help him up. He struggled to stand to greet her in return and slumped back into the chair with evident relief. For the brief moment that Helen supported his weight as he sat down again, she thought, 'So this is what it's like.' She met his eyes, smiled and said drily, 'He's worried you'll confuse me with one of his other women.'

Dai's Grandad chuckled. 'You're right to worry, boy. You don't have to be senile to find your love life confusing. Sit there by the fire so I can see you.' Helen sat. He fixed her in an unswerving gaze. 'Are you a vegetarian?'

She faced the inquisition steadily. ' No – and before you ask, I do eat beef.'

'I could tell that just by looking at you. A girl with a mind of her own. So when are you going to come and live here?'

'Grandad!' Dai warned. 'I've already told you, we're looking for somewhere we both like. People don't have to run the family farm any more.'

'More's the pity. This is the best place on God's earth to bring up children. You wouldn't want to bring them up with drugs and drunks on the street now would you?' He appealed to Helen, who didn't dare risk either 'Yes' or 'No' as an answer. Luckily Dai's mother offered a diversion by announcing that lunch was ready.

'You go ahead,' prompted the man Helen instinctively

152

thought of as old Mr Evans. At what age did that adjective arrive? Could you ever accept it being attached to your own name? As Dai led her to the dining room, she was aware of Dai's mother behind them easing his grandfather to his feet and supporting the slow, shuffling movements. This was clearly a special occasion room, clean, bare and unused, where even the Family needed instructions as to where they were allowed to sit. Having organised them all into places, Mrs Evans brought in bowls of cawl and Helen met Dai's father. He had somehow materialised in the dining room and was quietly and stiffly occupying his place at the head of the table, without Helen having seen him enter the room. He responded to Dai's, 'Dad, this is Helen' with a bob of his head and a request for bread, and her smile felt a little wasted on the water jug raised between them at a crucial moment.

Soup slurping took place in what would have been silence bar the inevitable clink of spoon and gummy gurgle. The hiatus before the main course was filled by Dai's Grandad.

'She isn't a vegetarian. And she likes beef,' he announced, presumably to his son, who acknowledged the comment.

Persevering on Helen's behalf, old Mr Evans added, 'Thank God. We had enough trouble with the other one's fussy ways. Do you remember, Gwen, when you offered her chocolate sauce and she read the label aloud?' He mimicked a high, disdainful voice.' Oh I couldn't possibly eat all these Es. What you eat is what you are.'

Mrs Evans' face sparked at the memory and she hovered at the table, oven glove in hand, as she put down serving dishes. 'Yes and I remember what you said too. You said, 'And is that greens and nuts you're eating, if you get my drift.'

153

Carried away now, Dai's Grandad could hardly finish the story for chuckling, 'and she were that mad, she says "I'd rather be green and nuts than a pig like you!" Do you know, I often wished we'd been eating sweetbreads cos I know what she needed . . .'

Dai cut across him, exclaiming, 'Mam! Grandad!' partly at the vulgarity, partly realising that open season on Karen might be in Helen's favour but it wasn't fair. It hurt too much to remember what it had really been like, especially at first, and he knew perfectly well he had encouraged exactly that partisan response. It suited him to hear ill of her, the 'I never liked her anyway' approach, but he knew it had not been like that at all. He promised himself that, although it was too difficult to set the record straight, at least he would not join in.

His father looked at Helen full in the face for the first time and gave her a smile full of pure mischief, speaking clearly over the others.

'Tact you won't get. Good plain cooking, you will.' Helen didn't think the cooking could be any plainer than the speaking. 'Hurry up woman – we're starving.' Noticing Dai wince, Helen started to relax. She reached for his hand under the table, squeezed it and returned his apologetic grimace with what she hoped was a reassuring wink.

Luckily – or disappointingly – food took all Dai's Grandad's attention and it was Mrs Evans who took up the conversational baton, more conventionally.

'Do you go out to work, Helen?'

'I run a shop – a hand-knitting business.'

'Not the one in the precinct is it?'

'Yes. Been there for – oh, it must be five years now.'

'What's business like?' This enquiry came, surprisingly, from Dai's father. Even more of a surprise, even to herself, was Helen's honest answer.

154

'Awful. If Christmas doesn't really turn things round, I'll have to cut my losses. I've been putting off doing the books and facing figures, but it looks bad.'

'But at least there's a steady income with Dai,' said his mother, intending to console and rubbing a raw spot.

Again unexpectedly, it was Mr Evans who spoke. 'You've missed the point, Gwen. For someone with a business of your own, something you've built up, nurtured, and then the world outside crashes round you – politics and economics and no fault of your own – it's like, it's like . . .' he searched for words, failed and finished quietly, 'I know what it's like and Dai having money is good for him but makes no difference. At least, that's what I think Helen might feel.'

'Oh you're right, you're so right.' Helen looked at him gratefully. 'And there's the women who do a bit of work for me. They rely on it what with the men's jobs being so dodgy at the moment. Steelworks, one of them.'

'Have you told them?'

'No.' She put an end to the subject. 'Anyway, Christmas will put it right. I didn't mean to be so gloomy. The beef is so tender, Mrs Evans – did you cook it in the Rayburn?' Helen ignored the signals Dai was sending her, confused herself that what she hadn't been able to tell him had come out so casually with strangers.

Dinner finished in a businesslike bustle of clearing away and washing dishes in the more relaxed atmosphere of the kitchen. Early in this process, Dai's father slipped away, but not before giving a general invitation. 'I'm cutting Walter's fields if you feel like walking down.'

Dai caught Helen's response and told him. 'It's fine for a walk. We'll see you later.'

Leaving Dai's Grandad to sleep and his mother to household chores, they set out across the fields,

155

accompanied by assorted dogs. Helen had borrowed wellies, which made occasional rubbery belches from the air pockets round her stockinged feet. She intended to get the hang of this country life but it would take time. After all, she walked for miles through town in her low heels – why did the farm have to be quite so hilly? You'd be hard pushed to find enough flat space to pitch a tent, not that she intended to pitch a tent ever again. She automatically stopped that train of thought and concentrated on Dai, who was worrying away at her business problems.

'I didn't tell you because I'm sure everything will be all right. It just sort of came out at lunch – forget it. What a glorious view. I'm not surprised you love it here.'

The fields dipped away in front of them to reveal the river valley and hills behind in every direction. Villages straggled the roads at rare but regular intervals, the defiant, plain squareness of houses visible even at this distance. It seemed impossible that people had built on such slopes, let alone doggedly pursued the linear route towards the next settlement. Close up, 'linear' would not have been the most accurate description, as hairpin bends with misdirected cambers made the rural roads interesting to drivers. Wisps of cloud crossed lazily overhead, forming shadows on a grand scale across the hills, focusing attention on different features as the light shifted and sunlight caught a sparkle of water or the movement of cars. Despite the panoramic view, gentler rises and falls in the countryside concealed surprises, and Helen caught her breath as a sheltered hollow was revealed. Nestling against slopes on two sides, a small cottage faced the open vista across the valley.

'Who lives here? I thought this was your family's land. What a wonderful place to live.'

When Dai could get a word in, he answered, 'It's been empty for years. Dad bought some extra land – oh about ten

156

years ago – and the couple who had lived here moved with great relief to a little bungalow in one of the villages. Access is awful and the facilities are pretty basic. Anyway, it was no use to my Dad and I shouldn't think he lost any money on the deal.'

'Let's look.' Helen didn't wait for an answer but disappeared into the cottage. Motes of dust danced in shafts of sunlight, slanting in through small, paneless windows. The kitchen contained an old stone sink, a free standing cupboard and two lethal-looking power points.

'Look at the floors!' Helen's voice contained real awe. 'They're quarry tiles in the kitchen and that's real stone flagging in the living room.' In her mind's eye, she saw what the cottage would be like. 'It's got electricity then?' Dai nodded. 'And water. It wouldn't have gas of course, but you could get Calor gas or do without. It's dry, which means the roof's intact and it smells like it could be renovated.' She wrinkled her nose, sniffing, with a professional frown.

Dai laughed. 'What could a townie like you know about house renovation?'

'Try me,' she retorted. 'I have accumulated expertise on such matters as the rendering on outside walls and the laws for plumbing in bidets.'

'Reading women's magazines,' he guessed.

'Just so,' she said with dignity, 'and a source of vital information, they are.'

'That was Welsh,' he pointed out.

'What was?'

'Sticking "they are" at the end of a sentence. You're becoming Welsh, it is.'

'No it isn't, I mean I'm not. "They are" made sense, not like "it is".'

'There you are, you've just done it!'

157

She glared at him and returned to more important matters. 'I'd keep the floors – they're not even chipped – but cover the wooden ones of course. If I had lots of money, I'd shine up a wooden floor in the big bedroom. I'd put in oil or Calor gas heating – a kitchen range, a Welsh dresser, make the kitchen cosy like your family's. It's worth double glazing and no maintenance of window frames. I'd keep the open fire. Warm colours for the fabrics, woven wool rugs, perhaps some rag rugs . . .'

'Exactly which room have I just decorated in your over-vivid imagination?' he teased.

Stopping in her tracks as she paced about the house, peering into corners and weaving her plans, she looked at him, taken aback, stammering slightly.

'I wasn't really thinking of us. I was just . . . creating, designing.'

'Like all those jumpers you make for yourself and sell to other people?'

She shrank a little bit and said nothing. His arms went round her straight away. 'I'm not belittling what you do – I think you're very creative. But we can get a place together – we can make our dreams real – somewhere like this if you want. Although,' he looked round with distaste, 'I must say I'd rather have something we could actually live in within the next five years!'

'OK,' she conceded, 'we'll look for somewhere. But I can't afford as much as you, and I want to be independent.' She already felt that events were accelerating way out of her control.

Standing still for a moment to point out the soundness of the wooden bannisters underneath odd, peeling strips of yellowed gloss paint, Helen felt her hands trapped in Dai's larger grasp, and his lips on the back of her neck. She relaxed against him, freeing her hands to stroke his thighs.

158

'Is this what you usually do after Sunday lunch with your parents?' she murmured.

'Any objections?' He turned her towards him and had successfully negotiated underclothes to reach her skin. Responsive to the gentle circling movements, she was starting to melt when a polite, breathy snort froze them both. Instinctively they parted, adjusted clothes and walked towards the sound. Helen couldn't help a sigh of frustration and Dai reached for her hand, squeezing it. 'Later,' he whispered.

The intruder was outside the kitchen, to judge by the soft sounds on the grass, so they went out through the back door, intending to pass the time of day. Their sudden appearance startled the ponies which had been snuffling curiously at the strange scents in the air. From a safer distance the seven Welsh ponies paused, heads raised, poised for flight as they regarded Helen and Dai.

'If I'd known . . .' said Dai ruefully.

'And it was such a polite sort of interrupting cough!' Helen laughed. 'Oh well.' She shrugged with resignation and moved towards the next field and the ponies. A large brown one neighed and made a short, aggressive charge towards her, while the others shifted restlessly. Helen stopped, shaken.

'It's all right. There's a colt. They're warning you off – that's all. I suspect that's a stallion.'

Dai was right. Helen could now see the leggy youngster half-hidden by protective flanks, its eyes large and luminous in the long, bony face. The snorting noises now struck her as threatening.

'What do I do?'

'Come back here . . . slowly. Come backwards if you feel safer.'

It was only a few steps but Helen felt very exposed,

159

particularly as the leading pony made another little warning run at her. She held Dai's hand again with a mixture of relief and irritation at her own helplessness. She had made sure that there were so few situations now which she could not handle, competently, without help, but the countryside still presented new challenges.

They gave the ponies enough of a berth so that everyone felt safe, but Helen was aware of the eyes following them.

'They live pretty wild here,' Dai explained, 'but if you take a young one and train her, you'll have a friend for life. They're hardy too.'

'I used to want a Shetland pony when I was little – my little pony, I suppose. Stereotypical girl – I wanted to be a ballet dancer and have a pony. If I'd been a bareback rider in the circus, I'd have had both.'

'Bad-tempered, Shetlands,' was Dai's professional opinion. 'You saying bareback reminds me. When I was a boy, I'd ride these ponies bareback, for a bit of fun.'

'Now I'm impressed. Go on, show me.' She mimed wide-eyed admiration but he refused to take the bait.

'No thanks. I risk being kicked often enough in a day's work. Besides, even at eleven, I knew enough to leave them alone when there were foals.'

Dai's father was cutting silage, sketching great arcs with the tractor, the engine rattling through the small noises of late summer. A row of swifts, swallows and house martins bounced like tightrope walkers on the telephone wire which ran along the narrow lane that bordered the field. Swooping birds added parabolas in the sky. Dai waved both arms to attract his father's attention, and waited until the tractor bumped its way to the point nearest them on its predestined path.

Will jumped out of the tractor and hunkered down in the grass, a position Helen found killing on the thighs but in

'You'd have' em anyway, whatever the windows were like. You did on your last place.'

'£20,000'.

'£35,000 and I'll take the JCB over the bit round the house to make a garden for Helen – if she wants one.' Helen's involuntary 'Yes, please,' gained bargaining points for Will, showing him just how much Dai's lady-love wanted the cottage. So much the better for Will.

Screwing his face up in pain, Dai said, 'I could go to £30,000, but only if we can pay you monthly like a mortgage. I'm not made of money you know.'

Will savoured his moment of triumph but couldn't resist a final pause and coup de grace. 'All right then, but at £30,000 that's leasehold not freehold.'

Helen held her breath. Surely Dai wasn't going to accept! Yet the scowl on his face didn't fool her. Somehow things had gone as intended. He growled at his father, holding out a hand, 'You'd make a profit from a church choir you would. If Helen didn't love that cottage, I'd tell you what to do with your bargain.'

Will's eloquent shoulders and head held high told their own story, as he shook on it with his son, who made a show of storming off with Helen.

'It was bought dear enough – we might as well go look at it,' he yelled for his father's benefit.

Utterly bemused, Helen asked, 'What was that all about?'

He lifted her and swung her round, losing one of her too-big wellies in the process. 'Darling mine – we have a house and my father has a little pride restored and a steady little income.' She still looked confused. 'Don't worry about it.' He kissed her. 'Damn – I didn't think about that!' He looked at her ruefully. 'You did mean it when you said you'd like to live in the cottage?'

'Yes, but . . .'

'Good. Then you can start planning all those wonderful designs.'

'Yes, but . . .'

'But what?'

'Oh I don't know. Nothing really.' How could you say *Yes but we're going too fast – something's going to go wrong – I'm scared.* She smiled, 'It's too good to be true.'

One last cup of tea was offered before they returned home, a ceremony which took place in the Evans' parlour. Gwen seemed a little ill at ease in the musty armchair; this was clearly another of those rooms 'for best' in which no one really relaxed. Gwen said as much, saying how cosy the kitchen was and how some rooms just never seemed to get used.

'I've never lived somewhere big enough to have that problem!'

'We call this the parlour but you'll still find people with old ways round here, who'll talk about their "laying out" room.'

'Laying out?'

'Yes, for when one of the family dies. I remember when Dai bought his house, his great Aunt Nerys said straight out what a lovely room their – drawing room they called it – would be for laying out. There used to be a jack of all trades worked from a shed in the village, doubled as an undertaker he did and if he was out there was a sign on the door said "Laying-out boards behind the door – help yourself!" Talk about do-it-yourself!'

Interested despite herself, Helen said, 'It's like another world. You must know so many stories.'

'Indeed. There's some characters around. Why, our

164

neighbour Mrs Williams Dderwen-teg . . .' Something intruded on Helen's concentration. Yet again, the birdsong was somehow wrong. One piercing note was being repeated over and over. Helen looked behind Dai's mother, through the window at the poplar hedge where a greenfinch fluttered and withdrew, repeating its cry. At the foot of the hedge was the fat black cat which Helen had seen earlier, curled in the kitchen chair. Now it seemed less fat, more like the predator she had forgotten it to be.

'Why doesn't the bird just fly away?' asked Helen, cutting across Mrs Evans' long story. Dai and his mother followed Helen's gaze and took in the situation.

'Gweneira reliving her youth,' remarked Dai with tolerance.

'It's probably a parent with a late clutch. They sometimes have a second brood, in this warm weather, or when they lost their first,' suggested Gwen, more sensitive to the concern in Helen's voice. 'I think it's trying to distract Gweneira from its young.'

'Can't you save them?' asked Helen. Dai threw her a quick glance and left the room. A low growl of irritation announced Gweneira's removal from the siege, then Dai returned with an armful of indignant cat. He shut the door to keep her in the room and distracted her by 'playing mouse' – walking two fingers in front of her disdainful nose and wriggling them.

'Her name means Snow White in Welsh,' Gwen told Helen. 'We thought it was funny at the time but the joke has grown a bit thin, especially as I don't know whether someone's calling for me or the cat.'

'How can you say that Mam?' teased Dai. 'If the tone is friendly you know it's for the cat!'

'That's not so funny,' responded his mother drily.

'Time to go, love.' Dai turned to Helen, who had

165

controlled the tears pricking and who mustered a creditable leave-taking.

They had barely walked through Helen's front door when she threw her arms round him, saying, 'It is later now. You promised.' Her desperation both worried and enticed him, but he didn't stop to ask questions.

Afterwards, he wondered, and later again that same night he began to understand what passions had shaken her with tears even as she lay with him. At the time he merely held her, innocently pleased with purchasing their dream home. While she slept beside him later, he organised builders and plasterers, planted a kitchen garden and put up shelves in his mind, until he too fell asleep.

Waking in the dark, Dai automatically checked his watch and reached for the phone. Three a.m. and it was not the phone which had woken him – no call-out then, thank God. He rolled over towards Helen and was pushed away with the clumsy, thrashing movement of someone in deep sleep. Her body was clammy with sweat, moving restlessly. Worried, Dai stroked the back of her neck with his finger-tips, hoping to reach her subconscious and soothe her without waking her. The result was an increase in reflex twitching. Dai dropped his hand and moved away a little, noting the symptoms of fever and surprised at their sudden onset. They always said that the more you knew, the more you worried, and Dai tried not to think of meningitis or rare and fatal toxoses.

Unable to fall back to sleep, Dai threw some clothes on, padded out to the kitchen and mixed some milk and Marmite. He paced around a little, drinking and dropping crumbs from the cheese and Marmite sandwich with which he was comforting himself. When a vet student on placement at the practice had once asked him how he coped with the stress of the job, he had absent-mindedly answered

166

'Marmite.' The student had felt patronised and insulted, and it had taken weeks before Dai had regained his trust by explaining that he had been joking of course. He had then given various text-book suggestions on healthy, balanced lifestyles as a means of coping with the unwanted adrenalin caused by stress. Dai had not been totally honest in that he also believed that a wonderful sex life helped, but Marmite was certainly a crucial factor. He wondered whether you could get the human form of BSE from Marmite.

Low mutterings and moans reached him from the bedroom and Dai decided if there was no improvement in the next hour he would call out the doctor. He walked back through to the bedroom, standing in the doorway as his eyes adjusted to the lack of light. A chunk of sandwich fell on the carpet and he bumped his head as he bent to pick it up, letting out an involuntary exclamation. Helen sat up in bed, covers thrown off, and seemed to look straight at him. The muttering became clearer. 'It was the cat. I didn't kill her, it was the cat. Rebecca.' The name was spoken with such pain that the rest of the Marmite sandwich hit the floor, un-noticed, as Dai moved instinctively towards Helen. Her face followed his movements and her eyes were wide open, unblinking, but unseeing. He sat on the edge of the bed and reached out to hold her. She kept murmuring, 'Rebecca' and held out her arms but at the contact, she flinched, shuddered and her eyes closed, only to open as she screamed 'Rebecca!' and came fully awake.

Shaken, Dai tried again to hold her but Helen evaded his arms, slipped out the other side of the bed and ran to the bathroom, where he could hear her retching. Dai prepared a potion, then knocked at the bathroom door, suddenly polite to this stranger.

'Helen? Take this – it might help. I think you have a temperature. Perhaps we should call a doctor?' The uncertainty in his voice was beyond his control. He rememembered the nights he had nursed loved pets, rendered even more helpless by his expertise, and unable to follow his own advice for emotion overriding common sense.

Her voice was a reassurance and yet seemed to come from a great distance. 'It's all right. I'm all right now, thank you. It will pass. Go back to bed and I'll be there soon.'

It will pass. So, this had happened before. Dai straightened the bedclothes, lay in the space of his half, listening. Too recently, he had tried to understand a man by listening to the sounds in the night, and the comparison added to his fears. Helen returned to bed, smelling of soap and perfume. She kissed him coolly on the cheek, then rolled away from him into foetal position and, for all he knew, went straight back to sleep. Dai did not go straight back to sleep. 'Perhaps it's a variant of epilepsy' was the explanation which, however unsatisfactory, finally allowed him to drift into unconsciousness.

10

Helen did not want to tell Dai. She did not want things to change, but it was already too late for that. He had been subdued at breakfast, said 'No, nothing' with artificial cheer when she asked if anything was wrong, and had avoided eye contact. She had eaten little, still feeling sick. Neither of them had made any reference to her behaviour the night before, and yet it strained the silence between them. Even his goodbye kiss had been more of a peck in the air. What had he seen and heard the night before? Her hands were still shaking from the force of the nightmare and she wondered how much Dai had been able to deduce. It had been months since the last visitation, and she had started to believe she might recover, to start a new life with Dai, but she had lost the right to happiness and she had been a fool to allow Dai and hope into her life.

All day long, while her hands sorted stock and served customers, Helen twisted the yarns of her life to shape a fabric she could wear with Dai. A fresh start had failed her and she could not face his wariness of her. Whether he spoke of it or not, something had made him doubt her and would maggot away, feeding on any nightmares, fattened on her silence. If she gave him some plausible lies, the maggot would eat at her instead until she was rotten to the core, until in the end she would tell the truth anyway. The only hope left was to tell him and to hope for understanding. Some hope!

She remembered watching a documentary on the rehabilitation of prisoners convicted for crimes such as rape, murder and paedophilia. A clinical psychiatrist explained that some of these men were completely different people who deserved a fresh start, and were genuinely horrified by the crimes they had committed. However, they nearly always failed in their attempts to form relationships because they felt the new partners had to accept them as they were and to forgive them. 'So you tortured and abused two children. Never mind darling – that's all in the past and I forgive you.' This was not what real people said. Some truths were too much for anyone to hear; some crimes could neither be forgotten nor forgiven. Helen knew this. She knew that the only way forward was to tell the truth and that she could not expect understanding, but at least she would have tried.

She wondered yet again why she had not just killed herself when it happened. When the psychiatrist had presented this as an indication of her will to live, a positive indicator, she had stared at him with contempt. At first her will to punish herself had denied her the ease of death and then, later, the timing was never right. The washing was in mid-cycle or – most painfully ironic – she was baby-sitting for her niece. It was because time and routine were numbing the pain that she had taken a razor blade and drawn it along the two silver stretch marks left by child-birth. Tony had found her, staring at the thin, bloody reminders of Rebecca and he had insisted on her seeing a shrink. Who had not understood. Talking to him she had realised that no one understood and it stopped mattering to her. She had started to live her solitary life, perhaps not so different from before, if you discounted Rebecca.

With no recollection of what customers she had seen that day, Helen turned the keys in the lock at closing time. There had been no miracle reprieve, and the worn tracks of her thoughts merely turned on how to tell him and rehearsed what to say. She had planned a special meal and, although her stomach churned, she would cook for him, share a bottle of wine, capture his smile for her memories, and then tell him.

The pungent Mediterranean aromas of garlic, olives and tomatoes filled Helen with a nostalgia for the future – a wistful longing for an illusion of the past, only in this case it hadn't happened yet. She could smell it so clearly though, a dream of France in which she and Dai were retired grandparents. Something comforting about being grand-parents; it meant you'd had children but you didn't have to think about actually having them. All this would be in the past and she'd be saying, 'Remember the night when . . .,' and he would smile with her.

For once, the kittens left her reverie and her cooking undisturbed. They formed a multiple-headed furry ball snuggling into a cushion on the kitchen table. Helen had eyed them with distaste that morning, reminded by the farm cat of their predatory nature. Now, they formed a chocolate-box portrait which allowed her to dream.

She stirred the chicken casserole, checked that the rice was drying out to time, and arranged some slices of kiwi fruit in an artistic pattern on a cheesecake which she'd made the day before. She looked critically at the table, which was laid carefully but lacked personality. Too late to get flowers. Inspired, she grabbed a handful of coloured pencils and jammed coloured shapes of dried pasta onto them so they looked like the produce of an alien planet. These she arranged in a plain white, glazed jug, which she placed off-centre on the table. Just as she finished her preparations, Dai walked in. He started to speak but she interrupted him with a long kiss and he accepted the welcome.

Her pencil arrangement crinkled his eyes and mouth, but all he said was, 'You've been working hard – it smells wonderful. When's it ready? I'm starving.'

'Now. Sit down. How was work?' It was as if nothing had disturbed the miracle of them finding each other and Helen wondered again if she should leave well enough alone. She glowed with her determination to do the right thing, high on adrenalin, wine and a strange feeling of heroic intent. Old lines of poetry came to mind, which Neil had once quoted to her and which she'd tracked down and copied, to keep.

He either fears his fate too much
or his deserts are small
who puts it not unto the touch
to win or lose it all.

If she lost it all, it would not be through fear. After the meal, she evaded Dai's attempts to move the evening

171

towards the bedroom, squirming out of his grasp to a safe distance.

'There's something I want to talk to you about, now, or I'll lose my nerve and it will always be between us.'

The way he looked at her would have boiled ice. 'You don't have to say anything. I don't care if you're a snake on Saturdays, I love you and nothing can change that.'

Even as she treasured the words of unconditional love, she was conscious of how easy it was to make bold promises in total ignorance. She held on to her resolve and told the story of her nightmares. She told Dai of her marriage and of the fireworks in St-Geniez, when she had felt so happy, and of the day after that . . .

Despite their intention to set off early the next day, they overslept, and Tony's temper was frayed as they bumped into each other, packing and taking the tent down. Rebecca too was fretful after her late night and Helen felt pulled in two directions, trying to help her husband and comfort her daughter. There was no need to be fussy with the packing, as they were only driving for five hours, then breaking the journey by camping overnight, so they didn't bother brushing down the tent or rolling it too carefully. Even so, the sun was high by the time they left St-Geniez and it was a sweaty journey in the French summer heat. Not until they reached the next campsite was there any vestige of the previous night's ambience.

Helen was wholeheartedly in favour of Tony's decision to go swimming before pitching the tent, and the three of them had dipped into the campsite pool with relief. The memories of the hours before it happened were engraved on Helen's mind. She could see her own toes, like swollen red sausages, wriggling in the cool water. And Becky, splashing

172

around in her water wings, screaming as Helen chased her. The pool was quiet, and Tony was making methodical circuits in an impeccable front crawl.

The campsite was small, with basic but adequate facilities, and shady pitches arranged randomly. An outer ring of new pitches was exposed to the full glare of the sun, waiting for its ration of saplings to grow, and Helen was grateful she had phoned ahead to reserve a place. She couldn't understand the urge to bake, grill or fry the human body exhibited by so many other campers – including Tony – and she sat peacefully under a tree, watching Rebecca talking to her toy dog, Heathcliff.

'Becky go swimming,' Rebecca informed Heathcliff, waving his stubby body in front of her face.

''Eath dog don't like swimming. There's sharks,' replied Heathcliff, alias Rebecca using her idea of a deep voice.

'Silly dog. There's no sharks.' Helen could hear her own tones in the way her daughter dealt with the dog's fears. 'There's Chinese. And they eat bad dogs.' Helen winced and wondered why children seemed to thrive on prejudice and fantasy. It seemed to have some connection with hating sprouts but she hadn't quite figured it out. So the afternoon drifted lazily to tea-time. When Rebecca took a nap and all was still, Helen noticed a goldfinch coming and going to a high branch above her. Patience was rewarded when two tiny beaks appeared, just visible over the late nest. Butterflies clustered on nearby buddleia like tiny flutters of blue sky or warplanes with camouflage circles.

Open-air cooking renewed Helen's joie-de-vivre completely, and sunbathing had restored Tony's good humour to the point where he cheerfully volunteered to do the washing-up. He disappeared with a bowlful of dirty dishes, heading for the row of sinks by the concrete toilet block. Rebecca sat on the warm grass in front of the tent with a box of small ponies, a digger and a teaspoon. She loaded the digger with sandy soil from a bare patch, then harnessed a pony who took the earth over to his friends, who were building a stable.

'Becky's thirsty,' she called, commanding

'Magic word?'

'Drink, please.' Helen went into the tent and started to mix a fruit juice with water from the cool box. She heard the car coming up between the pitches, perhaps a little bit faster than it was supposed to. Afterwards she wondered if she would have been in time if she'd run out then, but there was nothing to warn her. Nothing that is, until a woman screamed and the car stopped. Then Helen ran out, still carrying Rebecca's drink. She saw a metallic blue estate car beside their pitch, the passenger door near her swinging open and a man sitting in the left-hand side driver's seat. A woman, presumably the passenger, was running until she reached a tree and threw herself against it, head bowed and shoulders shaking. Heathcliff was right against a car tyre, trapped by it. His face would be a little damaged when she rescued him, and Helen thought how upset Becky would be. The car engine was still running and the driver revved, crunched into reverse gear and backed twenty yards. Helen watched the car, worrying that the passenger door was still hanging open and might hurt someone, then the engine was cut. Only when the driver unfolded from the car and stood holding his door, looking at her, did Helen realise what had happened.

In her nightmares, the crushed bits of body on the grass would reassemble and dance in mockery or dissolve to skeleton. The worst nightmares simply relived that moment, when she turned from the crazed stare of the driver to the thing that had been under the car. The thing that had been Rebecca, and not all the king's horses, nor all the king's men would ever put Becky together again.

With hindsight it was amazing how quickly the *sapeurs pompiers* arrived on the scene but everything seemed to happen in slow motion. Why the fire brigade? As if it were a cat stuck up a tree. Someone must have phoned but it seemed like magic, made the heart beat with the familiar belief in the power of uniforms. The police, too, in a small blue *deux-chevaux*. Blue seemed to be the colour. The gendarmes jumped out of their car and spread sawdust on the bloodstained grass, with professional detachment. As if it were a mess in the circus ring and the show must go on. At Helen's dry little laugh the gendarmes turned to her and one brought out a little notebook, taking details of name and nationality. Tony's return with a pile of clean dishes added to Helen's feeling that she was watching these strange people from very high overhead. She felt nothing watching Tony's mouth make fishy openings as a paramedic told him in toneless English that his daughter was dead. He was still repeating, 'But I don't understand' as he and Helen were gently ushered into the ambulance, leaving the gendarmes to question the others at the scene.

Tony and Helen were instructed to stay in the waiting room, while the trolley with its blanketed body passed through double doors and out of sight. Sitting on two hard plastic chairs, side by side, they contemplated a wall.

'If you'd taken better care of her, this would never have happened.' Tony's words injected slow-release poison into her frozen soul, but she felt nothing and couldn't speak. He might have been talking to the wall at which he gazed so steadily. 'I only left you for five minutes. If only you'd taken her in the tent with you – if it was so vital that you had to go into the tent at all.'

'She wanted a drink.' Helen's words were barely audible, remnants of a world in which Becky drank fruit juice with water in it.

175

Tony's bile continued to rise. 'Any caring mother would have moved her or put something tall beside her so she was safe. She should have been safe with you for Christ's sake. How could you let her get run over!' It was a relief when he dropped his head in his hands and started crying. At least the words would leave her alone, for now. It wasn't as if he were saying anything which wasn't echoed even more viciously in her own thoughts. She just didn't feel anything, yet.

A nurse came and spoke softly in French. Helen could not understand, her so she left and was replaced by another one with some English.

'They do things. It be ten, fifteen minutes.' The characteristic Gallic shrug of shoulders. 'Then you say arrangements.' The last word gave her difficulty and was pronounced with some satisfaction.

'You'd better phone home. Tell Mum, Dad, your parents. Get it over with.' It was understood between them that Helen had done it, so Helen could break the news. Besides, Helen had always written the birthday cards and bought the Christmas presents – this was just another family duty and she didn't think to question it. With great efficiency she dialled the international code and made two identical phone calls, first to his parents, then to hers, holding the phone away from her ear as the shock led to crying and then interrupting after thirty seconds to give the few cold facts they needed to know. She finished, 'I'll let you know about the funeral arrangements. Speak to you soon.' It was probably these cold phone calls, bitter in their own way as Tony's blame, which opened rifts which never healed. No one suffering the shock of bereavement should have to break the news to those whose pain needs careful words.

Eventually they were called to an interview room. It didn't take a doctor to tell Helen that Rebecca's mangled body was dead, but she watched him sign the certificate and pass it to Tony, whose hand shook. They were asked if they wanted to take the body home for the funeral; Tony indignantly said 'Of course,' and so they made 'arrangements'. Helen found it all rather ghoulish as they discussed plane flights and undertakers' phone numbers. The gendarmes took statements from both of them and told them they would have to return for the trial. The English-speaking nurse ordered a taxi for them and they returned to the campsite.

Helen could hardly drag her feet to the tent for the weight of shame she carried. A Belgian woman rushed over from her tent opposite, volubly and unintelligibly sympathising. As if at a signal four or five women appeared, gesticulating, hugging Helen, some even crying. She gave a set little smile, thanking them as if for an enjoyable coffee morning, 'Thank you so much for coming. The women cast dark glances down the slope, waving their arms at the blue estate car, which Helen now noticed was Dutch. Probably the only other couple speaking English, but they could hardly comfort each other. The Dutch tent was zipped up tight. Helen remembered the reflection of her horror on the driver's face as they both realised what had happened, what they had done. Neither could have prevented what they did not foresee. Both would have to live with the consequences.

Although it was early in the evening, the tact of mourning made campers withdraw into their tents, zip them fast against the tragedy outside, shush their little children and hold them close. Helen followed Tony into the empty tent.

It was best not to think, so she didn't. That made it possible to pack up a tent; to work round Tony in mutual silence; to ensure regular body maintenance with food,

177

drink and sleep; to organise their return home and then funeral arrangements. Not thinking allowed Helen to choose bud roses for a wreath and to remain upright while something turned to ashes. Not even in her frozen state could Helen tolerate the word 'corpse'. It was like 'beef' or 'mutton', a word designed to distance the living from the dead, to allow you to burn, bury or cook it. Corpses had no names.

Tony was 'coping better' – so everyone whispered for Helen to hear, and she silently agreed with them. He cried from time to time, then busied himself with work. He talked to the stream of visitors about all that Rebecca had been and done, such a bright, loving child. He shared his sense of infinite unfairness with every caller and gradually he regained control and talked less. He had spoken to Helen as soon as they were back home, apologising for the hurtful words, telling her that he had just been taking it out on her, that he hadn't meant it, that they needed each other more than ever. She had made the required gesture, holding him, telling him that it didn't matter. And indeed it didn't. Nothing mattered any more and his words had been the truth.

A week after the funeral, Helen had her first nightmare. At first Tony was relieved that she was 'letting her feelings out' but the intensity of her grief soon frightened him even more than her icy aloofness had done. His own nights were interrupted and he asked both his parents and parents-in-law for advice. Helen had rescued Rebecca's toy dog, which was miraculously intact bar the loss of an eye. He had been put through a wool wash cycle and now, slightly bobbled and one-eyed, Heathcliff shared the marital bed, it was to the dog that Helen clung, in the depths of nightmare or the whimpers of half-waking. She rejected all attempts to make her see a doctor and was humiliated by the knowledge that Tony was discussing her with others. The nightmares grew worse, and Tony asked Helen to leave Heathcliff somewhere else as he couldn't stand him any more. Beyond caring, Helen moved into the spare bedroom. At least it relieved her of the dutiful physical motions that he thought were necessary to their marriage. She had been beyond his reach for so long there was no point of contact now. If she had helped him, so much the better, but as he looked to the future, Helen's pain grew worse.

They were told how lucky they were that the trial took place so quickly, only a few months after the accident. Strings had been pulled because of the number of foreigners involved, whose whereabouts were unreliable, and the summons came to return to France in November. They did not feel particularly lucky.

Checking baggage through the kiosk at Manchester airport brought back Helen's frozen detachment. They must look like a couple going on their holidays – she was even carrying a tourist guide that Tony had bought her in a well-meant attempt to distract her. When they had read that the trial would be at the Palais de Justice, Orleans, Tony had made cheering-up conversation, suggesting Helen would enjoy finding out about the Maid. He had pointed out that life must go on, it wouldn't help Rebecca for them to fall into a decline and Helen should make the most of a trip to her favourite country, even in such circumstances. Helen politely agreed.

In a strange way, her respect for her husband had grown as she observed his patience and his clumsy attempts to use advice from family and friends to start her on the mend. After all, it was hard for him too and there were times when he would stare at a photo and fill up with tears. Helen acknowledged his grief, was always willing to put an arm round him if it seemed to be required, and remained alone.

Orly Airport in Paris impressed her with its glassy international façade, without revealing its nationality. The elevators took Helen down past the small concession shops to the rail link across Paris to Gare d'Austerlitz and Orleans. She remembered to get tickets date-stamped before the journey, then slumped beside Tony as the window panned the industrial hinterland of Paris.

The train ran parallel with a busy main road much of the way. Helen responded automatically to Tony's request to know what this one was called. In the past it had been Helen who delighted in the romance of French motorway names, l'Arlesienne, la Languedocienne, l'autoroute des deux mers, but now she merely pointed out that this was only an N road. Glimpses of forest and the inevitable battlefield and war memorial could be glimpsed through the November mists as the train pulled into Orleans. It seemed strange to stand, cold and bedraggled in the drizzling rain, in a land Helen associated with sun and relaxation. Or rather had associated.

The hotel they had booked into matched their spirits but provided somewhere to wait, which, as they soon discovered, was the main activity. Their ordeal testifying at the Palais de Justice took up only twenty minutes (for Helen) and five minutes (for Tony) but the gendarmerie asked them to remain 'within call' at the hotel, when not waiting in the court itself. The trial dragged on for two days, mostly because of judicial involvement in other more important affairs. There were delays in starting and an early finish on the first day. Leaving the court, Helen had felt someone's eyes on her and she had turned to see the Dutchman's haunted stare. She wondered if her face too had stuck in the same expression forced on it four months earlier, when the wind had changed.

The court's verdict, as relayed to Helen and Tony by a

gendarme, was manslaughter, with a three-year driving ban and a fine. They were advised that they could press civil charges if they so wished but although Tony hoped 'that Dutch bastard' would suffer all his life, his vindictive feelings sought no financial compensation. In this he agreed with Helen who found the idea both futile and repellent, with its suggestion that money *could* compensate. She could not however share Tony's wholehearted blame of the Dutchman. She did not want him to suffer all his life and yet she believed that he would, as she would. No punishment for either of them could be worse than the knowledge of what they had done.

As soon as they were back at the hotel after the verdict, Tony slept, drained by the tension. Helen took a turn around the block, her hood up against the continual drizzle. She stopped at the newsseller's stand, her attention caught by the headline *CAMPING FATALE* in the local paper. Quickly sorting through the necessary change, she bought her copy of *la nouvelle republique du centre-ouest.* Sure enough, the leading article was an account of the previous day's trial. Helen skimmed it rapidly but couldn't take it in for the feeling that everyone must be looking at her and pointing.

She rushed back to the hotel bar, sat on a plastic corner bench away from the cigarette smoke and growl of conversation from the barman and a swarthy man on a barstool, and started to read. Her memories of the accident expanded to allow new details to take their places. The Dutchman had not seen the little girl as she was sitting down, and so small that his bonnet had hidden her from view as he drove up. His wife had screamed because she had seen Rebecca the instant before the car had hit her. The man, Johann Geldt, had jammed on the brakes and his wife had jumped out of the car, running in shock. Strange to have a name to go with the face Helen knew so intimately.

It had been too late. Where had the little girl's mother been, the paper asked, and replied that Rebecca had been left alone while her mother was in the tent. The poor father had returned from washing up dishes to find his cherished daughter dead.

Gripped by morbid curiosity, Helen read on. There was an interview with Monsieur and Madame Berne, the camp-site owners, who explained that they had rearranged their campsite geometrically to prevent such a tragedy happening again. They emphasised that their campsite had been safe before, but of course it was vital not to leave such a young child alone, and with cars around, however slowly they were travelling . . . They said how sorry they were for the poor Dutchman and his wife who had been shocked at the time by a tragedy for which they felt responsible.

The paper's verdict was quite clear even to someone with Helen's level of French, and differed considerably from the court's. Below the main article were interviews with 'ordinary women' of Orleans.

> *16-year-old Martine Albert said 'I'd never leave my child alone. If you have a baby, you should look after it, like Maman always looked after me.' 38-year-old mother of twins Angélique Sèves said, 'If I met that mother, I'd spit in her face. She should have been on trial, not the driver.' 94-year-old grandmother of nine Cecile Duval said, 'In my day, women like that would have to leave the village. No one would speak to them.'*

A small advertisement for the next day's paper promised *'Full details of mother's testimony and court verdict in baby-killing.'*

The thinking part of Helen suspected that the article was prejudicial to the verdict and therefore probably illegal. The feeling part gave up. By the time the next day's paper came out, Helen was back in Leeds, but her imagination presented her with her own words, subtly changed, confessing her guilt over and over.

Heathcliff and Helen did not return to Tony's bed. Shortly after the incident with the razor blade, Tony himself started spending nights away from the marital bed. She was glad for him, and when he hesitantly suggested that perhaps they would both benefit from a fresh start, she took the hint and drifted with a few belongings, first to her parents' house and then to her sister's. Neither had worked out, so she had tried for a fresh start herself and here she was. Dai knew the rest himself.

Helen looked across at Dai, sitting on the sofa where she had deliberately not joined him. To her surprise he was smiling somewhat foolishly and looking relieved.

'Is that all!' She looked at him in disbelief. 'I'm sorry – that was tactless. I mean, that's something which will heal in time. We're all right.' He moved to touch her but she remained tightly upright, unyielding, and his arms dropped. She watched him as he leaned against a window sill. He was totally in shadow, silhouetted against the fading sunlight. His voice came from the darkness of his face as if the scene were poorly dubbed. She told herself that it was natural to see Dai as a stranger after revisiting all she had been through. The sick feeling of unreality still lingered, and must be affecting her reactions. She concentrated on what he was saying.

'You've been through so much. You mustn't blame yourself. I am sure you were a wonderful mother.' He sounded like her mother or, worse still, like Tony. 'Cashmere thinks you still are.' Dai smiled at the kitten which had jumped as high as it could up Helen's legs and

183

was now systematically working its way up her body, using its claws as crampons. It reached Helen's neck and settled, so ecstactic it choked on its own purr, coughed and started rumbling again with its eyes half-closed. Helen automatically unhooked its claws from her skin and stroked it with her forefinger. 'Accidents happen to anyone and there's nothing you can do about it.'

She could not discipline her response to the clichés; she was too close to the events she'd lived through. 'What would you know about it?' she demanded bitterly.

He returned to his seat and she could see his serious expression, presumably as he considered his own experiences. When he spoke again, it was with some difficulty. 'It's part of my job to make life or death decisions.'

She was dismissive, unable to control the urge to jibe, to rebuild her defensive walls. 'Yeah, you've told me, like whether to send a lamb to the slaughterhouse now or two weeks later.'

He was clearly taken back but ignored the tone and continued quietly. 'I was thinking more of the judgements you make over treatment, or in the operating room, particularly with people's pets. Every vet has stories he doesn't want to tell, wrong decisions.'

'So what's yours?'

He met the challenge in the same quiet tones. 'There's more than one. You can drive yourself crazy thinking of the new medicine that you hear about after the animal died, or a fatal allergic reaction to a vaccination you recommended. That's where the partnership helps – you share the feelings and stop looking for blame.'

He looked directly at her, offering such a partnership. Doggedly, she pursued him. 'All these generalisations. There must be one time you remember.'

184

'As I said, there's more than one. There was a spaniel, when I'd been practising about four years – long enough to get careless and not long enough for experience to weigh in on my side. Beautiful eight-year-old bitch in with sickness and diarrhoea, no temperature. The owner was beside herself with worry, typical overreaction of neurotic middle-aged woman.' Helen made a sound of protest.

'I know, I'm not proud of the stereotyping – in fact that made two wrong diagnoses, and really listening to the owner is part of what I've since learned. What they don't tell you and don't know, as well as what they do. Anyway, that was how I thought, then. I'd seen so many pets like that – stomach upset, nothing more. So I prescribed twenty-four hours' starvation, water only, to clear the system, and promised her dog would be right as rain. Hysterical phone call at eight the next morning – the woman had got up to find her dog dead, froth all over its mouth. She wanted a post mortem, kept saying, 'You told me she'd get better. How could she die of a stomach upset?' Post mortem showed up poison – lack of food had made it act more quickly. I should have noticed the classic symptoms – dilated pupils, drugged look and gait. If I'd been younger, I'd have been more methodical and spotted it. David handled it for me, fudging over the error with diplomatic explanations that any vet would have been misled by the symptoms. I wish I could say that's my only mistake, but it wouldn't be true.' Dai gave a rueful smile. 'Don't go putting off all my clients now. As I say, it's that responsibility for life and death, too heavy sometimes.'

'Yes, it must be hard,' Helen's mouth said politely. *Look at his complacent normality! As if you could compare a dog's death with her daughter's. Or his mild feelings of guilt, which made him feel a little uncomfortable at times with what she went through.* He had no idea and she had

185

been stupid to think he might understand. She'd have preferred horror and revulsion, acknowledgement that this mattered, anything other than this trivialisation. Melusine had screamed because her husband had seen her as a monster, looked at her serpent's tail and said,

'How about a cup of coffee?'

'Yes please.' Helen switched on the television where the TV news announcer tried to reinforce Dai's message that Helen was not responsible for all the evil in the world. Dai reappeared with the coffees and watched the news. There had been a serious train accident in north Wales, details of which were just reaching the newsroom.

'Don't you just hate it when they do that!' exclaimed Dai.

'What?' Helen was barely concentrating.

'Gwhy ned,' mimicked Dai, imitating the pronunciation of the announcer. 'Someone who can't say Gwynedd shouldn't be allowed to read the news for England and *Wales*. It's as if they're proud of their ignorance, the way they look down their noses as if the word is too barbaric to be worth taking the trouble to say.'

Helen's mouth said, 'Same with Asian names.'

After a little more non-conversation they went to bed, where Helen accepted Dai's enthusiastic lovemaking, then lay awake most of the night.

The next morning she asked Dai to contact Mrs Rees about the kittens. 'They're strong enough now and she said she wanted them if I could get them past the suckling stage.'

'Is something wrong?'

Pause. 'I'm a bit tired. The kittens are fine. I just think it's time they went, that's all.' *Too much responsibility. It's not working out.*

Mrs Rees came with her two children, who grabbed a

186

kitten each and were cautioned by their mother to be more gentle. Helen had to keep her hands firmly holding her arms to prevent herself clipping the squabbling duo about the ears, but she trusted Mrs Rees. The woman's eyes filled with tears as she stroked Tibby's kittens and thanked Helen.

Helen couldn't resist asking, 'What are you going to do with them?'

'We'll definitely keep one, but I don't know which yet. This one's pretty.'

'I've been calling her Cashmere – she's my favourite.'

'What a pretty name – don't you want to keep her? You could, you know. If it wasn't for you . . .'

'No, no . . . it's better not.'

'Well, I'll find good homes for them, you may be sure of that. Come on Lindsay and leave the lady's things alone! Adam!'

The house seemed quiet, kittenless. When Dai arrived home from work, Helen's face told him that there was another serious talk in store. He was tired and his heart sank. He tried to stave it off.

'Mrs Rees must have come then. I miss the sound of kittens yowling for food and their welcoming claws in my shin.'

'Yes, it's strange without them, but I'll get used to it.'

I. She'd said I. He sighed. 'There's something wrong. Do you want to talk about it?' He knew he hadn't found the right response to all she'd told him. He didn't know what the right response was. He'd just hoped that patient day-to-day loving her would speak for him. 'It's that snake-tail showing again, isn't it?'

'It's not funny, Dai!'

'No, I know, but I don't know what to say. I don't know what you want me to say. You seem to be putting distance between us for no reason.'

187

'I'm sorry.'

'I don't want you to be sorry. I want you to marry me.'

'You're a nice man'

'Nice! What on earth does that mean?'

'But it's no good. I'm no good. I can't make this relationship work. I'd rather end things now, so at least we have something good to look back on.'

'You're joking!'

'Do I look like I'm joking?' He had never seen her so subdued.

'Tell me what I've done wrong!'

'It's not you. Let's just leave it there, can we?'

'This is crazy.' She gave an ironic little smile that twisted his heart but there was no reprieve.

'Perhaps you need space for a while.' The ironic smile deepened. 'I'll move back to my parents for a bit. But I'm not giving up – I'll be there. Think about it, please.'

'Don't you think I *have* thought about it! Don't waste your time waiting – get on with your life.' She even kissed his cheek coolly, then walked to the door. 'I'm going out for a while. There's no need to take all your stuff now – I'm not going to bar you from the house. You can collect things whenever you want, but perhaps you could leave your key.' And she went. If only he'd had something concrete to fight against it would have been easier. What exactly was he arguing against? He just knew she was utterly wrong. An hour later Dai was back at Brynglas.

'Christ Almighty, not again,' was his father's only comment. Even his mother seemed somewhat unsympathetic. Dai avoided his grandfather and went up to his bedroom.

Helen almost left the phone ringing but her prepared speech was unnecessary when she found Neil's voice on the other end. She didn't tell him about Dai, not yet, but at the end of the call she asked, 'You know the guy who wrote *He either fears his fate too much . . .*'

'Marquis of Montrose – what about him?'

'What happened to him?'

'A royalist. Supporting Charles the Second he landed a small army back in Britain. They fought against tremendous odds.'

'And?'

'Wiped out of course. Why.'

'Just wondered.'

11

'I suppose you'll want to go back on buying the cottage.' Dai hadn't thought about it but the response to his father's question came quickly.

'Of course I'm not going back on it. I need somewhere to live and besides, we shook on it.' There were other 'besides' that Dai kept to himself. And besides, Helen and he would be there together one day. And besides, he was bailing out his Dad financially without seeming to. And besides, physical work on the cottage would take his mind off the emotional tangle he seemed unable to unravel. He was torn by two opposing convictions, both equally strongly held. In time, Helen would realise that their relationship was too important to end for a delusion, a chimera. On the other hand, she had looked at him as if she now saw him clearly, without the glamour of love, and the quiet resignation with which she had dismissed him had left a sick finality in the pit of his stomach.

'And if you want my advice,' which Dai didn't, but it was so rare for his father to give any that he held his

189

tongue. 'Don't patch the cottage – gut it, starting with plumbing and electrics. Rip 'em out and start fresh from the inside out. And allow four times as long as any workmen say they'll take, even if you know them.' Will gave a rueful smile. 'In fact, especially if you know them. They think you'll put up with more.'

Whatever daylight hours were left outside work and eating, Dai spent at the cottage. He booked in the water and electricity boards, telephone engineers, a plumber and building contractors. At first, he was frustrated by the laxity of timekeeping, appointments being kept within a few days or, occasionally, not at all. Any suggestion of impatience on his part seemed somehow to delay work even further, and he soon accepted the inevitable commitment to seven jobs on the go at any one time which characterised the workmen. His expectations fell to the point where he was actually grateful if they let him know when they weren't going to turn up. When he found the electrician to be prompt, efficient and incredible value for money, he kept shaking the man's hand and thanking him.

His days became increasingly complicated once a new front door, which locked, was put in place. From this point on, he had to make arrangements with keys whenever workmen needed access to the cottage interior. His parents were willing to help out but there still seemed to be an exhausting ritual of contacting builders and rearranging his calls so that he could drop into the cottage en route. Whenever he could, he joined in, if only by sitting against a wall and asking questions. He ripped out old wires and pipes (following his father's advice), hacked off rotting wood and took a claw-headed hammer to crumbling mortar until the bare carcass of a house was ready for whatever job was next on his priority list.

Unfortunately, his carefully worked-out priority list did

190

not quite match up with his workmen's agenda. A wet week prevented the builders rendering the exterior on schedule and they arrived at the same time as the double glazing company. Dai wasn't even there for the ensuing squabble over which men were harder pressed for time and more constrained by factors outside their control, but he heard varying accounts afterwards. Inevitably, the upshot was that everyone refused to start work without a guarantee that they would be the only ones on site, so the two vans drove off at high speed leaving Dai to wonder that night at the lack of progress and eventually, through persistent phone calls, track down the reasons why. More phone calls established a new order for the work, with margins for weather, other commitments and what Dai could only call the L factor (Life!). Increasingly wordly-wise, Dai could only marvel that the habits of continental workmen had seemed quaintly humorous in popular fiction. Why go so far when you could study the species locally?

Dai kept to his resolution to leave Helen space and time, and had sent only one card affirming his commitment. He poured his love into a cement mixer, into turned newel-posts on new bannisters, into a slate hearth and an artexed ceiling. He eased his pain knocking down an old wall with a sledgehammer, fighting mud in the autumn rain to unblock drains and adjust the angle of new plastic guttering. He sliced a storm-split tree and dried out a round two inches thick as a nameplate. After a few practice attempts on some scrap wood, he traced the pencilled letters with a blowtorch, drilled two holes at the top and attached a chain. The sign *Brynglas Fach* was then hung ceremonially from two masonry nails in the newly whitened rendering. The compliment was not lost on Dai's father, who regularly inspected progress in 'Brynglas junior' as he went about his work.

Will nodded at the sign. 'That'll please the postman. On a wet day he can ignore the 'fach' and leave your mail with us. How's the electric?'

'Perfect – come on in and have a look.' Dai left his struggle with a paving slab and led his father into the cottage. 'There.' He indicated the walls with pride. Luckily, Will was a practical man, who was able to nod approvingly at the mess of wires hanging from ceilings and out of walls, for lights, cooker and power points.

'It's coming on,' Will agreed. 'But leave it a bit yet before you ask your Mam down.' They shared a look and a shake of the head which expressed their mutual experience of female insensitivity, that inability to recognize a perfect soldering job or a good piece of hardwood, combined with an obsession with decor. Dai felt the familiar pangs that his woman would not be visiting. Not yet, he told himself, not yet, and he returned to wrestle even more fiercely with the paving slabs in the front path.

Fresh air and manual labour, on top of his usual heavy workload in surgery hours, rounds and research, strained every muscle Dai possessed. He even slept well, having perfected the sleight of mind which allowed him to postpone thinking about Helen 'until tomorrow'. His dreams were less well regulated and frequently forced 'tomorrow' on his brain in the early hours of the morning. For all he was aware, he had never had dreams before, and he would have been grateful to retain his habitual and comfortable distance from his subconscious. Instead, he found his first thoughts on waking dominated by bizarre images. Some could clearly be attributed to his conscious concerns even if oddly presented, as when Helen teased him with a game of strip scrabble only to accumulate swan feathers as she lost clothes, eventually vanishing in cartoon-genie style into a stoppered tomato sauce bottle, from which he was still trying to shake her as he awoke. Other dreams he could not begin to translate or account for, except by the feelings they left him with – happy, guilty, nostalgic. He felt worst after the happy dreams, as though something had been regained in sleep and lost again in waking. It was just as well dreams – and the feelings they aroused – faded quickly. Dai prescribed more work for himself until at times he was so tired he felt himself to be dreaming all the time. On one particular morning, Dai woke full of deep and terrible regret, which regained perspective as he realised it should be attributed to him having gone off to the pub while his mother's lovingly baked cake staled – on his seventeenth birthday. Only through these recent dreams had Dai become familiar with guilt. It was an emotion usually associated with other men's wives and with which he was impatient. 'Either don't do it or don't feel guilty about it' was a philosophy which had been particularly useful following an instinctive kiss. As he saw it, only guilt was keeping Helen from him, so he found it impossible to consider their separation as anything other than temporary. He did, however, think it might be helpful if he could develop some understanding of her feelings. Which meant taking guilt more seriously. Perhaps, he mused after his birthday cake dream, he had suffered from a less accommodating conscience when he was younger, and he tried to recall other occasions when anything like that feeling – 'I'm so awful, how could I have done that, there's nowhere to hide my shame' – had touched him.

He had already told Helen of the professional mistakes, but they were part of the responsibility he shouldered daily and shared with other vets, accepted as the downside to the days he was thanked for performing miracles. He did remember a fiasco involving a newborn chick, when he was twelve, that had left a raw spot. He had hatched a batch of eggs in an incubator, carefully monitoring the temperature and the automatic turning, having lost one batch during a power cut. On the first occasion, his curiosity had led him to check how far the eggs had developed and although he had felt sick at the smelly greenish albumen and the dead half-formed embryos, he had also been fascinated, and had stored up the scientific information in that part of his mind which also retained the anatomy of a dead mole, a sheep's skull and other boy's treasures. The second batch of chickens had delighted him with their determined assault, bulging through the interior air sack to peck a crack and force their wet way into the greenhouse environment of the incubator. As they dried out into the fluffy cheeping Easter chicks images, Dai noticed that one chick had a badly crippled leg and was being knocked over and crushed by the others.

His mother had told him to put it out of its misery; chickens were vicious with each other even when fit to compete in the pecking order. Dai had watched the cockerels spur blood and fly at each other's eyes, the fatigued loser being fair game for the whole run, and he knew she was right, but he was too stubborn to accept it. She let him learn the hard way. He had separated out his little crippled chicken, hand-reared it for a fortnight in a cardboard box in his bedroom, where it weakened and died. Its death smelt like the murdered embryos and he took to heart the message that if you play God, you take on the responsibility for a kind death. That knowledge had steadied his hand as a vet, time and again. Even as the feelings of guilt revived in Dai at the memory of the chicken, so did his knowledge that what he had done and learned was part of what he was, and guilt had no place in that. He gave up. However much he loved Helen, they were different people and he could not begin to share her guilt.

'Dai! Can you help a minute?' His mother's voice called him to the kitchen. 'Can you get those things off the top shelf for me?'

'Autumn cleaning?' he teased.

'And so will you be when they finish that house of yours. Load of old mess workmen leave. It'll take you months to wash the dust off the walls and windows – it gets everywhere.'

'A little bit of dust won't hurt. It works homeopathically you know. They've proved that people are less likely to have asthma if they have a regular intake of dust and house mites and all those little bugs that live in even the best-kept houses.'

'Get off with you.' She flicked his fingers off her shoulder where they were making little spidery movements. 'Be serious, Dai. Your Grandad's not very well. You should spend more time with him. He enjoys your company.'

Dai stepped back, no longer familiar. 'I'm not twelve to be told what to do. I'm busy.' He softened the instinctive irritation in his voice. 'I'll try and sit with him a bit when I can. All right?'

'That's all I'm asking.'

All! All! thought Dai. These women were all the same. *All* they ever wanted was something from you that you didn't want to do, give or be. Why couldn't they leave a man be? Even Helen, though she hadn't said it, wanted something else from him. Guilt, for God's sake. Why should he try and understand a feeling that was so pointless at best, destructive at worst, and either way not something he had a bloody clue about! He supposed he'd better sit with his Grandad some time. Perhaps tomorrow, or the next day.

Four days later, Dai sank into a chair in the tropical warmth of the sitting room and steeled himself for audience participation in the television news. However, his grandfather was comparatively subdued and it was Dai who felt the urge to hurl abuse at the screen. One item focused on the tragic death of a two year old who had wandered onto a railway line while his mother was on the telephone. 'She hadn't even noticed he was missing,' read the news-reader.

'It probably only took one minute,' Dai yelled, newly sensitive to the implied criticism. 'You can't bloody look after a kid every second you know. It could have happened to anyone!'

Dai's Grandad took a tranquil puff on his pipe, steadying it with a hand that shook as he rested it back on his lap. 'I remember when you were two,' he said. 'Right little devil. Your Mam was calling 'Dai, Dai,' right throught the house. She had you drowned, battered and murdered in her mind till she heard you crying in the little cupboard. You'd hid in there to play a trick on her, but someone must have pushed the door to and you couldn't get out. Can't have been more than five minutes you were gone but your Mam tanned your bottom 'til it was red, just from her worry and relief. Funny how you always do that, hit someone or shout at them when they're safe. She was shouting 'Dai, Dai' – comical really, but she didn't think so.'

A news item on illegal immigrants attracted Lloyd's attention. 'You know the most precious thing you've got, Dai?' The portentous pause tempted Dai to make several facetious answers but he restrained himself.

'Go on, surprise me.'

His Grandad laid the pipe to rest in its little stand, his hand shaking a little as he pointed at Dai to emphasise his point. 'My Dad told me and I'm telling you. Someone offered him money when he went up to London and said they would buy it off him. Mind you, it was how it was in those days that he thought he had to take it with him to get to London. Anyway he said "This is my most precious

196

possession." His passport, it was, his nationality. All this fuss about being Welsh is a pity if you ask me. In my day it was easy enough to speak Welsh and we had to work hard to get the English good enough, and now all these college professors are talking of throwing it all away. A British passport!' extolled Lloyd. 'My Dad fought in the war and he knew what people would do to get one and he knew it for the treasure it was.' The pipe made its faltering way back to his mouth and the small puffballs of smoke danced with dust motes in the beams from the setting sun.

'Another tragedy at a local beauty spot where last week a woman walking her dog found the body of Terry Rattigan,' intoned the newsreader. 'Today a mother was walking the shore with her two small children when Gareth, aged four, slipped and was caught in the stream which joins the sea at that point. Despite frantic searching, the body has not been recovered and it is assumed that the boy has been carried out to sea.'

'Hanged himself, Terry Rattigan,' commented Lloyd with relish. 'From a tree below the castle. I feel sorry for the woman who found him. Imagine! You're out for a walk with your dog on a lovely sunny day. Is that a rabbit, King? What's all that barking for? And then she looks in the bushes and it doesn't bear thinking about, does it. Terrible thing, depression.'

But Dai was following his own train of thought. 'Always the mothers to blame. You can hear it in her voice.' He raised his own, growing angrier and imitating the newsreader's voice. 'No decent mother would allow her child to get swept out to sea.'

'That's true,' Lloyd assented blithely, earning a withering look from Dai which was totally wasted. 'She should have been more careful.'

'An eleven-year-old boy died in North Wales today after

197

being run over by a tractor which his father was driving on the family farm. It was described by police as a tragic accident.'

'You learned to drive in a tractor,' observed Lloyd. To his amazement, Dai jumped up and down in his seat, raising both arms in the time-honoured gesture of sporting victors. 'Yes, yes, yes!' he crowed. 'A man whose unbelievable stupidity kills his son! A man to blame! And the man will have to live with that all his life,' he declared vindictively.

'I think you've been working too hard,' was the kindest remark his grandfather could find.

'Food's on the table,' announced Gwen, coming to help Lloyd rise from his chair.

'Your son's mad. He's shouting at the telly and laughing at all the bad news saying he's glad.'

Gwen cast an amused glance at Dai, as if to say, 'We know who's going mad, but make allowances.'

Lloyd caught the look and said sourly, 'I might be getting older but I'm not *twp* yet. The blackbird sees its babies white but I know that boy's cracking up. You'd better see someone before it gets worse,' he advised Dai.

'Perhaps you're right, Grandad.' *But there's only one person I want to see.* And shouting at a television was unlikely to help. After his meal he went out to the yard and split wood till his arms and brain were numb.

Dai had worked with his partner for long enough to establish a good understanding, despite David's reserve. They were a good team who capitalised on each other's strengths and watched each other's backs, looking for the signs of strain or complacency which led to mistakes, double checking and reminding each other, training the nurses to do likewise. Dai had learned to listen to his instinctive gut reaction to a patient – and its owner – and then apply all his training and experience. David was more coldly analytical, precise in observation and deft in surgery. They both responded to a challenge, but whereas Dai could find satisfaction in curing a commonplace complaint, David needed the exceptional – a new and difficult surgical technique, a rare blood disease – to provide professional highs. Dai had sometimes accused him of deliberately looking for difficulties 'to make life more interesting,' and David had acknowledged with a laugh that he would be happy to cure ear-mites with brain implants.

Both men were open-minded, shared their views on current research and considered how to improve their practice. Dai had experimented with homeopathic medicine and was willing to investigate some of the folklore cures from his farming childhood, while David tended to be the one who introduced new medicines, cautiously. They compared notes and always followed through a course of action the other had decided upon, if they swapped clients by chance or lack of client preference.

After the initial conversation telling David that his marriage was over, Dai found work to be pleasingly devoid of personal tension, somewhere he was in control and in harmony with his colleague. It therefore came as something of a shock when he headed towards the Interview room he used as a den for his paperwork and Sarah said, 'Oh, Dai? David said he's sorry he's left your drawers in a mess – he needs to talk to you.' Dai looked at the pile of papers on his old desk, and at the top drawer, still slightly open. He pulled it further out but he already knew what he would find. The envelope addressed to the Ministry, containing all the details of his father's illegal records, was missing. There could only be one thing that David wanted to talk to him about.

'Why don't you try highlights?'

Helen's reflected face grimaced at Jane, who was holding out a chunk of hair and snipping at it. 'In my life or just my hair?'

Her friend laughed. 'Sometimes one leads to the other.' She held out another chunk and compared lengths critically, pulling the wiry tendrils straight.

'Don't be too fussy – it just curls back up into a mess, whatever you do to it.'

'Professional standards to maintain. Anyway, if I undercut the back a little, it'll curl under for you. You should use mousse, you know.'

'I should do a lot of things,' said Helen drily, 'but I'm not going to start now.' Jane shrugged and concentrated on shaping the springy back edge. 'You'll have to stand for this bit.'

Around them eternal verities were confirmed; that this inner sanctum for women was preserved as strongly by brush strokes as any mason's lodge by a funny handshake, and that young hairdressers always go out on the town on a Saturday night.

'Don't they drive you potty?' asked Helen, gratefully sitting again. She always felt like a naughty child standing in a corner when Jane was trimming the back.

'Goes with the job. Wallpaper chat and wallpaper music. I think of it as psychotherapy. When I'm training a new girl, I tell her, "Make your customer feel pampered. If she wants talk, talk; if she wants peace, silence is golden." We had a girl here on work experience who wouldn't open her mouth – never make a hairdresser. The scissors stuff you can learn – personality needs something there to start with.' Jane surveyed her handiwork with pride. 'Though of course there's scissors stuff and there's art.' She bent down and whispered in Helen's ear. 'A hair root is the most sensitive

200

erogenous zone you know – direct route to orgasm.' She stood back and smiled innocently as Helen hastily uncrossed her legs and shook her hair. 'For some people.'

'I said it was a good way to start the day, but that's not quite what I meant,' Helen attempted to clarify, but gave up, her composure ruffled for once.

'I won't give away any more tricks of the trade!' Jane gave a last tickling flick of brush to sweep stray clippings from the skin, then whisked the garish plastic gown from Helen's shoulders. 'Ten to nine – have a good day.'

Indulging in an early morning appointment with Jane had lifted Helen's spirits, but it was always unsettling to face your own image in the relentless strip lights, particularly with an unflattering cap of wet hair pasted about a face that seemed all bags and hollows. Once her hair was restored to long red froth, she could hide behind it again.

To give up someone you still love is an act of either great courage or even greater stupidity, and Helen's view of her decision had alternated between the two verdicts over the last ten weeks, while clinging to the decision itself. Indeed, she was now incapable of making any decision, however trivial, without misplaced agonising. A weary numbness had replaced feeling, and she stumbled from day to day, unable to recall her reasons for finishing the relationship with Dai and yet convinced that those reasons had been incontrovertible. They must have been or she would not have taken such a decision. QED. She did however know how to survive when all feeling had gone. She forced herself through daily routines, forced herself to go through the motions and contact her friends, until – as she knew would happen – she would sometimes smile and chat naturally. Life went on, and losing Dai merely reinforced her conviction that she was one of life's losers. That didn't stop you sneaking the little pleasures – coffee with a friend, an Inca motif in red and gold, a heron in flight – but some things were not for the likes of her. She was different, marked by fate and she knew it, but she would not spend her life with her nose pressed against the glass wanting others' sweeties. She would settle for the little pleasures.

Helen bumped into a burly middle-aged man who merely grunted, glared, adjusted his route and froze her apologetic smile and half-spoken 'Sorry'. She rubbed her side where he had whacked her and realised that it had not been her abstraction which had caused the collision so much as his sudden change of course.

It was to be that sort of a day. Once Helen had turned the corner, she could see that access to her shop was cordoned off by the police, two of whom were in the doorway of the picture-framer's next door. The picture-framer himself was sweeping shattered glass into a bucket, watched by a small knot of passers-by – people who *would* pass by, if there were any risk of them being asked to do something, Helen thought grimly. If she'd had a handbag, she'd have clutched it with both hands as she elbowed her way between an open-mouthed couple. 'Excuse me,' she started, trying to catch the attention of either of the police.

'Sorry, Madam, as you can see, this area's out of bounds to the public for now.' His long-suffering tone told of countless years stating the obvious to the ignorant.

Helen's hackles rose. Her voice was the quintessence of Standard English when she spoke with all the hauteur she could muster. 'This is my shop, Officer. If there has been a break-in, it would be civil if I were informed. If not, then I would like to enter my own premises in the customary manner. If that doesn't inconvenience you, of course.'

A level brown gaze regarded her coolly. 'There's no need to be like that, Madam. We have a job to do and you're not the first to be annoyed you can't get past.' His partner

202

snapped down the aerial on her walkie-talkie and cut through the tension. 'Yeah, but she's the first one with every right to an explanation. Come on, Gareth, remember 1% of the population have brains.'

Surprisingly he smiled. 'Yeah, but you think that's just the women.' Automatically, Helen thought, 'Nice smile. So policemen do have a sense of humour.' She felt obscurely guilty for her manner – after all, hadn't she felt much the same about the onlookers? – and envious of their easy partnership, she who worked alone.

The woman PC moved a cone to allow Helen into her shop, which she was relieved to find intact.

'I'm PC Wardell and my partner is PC Gareth Evans.' PC Wardell had followed Helen into the shop and produced the inevitable notebook. 'There's been a break-in next door and I need to ask a few questions. Are there any signs of an intruder being in your shop?'

'None.' Although it did look as if someone had thrown balls of wool in the air to see how big a pile could be formed when they landed. She must tidy up and put some creative energy into the business.

'Did you notice anyone hanging around outside yesterday? Or over the last few days?'

Pause for thought. 'Not that I noticed.'

'Any strange customers? Particularly someone who browsed but didn't buy anything?'

'You mean like the man who wanted me to knit him the Prime Minister's face on a balaclava?'

Grey eyes narrowed. 'You're joking.' Stated flatly after consideration.

Helen sighed. 'I'm sorry. Yes, I'm joking. I find many people strange but I haven't noticed anyone carrying a brick . . .' A warning glance stopped her continuing with a burglar's profile, 'or anything that seems relevant.'

203

'It was unlikely but it's worth asking, just in case.'

'I don't think I'm any good at helping the police with their enquiries,' Helen said ruefully.

'Not many people are.'

'What's the damage?'

'Apart from a large, expensive window which will be a security risk until replaced, whoever smashed it went into the shop, presumably looking for cash and valuables. I would guess our man was a bit frustrated by finding no cash and only a load of picture frames, so he carried on smashing and trashed the place, fittings and all. It probably took place last night but it's hard to tell when there's no alarms fitted. Mr Griffiths discovered the break in when he arrived this morning and called us.'

The paradoxical professional intimacy of 'our man' jarred on Helen. Poor Mr Griffiths, facing the violation of his craft as well as his premises. How many people had walked past the smashed glass? If she had been working late, or if the policewoman were wrong about the time, perhaps Helen could have been here when the crime was actually being committed. She shivered. What else would 'our man' have added to breaking and entering? 'Is my shop at risk? Could I be next?'

'To be honest, last night's effort won't have encouraged our man to break into another little shop with nothing of value – no offence, but wool and loose change don't exactly tempt your average petty criminal – and probably cuts and bruises for his pains. On the other hand your security is nil, no alarms, no shutters and a whole pane of glass waiting for the first drunken yobbo who can't resist a smashing time. Which is probably just what happened last night.'

Chastened, Helen looked at her shop window where she had spent so long arranging a display of winter woollies with plastic snowflakes dangling on threads to create the right ambience. She now saw a vast expanse of glass with an invisible instruction label on it – 'Break me' or perhaps (she was starting to understand the psychology of it now) 'DON'T break me!' Neil would understand.

'Could it have been youngsters?'

'Could have been. But it isn't always. Alcohol brings out adolescent behaviour in all ages.'

The old-fashioned doorbell tinkled as PC Evans entered. Helen had considered the doorbell to be a security measure, letting her know someone was in the shop, but she now felt naïve. The policeman's deep local accent was inexplicably reassuring and again touched the vulnerability in Helen, although it was his partner he was addressing. 'I've finished next door and opened up the area again. Good news from base – no luck with the beat officers but video surveillance has caught it.'

'Time?'

'They watched from pub chuck-out onwards, as you suggested. Spot on – 11.20.'

'Description?'

'Three youths, male, one clearly visible, about fifteen or sixteen. You can see him looking round then throwing a bottle through the glass. Then the others join in.'

'Good.' PC Wardell gave a satisfied smile. 'Thank you for helping us with our enquiries Miss,' she checked her notebook, 'Tanner. I don't think you'll be bothered by that bunch but I strongly recommend that you have a security risk assessment, install alarms and check your insurance.' Helen's heart sank, both at the implicit threat and at the likely costs.

'How can you be so sure you'll catch them?'

'Modern technology.'

'And local knowledge,' added Evans. 'We'll scan the image from the video onto computer and pass it to the local schools

205

and colleges. The boys are probably still at school – or just left. Some schools even have photo-rolls of pupils and will match automatically, others can compare manually. Either way, we'll have a trace and a match within hours. If it was someone older we could spread the net wider . . . Computer-aided identification has really helped us in the job.'

'What will happen to them?' asked Helen, suddenly seeing Neil, with his problem-solving frown, wondering where he had gone wrong and compiling new teaching resources on alcohol abuse and respect for property.

'Not enough if they're under sixteen. But we're cracking down as hard as we can. Zero tolerance, like it says in the papers.' Helen hoped they weren't from Neil's school.

'We'd better be off. Goodbye, Miss Tanner, and please take the security advice.'

'Or you'll see me again!' Helen's attempt at humour fell flat.

Locking her own shop, Helen went next door and prescribed a cup of hot, sweet tea for the second time that day. She not only made the tea, but she sat with Mr Griffiths – Simon he turned out to be – and heard that he'd been intending to retire and this was the last straw. She urged him to think it over, not to make a decision when he felt low, but she suspected he would close shop and be much happier making frames for friends and acquaintances with none of the risks and overheads of a small business.

On her way home from a day's work which Helen preferred to forget, she bought a local paper to see if there was any report of 'her' burglary. A preliminary flick through showed little news, and a more detailed read, curled up with (yet another) cup of tea, revealed just how little.

Bored, she closed the paper and reached out for her cup, when suddenly the phone rang. Her heart lurched painfully in anticipation of Dai's voice.

'Helen?' Neil spoke hesitantly. Not Jimmy again? If it were, she'd say no. 'There's something I'd like your opinion on. I think I know what I want but I need to say it to someone I trust, to hear if it's true.'

'Shoot.' Helen shifted to a comfortable listening position.

'I've got the chance to go to Alsace for a year, on a teacher exchange. I'd teach English at a college there and my partner would come over here and teach my French and German classes. It'd be a bit of an adventure, and good for my teaching – improve both my languages and give me a broader view of education.'

'You don't have to sell it to me – sounds great. Do you want an assistant who speaks fluent English, some French and has exceptional designing skills?' And is going to be even more alone. 'So what's the problem? Your Mum?'

'Yes and no. You know what she's like. She told me I must go, that a year's nothing and I should make the most of my life. She says she'll enjoy having an attractive Frenchman to stay who'll appreciate her cooking.'

'She's right. So he'll stay with your Mum?'

'Yes.'

'Where will you stay?'

'That's the other thing – it's a swap, which is all well and good if it's a single man in a flat, but I'm a bit wary of someone else's family.'

'Well it's unlikely that a married man will just abandon his wife – with or without kids – so either there won't be one or she'll come with him. Odds on it'll be someone on his own. The details will sort themselves out – just say yes.'

'Oh, there is one other attraction.'

'Yes?'

'It's a stork habitat – they've re-introduced them virtually from scratch and I can do voluntary work at the Rehabilitation Centre, through the RSPB.'

'Now I get the picture!'

'If I go . . .'

'When you go . . .'

'Will you do something for me? Keep an eye on my mother and keep in touch with me? I'd like that anyway – I expect you over for a visit – but I'd never forgive myself if anything happened to her while I was away.'

'I can certainly pop round to your house now and again, but I warn you that I'll sit on your chair and I'll seduce your Frenchman!'

'Deal. I haven't quite made the decision yet but I'm getting there. I'll call again soon.'

''Bye.' So even Neil was adventuring, leaving her to look after his mother. People had to move on in their lives, change was inevitable. Had Dai moved on? Of course, she hoped he had and if he hadn't, perhaps a gesture of goodwill from her would spur him on. A last present to make it clear to him that although it was of course over, it had been special, important and they should remember each other with affection. What a noble, generous gesture such a present would be. It never crossed her mnd that if he were getting over her, a present would be a cruel reminder that would set him back. Instead she thought long and hard about an appropriate gift until she knew she had hit on exactly the right choice.

12

Dai had no time to think through what he would say to David, who had clearly been waiting for him – as well he might. His fine features looked drawn, a trace of worry evident to someone who knew him well. He closed the door carefully and pulled a chair over to Dai's desk – a long conversation, then.

208

'I'm sorry, David, I should have talked to you,' Dai began, hesitantly, but his partner ignored him, intent on his own train of thought.

'This is likely to turn nasty, Dai. It's important we present a united front although I realise how difficult this is going to be for you.' David had not looked directly at Dai once but was studying the corner of the desk.

There was an awkward silence. What was Dai supposed to say? *That's all right, it's only my father? It needn't turn nasty – I've just been slow sending away the details, but it will go now?* Now that it was too late he knew that he did not want that letter sent. He passionately, unprofessionally wanted to protect his father. There was, however, a practice to maintain and there had been hundreds of times he and David had empathised with farmers for breaking laws over exports, breeding, medication – you name it – but they had supported each other in making professional decisions. Dai had already been through this line of thinking and reluctantly he returned to the same conclusion, which led back to his reason for writing the letter in the first place; there were usually good personal reasons for breaking laws which were frequently stupid, but he could not turn a blind eye, even for his dad.

'I'll do whatever you think is right. But I think you're worrying too much about the practice – unless it's more widely known than I thought?'

'The TV programme last night has really put the cat among the pigeons.' David gave a twisted grin. 'Sorry, poor choice of words – it's the cats that are the problem. I really appreciate your support. Especially,' he swallowed and looked straight at Dai for the first time, 'when you warned me.' He waved some leaflets at Dai. 'I wish I'd never seen these.'

Cats? Support? 'I think I've missed something,' Dai ventured cautiously.

'Sorry – I thought you knew. Mrs Radwick brought Cranford Crystal in last night, dead.'

'The black Persian?'

'That's the one. I haven't carried out the p.m. yet but Mrs Radwick was hysterical. She'd just watched *Know your rights* on television, which had shown French pet owners whose perfectly healthy cats had died after being prescribed Tibodrine. This is our second death, and I'm beginning to think you were right about allergic reactions in the Higgins and Denton cats. No, let's be honest, I'm damn sure you were right, in all your misgivings before the trial and in your diagnoses afterwards.'

So that's what all this was about – Tribodrine, the new wonder drug to prevent fleas by vaccination. The leaflets David was waving had been stuffed in Dai's drawer because he'd had one of his instinctive reactions against the drug. He'd argued against its use, citing the lack of extensive trialling, the triviality of the problem it was designed to solve, the potential risks of the chemicals involved. David had countered with references to reputable scientific support, a reminder of the secondary consequences of flea infestation and a dismissal of Dai's reaction as his standard response to new medication. If Dai's instincts had prevailed, the practice would never have introduced the vaccine against feline leukaemia, a highly successful measure against the cat equivalent of AIDS. As always, the dispute had remained private and on this occasion David had won. Although Dai did not recommend Tribodrine to clients, he gave it on request and made no adverse comments when David's clients praised its efficacy. He did however note what he considered to be extreme allergic reactions in two animals and he collected any information on the use of the drug further afield, just in case. Among the leaflets David was holding was an article by a French vet

210

expressing the same misgivings as Dai, but the evidence was inconclusive.

'The allergic symptoms could easily have been coincidental rather than a consequence of Tribodrine, as you pointed out. The first death was of a twelve-year-old cat – again a mixture of factors to consider. There has been nothing published to suggest the drug is dangerous, until this television report last night, so there's no reason to blame yourself. You just think how many Vedro flea-sprays we sold – it must have been hundreds – until it was pronounced unsafe and taken off the market, but we didn't have one problem. All drugs carry risks – you know that.'

'I just wish I'd listened to you sooner, that's all.'

'So I was right this time – so what? Anyway, we don't know that for sure. Let's wait and see. What do we need to do?'

'The p.m., obviously. And report to Mrs Radwick.'

'I'll do both,' Dai volunteered. 'And if she's lost faith in the practice, I'll ask her in advance if she wants another opinion – I could ask Sonia. It might help if I tell her that because she's raised doubts about the safety of the product, we'll withdraw it straight away and write a report.'

'That sounds constructive. Perhaps we should get in first – go to the press, express our doubts . . .'

'Yes, but make it clear how much scientific evidence has supported Tribodrine, give some of the dangers of fleas, mention possibility of risks, side effects of all medicines . . . Oh – and include Mrs Radwick. It might help her to campaign, ensure others don't go through what she has, that sort of thing.' David was focused again, the shadow lifting. 'Not only does that sound like the right professional thing to do, but it might also prevent some thoroughly unpleasant local news items about us. Thanks, Dai. You could have done an "I told you so".'

Dai shrugged 'Hindsight's a wonderful thing. You today, me tomorrow.'

'Still, thanks.' David stood up to leave. 'By the way, this was in your drawer. I was going to put it for posting but I wondered if it was one of those things you'd left so long it didn't need to go any more?'

Dai couldn't read his partner's face. Did he know what was in the letter? 'You're right. That's exactly what it is.'

'I'll shred it then.'

'Fine.' Dai contemplated his feet as he listened to the whirr of the small machine shredding his careful, cruel words for future use as hamster bedding.

At the end of a hard day, Dai found his father manoeuvring a JCB, turning over the earth around the cottage and preparing the ground for what Dai still thought of as Helen's garden. A fresh sense of her absence caught him unawares after a day too busy for brooding, and he wondered for the first time whether he should steel himself to forget and move on, instead of this painful waiting, hoping. He gestured to his father, who completed a circuit and switched off the digger.

'It's looking good. Thanks, Dad.'

'First run only. Leave it for the rain and frost to break up the clods and I'll fine-rotivate it for you. Call it a Christmas present.' He gave a breathy chuckle which reminded Dai of his grandad. He had never thought of Will as getting older.

'Difficult day today Dad. Lot of paperwork to do.' He gave a sideways glance at his father. 'Too much paperwork these days. Letter to the Ministry about your register got destroyed in all the mess. No point making a fuss now. It's not as if you're still fudging the books.'

Will heard the question in the statement. 'The books are right,' he said quietly, 'and before you ask, yes, they'll stay that way.'

212

'Well, there we are then. Two early Christmas presents. Tell Mam I'll be up for food about nine. I want to sit on my own for a bit.'

'I'll tell her. See you later, son' There was no thank you, any more than there had been any pleading. Either would have acknowledged an unthinkable favour. There was however, an unmistakeable spring in Will's step as he walked back to his mechanical yellow beast, and his shoulders seemed less bowed.

Dai knew he should have felt guilty, but as far as he was concerned, fate had intercepted his honourable intentions and so be it. He sat on the borrowed rug in front of a two-bar electric fire in his nearly-finished sitting room. There is a limit to how long you can contemplate bars of heat, and Dai was ready to leave when he heard a van or lorry draw up outside. No workmen or deliveries were due, for a change, but it had to be someone to see Dai or someone very lost so he wearily rose to sort it out.

'Yo! Anyone there? Bloody Interflora here – with a difference.'

Wandering around the cottage, trying to work out where best to try for a response, was Gardener, the pig farmer.

Dai sighed. He had occasionally had to deter clients who pestered him at home, and he hated their righteous indignation as much as his own feeling of being under siege. 'I'm sorry, Mr Gardener, but if there's an emergency the surgery will contact the duty vet – and it's not me today, I'm afraid.'

'You've got got it arse backward, so just come and get the flowers and I can go home. Oh, and there's this,' was the strange response. Gardener presented Dai with a scruffy piece of paper on which was written, 'Goodbye, but I won't forget you – Helen' – in what was presumably Gardener's handwriting.

Bemused, Dai said, 'I haven't got a clue what you're on about.'

'It's clear enough. Some mad woman has sent you some flowers. She talked me into delivering them.' Gardener was spluttering with laughter at a joke only he could see. 'And I'm unloading them now, so come and get them.' Dai followed the farmer round the corner, where a landrover and horsebox were parked in the lane. An unmistakeable bray announced the contents of the horsebox and Dai watched as Gardener unlatched the tailboard and coaxed a reluctant donkey down the ramp. Most of a bunch of chrysanthemums were trampled underfoot in the trailer but the donkey still retained some battered specimens threaded in its mane. It regarded Dai balefully, big brown eyes half-hidden by a long fringe.

'She insisted on the flowers. Completely mad. But I've been hoping someone would have him before Christmas, and I couldn't hang on much longer. A vet's a real bonus. She said you'd got the right kind of place for Morgan, and your Dad's ponies for company.' He looked around, appraising the property. 'Not bad. Still a bit to do. Want a pig or two?'

'NO! No, thank you but definitely no.' How much had she paid Gardener? Could he say no? He looked at the donkey, which returned the stare, ruminating. 'When did you last check his feet?'

Gardener looked less comfortable. 'A while back,' he said vaguely. 'I mean we thought he'd be dog food as like as not. You know there's no slack for vet's bills for pets. Anyway, I've done what she asked. I'll be off now.' The tyres splattered some mud as the horsebox bumped off down the lane, leaving Dai holding a rope and contemplating his lover's present.

214

Ten minutes after the phone call, Helen was still shaking. She wanted to call him back, to say yes, she did want to try again; yes, she missed him terribly. It had never crossed her mind that he would consider the donkey to be an invitation to make contact, and the shock of hearing his voice again had numbed her into a frozen, monosyllabic response. He certainly would not doubt that it was over after that phone call. Well? Wasn't that what she wanted? She couldn't help smiling through the tears when she recalled his description of the donkey's arrival. She could just imagine his face as the gift-wrapped beast was unloaded. And how like him to call it Bogart. He had always preached that an animal should choose its name, and she could imagine his careful experiments to find a name that the donkey liked better than Morgan. He would have fixed the donkey with one of those serious, considering looks he had so often used on her, until he found a few names he thought were suitable. Then he would have tried them out on the donkey, watching for a sign of recognition – a twitch of a tail, the blink of an eye or toss of head. He'd have followed up their choice of name with its use, accompanied by a carrot, an apple, some endearments in Welsh. She ached for the endearments. Oh lucky, lucky donkey. The phone rang again while she was still reaching for it in her mind.

'Helen?' Charlotte's voice.

'It's me. What's new?'

'Actually there is something new.' Shy, hesitant. 'I'm pregnant.'

'That's wonderful!' Helen churned with pain and struggled to say the right things to her friend. 'I take it that you finally made up your mind?'

'We've been talking about it for so long, I didn't know what I wanted any more so I just thought I'd let fate decide and I stopped taking the Pill. I feel great. Dan's like a little

215

boy. He wants to paint the back bedroom and buy a train set.'

'When's it due?'

'August 23rd.'

'So you're . . .?'

'About three weeks pregnant!' The pride was unmistakeable.

'I'm not surprised you feel great!'

'Don't worry – I'll tell you all the details so you know what it's like in case you find the right man and want children. I'll call you again – I've got so many people to tell!'

'I'll look forward to that.' Helen's dryness was wasted.

'It's going to be so much fun sharing this with you and the others. 'Bye.'

''Bye,' said Helen but Charlotte had already rung off.

Helen pulled the phone out of the socket and wondered if it was time for her to leave Llanelli. Her urge to contact Dai had vanished, defeated by what separated her from normal, happy people like Charlotte. This was not the time to go, with Christmas orders to make up. She might go in the spring. She would have to consider the future of her business whether she stayed or went. Despite the increase in customers, she would have trouble breaking even this year. The town's only central wool shop had closed, an indication that the hand-knitting boom was over. Small village wool shops still remained, as did those in more affluent areas, but all the signs indicated that her craft was an expensive luxury that Llanelli could not afford – which meant that she could not afford Llanelli. She had already toyed with the idea of extending her design skills and her brush with the police had suggested a possible way forward. Perhaps it would also fill some of the raw emptiness of her spare time.

So Tuesday evening saw Helen enrolling for an adult course in Basic Computer Design, courtesy of the local tertiary college. She faced her screen and tried to produce the same bleeps and buzzes aroused by her classmates as they followed the tutor's instructions. Once she understood what it meant to double-click on a mouse, there was still the problem of physically carrying out the instruction. At least there was a concrete objective and no time to think.

Neil was encouraging when she discussed her course with him, although somehow the conversation kept returning to Alsace. They were stationed in Penclacwydd's main hide, in the fading daylight of a November Tuesday. Birds over-wintering in the estuary had been arriving in windswept drifts over the last month. Hundreds of lapwings were visible through Neil's telescope, their oil-slick plumage dulling to black as the light greyed. The lapwings' calls echoed eerily as the mists came down and Helen realised how easily peace could become loneliness. The notes of a solitary curlew bubbled up from the marsh but already the visibility was too poor to find it.

The coffee was warm and welcome. Helen grasped the mug in both hands and shivered. You didn't notice the chill until you left the hide and came back to the well-heated Centre. It was probably just the weather but Helen couldn't shake off a bleakness of the soul that was untouched by Neil's cheerful plans for a year abroad.

'When are you actually going?'

'Summer holidays, I hope, so I can work in the reserve before term starts in September.'

Perhaps she'd have moved on by then, an unpaired bird seeking richer feeding grounds and a warmer clime. What of her promise to keep Neil's mother company? What of it? A friendship was just another hostage to fortune if it meant too much. Better to enjoy it while it was there and leave go

217

when it was time. She'd stop French lessons and slough off the last remnant of someone who no longer existed. Neil was talking about storks. 'They're still endangered, despite all the work of the Centre, but there are signs of them nesting in some of the villages as well as at the Centre itself. Of course, it's essential to get rid of the migratory instinct. Most of those which fly to Africa get shot and a few are killed by telegraph wires. Even if we could persuade people to protect them, it would be too late, the numbers are too low now.'

'Why bother?' asked Helen gloomily. 'What is the point? Evolution at work says end of stork.' She made a throat-cutting motion with her hand. 'It doesn't really matter.'

Neil responded to her mood rather than to her words. 'What's up?' It was understood between them that Dai was a taboo subject and Neil respected her privacy. However, she suspected him of ascribing any moodiness to the end of her love affair, which irritated her deeply. The fact that Neil had expressed no such belief made no difference to Helen's reaction.

'Not what you think,' she responded sharply. 'If you thought you were going to be out of work after Christmas you might be a bit worried too.'

'That bad?' She nodded. 'I guess for all its problems, teaching's still relatively secure. People do keep having children. Although when you look at some of them you do wonder why . . .'

Helen shrugged. 'Anyway, I'm looking at ways of branching out, meeting the new market needs – if I can work out what the hell they are.'

'Let the computer work on the mathematics, the symmetry and the proportional scale; you provide the art. And you'd be surprised how much of that the computer can do for you with appropriate software.' So Helen had been told when she insisted that her keyboard skills would improve faster if she were working towards a practical goal. She wanted to design a glitzy evening top with a motif of birds of paradise. She experimented with size and positions of the bird, using the computer and a lot of help from her tutor, and then considered the latest draft. One bird swirled down the left front like an elegant corsage while the short cape sleeves were the tails of two asymmetrically placed birds dramatically dominating the back. The top would be a long tunic shape to balance the bold design, and she would knit it in fine metallic yarns, brilliant emeralds and reds on a gold background. There was one particular customer, the Indian wife of a local businessman, who had a weakness for rich colours and would be willing to pay the inevitably high price for such a garment.

If only, thought Helen, Christmas orders could all be like this. Her fingers were sore and her brain was numb from incorporating violent robots and sickly pink ponies into jumper designs for small boys and girls. Her window display included the olive mohair and silk design she had created months earlier, and which was still her favourite. She was both relieved and insulted when customers looked it over, said it wasn't quite what they wanted or quibbled at the price, leaving the jumper still unclaimed. Continuing after hours in the shop, or at home in front of the television, Helen drew birds of paradise. She collected pictures and descriptions from natural history books and magazines. She made sketches and ripped them up, knowing they weren't right and not knowing what 'right' was.

She screwed up another ball of paper, threw it at the bin and looked through her collection of stimulus material one more time. Her friends' help had been enlisted and there were one or two more references for her to read 'for inspiration'. She quickly discarded 'Ode to a skylark',

219

wondering wryly which of them thought a skylark 'close enough' to a bird of paradise. An article about a boy who kept a parakeet followed the discarded sketch to the waste paper bin. The next item looked too long and a very unlikely source of inspiration; an autobiographical account of living in a harem. She opened it at the marked page. 'Chama had to wait for months to get the exact red silk she was looking for and then the matching blue a few weeks later, and even then the colours were not quite right.' With growing excitement, Helen read of war waged with embroidery, where a powerless woman 'had to keep her birds buried deep down in her imagination' and reproduce traditional designs, where a woman could dream of 'a fabulous one winged green bird' representing 'the wings inside her'. Peacocks merged with birds of pardise in Helen's imagination until she could see her fabulous birds and she started drawing and visualising colours once more, thinking of harem women's dreams of freedom.

Two hours later, Helen was conscious of a stiff neck and looked up from her work. She couldn't believe how much time had passed while she had been absorbed in the curve of a tail and sweep of a wing. She stacked her sketches with a sigh of satisfaction, defying any computer to match her art, and she settled to watch something undemanding on television, which had been a mere visual backdrop during the evening. She turned the volume up and channel-hopped, lingering when she heard mention of Temple Newsam. Surely that was a stately home near Leeds somewhere? Sure enough, the presenter was showing the treasures inside a mansion and telling historical anecdotes. Helen let the commentary drift around her consciousness unil the word 'birds' caught her attention.

'. . . and Isabella, Lady Hertford, took these priceless works of art and cut out the birds. She then covered the

Prince of Wales' wallpaper with multi-coloured flights, to the horror of the artist. When he found out he immediately cancelled her subscription to his books . . .' Eighteenth century? Nineteenth? Another harem lady, thought Helen, dreaming of freedom. Through Helen's own dreams that night flew veiled peacocks with jewelled tails, carrying her with them high over the earth, to see the world growing smaller, more distant until it vanished and left only stars and soaring flight.

'Now!' Dai jumped sideways at his father's shout and the branch fell neatly where he had been standing. Dai automatically bent to drag the branch out of the way and found he could not shift it. His father laughed. 'I know. It still surprises me after all these years. You see them waving in the breeze as if they're light as air, then you take the strain for one branch. You remember pretty quick that it'll kill you if it hits you.'

'Now you tell me! So how come I'm the one on the ground?' grumbled Dai.

'Cause I'm not so green as I'm cabbage-looking,' was the response from up the tree. 'Come on, then. We've another three branches.' Dai unhitched the rope from the fallen branch and threw it up to his father. Will tied it firmly around another branch, threw the end down to Dai, and they began the process again. Will sawed and Dai pulled on the rope, opening the cut to let the saw bite deeper until the crack of rending wood led to the shout, 'Now!' and Dai jumped well out of the path of the falling branch. Once the fourth branch was pruned, Will climbed down and the two men dragged the debris clear of the trees. Limbless, the beech tree no longer threatened the telephone cable, but the naked new wood gleamed flesh-coloured at the severed ends.

221

'It looks odd. Like an amputee,' observed Dai.

'To a vet, maybe. To me it looks like a hedging tree long overdue a trim. If I'd thought it mattered, I'd have kept this hedge in better shape. He pointed to the mixture of blackthorn, beech, hazel and holly growing along the side of the lane which led to Dai's cottage. 'Better to prune in early spring when the sap's rising but before leafing.'

'Do I need to paint the cut ends with something?'

'You could give them a tar wash if you like but I wouldn't bother. Beech is tough enough. It's not as if it's a fruit tree.'

Dai shivered. 'I hadn't noticed the cold. Come in for a bit.' Brynglas Fach now had a Calor gas heating system fully installed and was maintained at a cosy temperature. Dai had picked up a few items of second-hand furniture to make the place habitable, but had given up on home-making after that. There were still smells of new plaster and sanded wood, and odd tools abandoned by unfinished jobs but, like the pile of dirty dishes, Dai just ignored them till his next burst of energy arrived.

'You can get a stack of logs from today's work.' Will nodded at the empty grate, no longer housing the little electric fire which had been the only source of heating. Dai had kept the old cast-iron fire-place, which Helen had so much admired, but had replaced the broken tiles and he was pleased with the effect. He had also splashed out on wooden flooring in sitting and dining room, although he'd quickly put down cheap rugs to cover the stains where he'd left mugs of hot coffee and plates of takeaway food. He'd tried to carry out the ideas Helen had had when she'd first seen the cottage, but he could no longer see the point of it. He despaired of her ever seeing the cottage, never mind living in it, and he saw no point in buying the kitchen dresser or in decorating. When he'd phoned her, his hopes raised by her present, she'd been cold enough to freeze hell.

222

'Cup of tea?'

His father's lazy, 'Ie', the colloquial Welsh equivalent of 'Yes', reminded Dai again of Helen. He took the Welsh language for granted and had never thought it odd to speak a language that had not one word for yes, but many. 'No wonder the Welsh have a reputation for being devious,' she'd teased, 'when it depends what you say to me as to which yes-word I should say back!'

'It's simple,' he'd said, 'just reflect the question in the answer. I say, Do you love me? and you say 'I do'.'

'What if I don't?'

'Say 'I do not'. Anyway, you do.' He'd tickled her feet 'til she agreed.

'Enough! And if I do, I want to say a straight yes.'

'You are saying yes, the Welsh way.'

'Ah, but the Welsh way is too complicated.'

He'd shaken his head. 'Not if you're Welsh.' He missed her. She'd come from a different world and made his seem rich. How drab it was without her. He made his father a cup of tea.

'I'm thinking of diversifying.'

'Not ostriches and kangaroos, Dad please!' There had been all kinds of recent experiments in farming and the produce 'designer meat', a fad that Dai sincerely hoped would be short-lived, for the sake of the ostriches, the kangaroos and the local vets.

'What do you take me for? No, I was thinking more of turkeys . . . I haven't thought it all through yet, but I've relied too much on the cows. The Welsh Development Agency is offering grants for starting local crafts, but I don't know . . . I just don't see me and your mother making wooden stools to sell in our tearoom on Mynydd Sylen.' Dai had to laugh at the image of Will whittling a rustic image for the tourists. Apart from the artificiality of

223

converting a working farm to suit a fantastic stereotype, there was the sheer impracticality of it. Tourists on Mynydd Sylen? Not for all the blarney in the local press about Llanelli's golden coast and unique amenities. He could almost hear Helen's dry comment, 'Well, be fair. Unique, they are. Good, they're not.'

'Don't rush into anything, Dad. This crisis will pass.'

'This one will, but I don't want to be caught like this again. Booth in Five Roads is making a 'Leisure Lake' stocked with trout, so he can charge a fortune for limited fishing rights. Rees down the road is thinking of selling up, but it's not a good time to sell. I'd buy some of his stock but I daren't spend money on that sort of risk at present.'

'I'll ask around, find out more about what the others are doing. Just don't rush into something,' Dai repeated, not knowing what advice to give his father. They both knew it was not an easy time to be a farmer. 'How's Bogart behaving?' he asked, to distract his father.

'He's put on weight and the ponies have taken to him all right.' Bogart was running free with Will's ponies, all now wearing winter blankets and with the option of an open-sided shelter where a regular supply of fodder attracted them and gave Will the chance to keep them tame enough to show when he wished. Dai and his father had strengthened fences to make sure the animals were safely penned and could no longer get into the cottage garden, although they grazed alongside it. 'You'd better keep up the talk and treat routine though. When he gets that look in his eye, I wouldn't want to argue with him.' Dai's 'treat routine' consisted of a carrot or apple each time he called Bogart or walked by him in the field. It had not taken Dai long to find the special place on his muzzle to smooth while sweet-talking the old donkey until he bared his worn yellow teeth

224

and snorted with pleasure. That did not, however, mean that Bogart was biddable. He was, after all, a donkey.

'I hope you're not turning him into a roly-poly pudding pony?' Dai eyed his father suspiciously. They had fallen out in the past over the weight of Will's ponies. Everyone in the show world knew that a bit of fat hid a lot of faults and no amount of Dai's criticism of unhealthy diets could prevent Will fattening up a pony before a show.

Will brushed off the comment. 'They're all skin and bone this time of year. I don't know what you're worried about. To say the truth, it's good to have a donkey at Christmas. There's something homely about them.'

Christmas? Was it nearly Christmas?

'Which reminds me,' Will continued, 'your mam asked if she could pinch some holly from by your cottage. There's more berries by here and three weeks is close enough to risk the birds beating us to it.'

Three weeks to Christmas? 'Yes of course – help yourselves.' Dai was dreading Christmas, the loneliest time of year. So was Helen, for the same reason and more.

13

Helen brushed the yellow gobbets of thawing snow away from the shop door and tried to shut out the jolly loop of Christmas tunes audible from the shop next door. Is this the best you can do? Two shopping days to go and a wet flurry of flakes had raised hopes of a white Christmas. Possibly on the hills there might be. On Mynydd Sylen, where Dai was, there might be. But not here, in the coastal concrete zone of Llanelli shopping centre. Here there would be the tidemarks of rubbish swept in wavering lines by the brief fall of snow. If Helen were to visit the beach, beyond the warehouses and the disused docks, there would be the same dirt curves on mud sands. Whether in town or on the beach, Helen could feel herself sinking in Llanelli's black mud, sinking into a bottomless hole that swallowed her fragile hopes for the future and belched them up stinking. You could import all the white sand you liked but the tides would always uncover the oozing, squelching essence of estuary.

Time to move on. Survive the drabness of winter and move with the restless surge of sap rising in spring, well before Charlotte's baby greeted the world and his 'Auntie' Helen. Meetings with the girls were less frequent, a subconscious response to Helen drifting away, but she could not politely evade Charlotte's excited details of pregnancy. Every conversation tangled Helen on the barbed wire of memories, and her friend's innocent affection merely poisoned the wounds.

'Do you think Dan will be a good father?'

What do you say? 'Yes, of course he will. You told me how excited he was about the baby.'

'Yes but he likes his sleep and his nights out with the boys.'

'So do you, like your nights out that is. There's bound to be changes for both of you.'

'But you don't know what it's like, Helen. You haven't had a baby. That's why I'm telling you everything, so you'll be well prepared. I've been talking to Sarah next door and she says the baby changed her life without making any difference to her Gareth. And as for sex – she says she's so tired she can't be bothered.'

Helen drew a deep breath and told herself not to care. It

226

was vital not to care. It kept you alive, not caring. 'If you think about it,' she said, 'we want a lot. You want a man who sends your nerve ends electric and can be relied on to do the washing-up and change the baby's nappies.'

'Speak for yourself.' I am, oh I am. And I'd found him. 'I just want a cuddle now and again, plus some help around the house.'

'I'm sure Dan will be fine.'

What did she want in a man? A good fit. She smiled at the ambiguity but liked the phrase more for it. A fit of sharp edges against curves, mind and body. And a leap of the heart that made life. She sighed. Had Charlotte's baby been made with a leap of the heart? She doubted it, but the baby would have a normal, loving family. She wanted too much. She missed Dai. Lack of sex, that's all it was, and the strain of not remembering motherhood.

The shop was not providing enough distraction. Helen's exotic birds had winged into glittering display on a tunic which had sold at twice the average price of her stock and taken five times as long to complete. Helen imagined her creation stunning St David's Hall in Cardiff where her customer was attending a Christmas Concert. She often wished she could follow the fortunes of her garments, hear any comments they attracted, visit the world they entered – particularly the special occasions. Her few regular customers would pass back compliments and she would wish she had heard the visiting Royal on walkabout saying, 'Lovely jumper – where did you get it?' She still fantasised about being 'discovered' but the accounts were looking gloomier than the weather and she was already marking down remaining stock for the January sales. Impatiently, she moved some Christmas cards out of her way, wincing as she caught the festive message from 'Sian and family'. Neither Sian nor Glenys had said anything about the

227

reduction in their work but they must know what was coming. If they did, perhaps it wouldn't be so hard to tell them. How Sian 'and family' would manage, Helen couldn't imagine. Little as she earned, it enabled Sian to buy wallpaper – a roll at a time – or treat the kids to a day in Tenby. Since Mike had been made redundant from the steelworks, there had been few treats. Sian's problem, Helen thought; Sian's problem.

Nothing forewarned her, when the shop-bell rang, that this customer would be any different from the previous three who had been trying to get last-minute presents at sale prices and had been offensive when Helen had told them that her sale started after Christmas, regardless of the fact that Living and Marks and Spencer's had reduced goods in already. She was therefore slow to look up when the bell rang again but the voice brought the colour to her cheeks.

'Déjà vu. I'd like some kind of fluffy jumper for a woman about your size.'

'Why are you doing this?' Helen looked at Dai, pleading with him to go away, leave her alone, not put her through this. Why was he here? Was he trying to tell her there was someone else? Surely he couldn't, he wouldn't buy one of her jumpers for his new girlfriend.

'For your wife?' she asked acidly, slipping his steady gaze.

'No, that remains one improvement the year has brought.' His tone was quiet, serious. He started to say something and then changed his mind. 'If you must know, it's for . . .'

She cut across him, speaking at the same time, 'These ones here are popular . . .' She laughed nervously. 'Sorry. What were you saying?'

'It's all right. I know which one I want – I'll have that one.' Helen regretted leaving 'her' jumper as the window centrepiece. She'd promised herself that if it didn't sell before Christmas, she'd treat herself to that jumper as a present. Trust Dai to want the best and assume that this must be it. She tried to hide her resentment as she carefully unpinned the olive mohair sleeves from their pose on backing paper. The intertwined Celtic cross motifs in gold twisted silk struck her anew with their combination of artistry and fine workmanship. She handled the jumper with care, wrapped it in tissue and tried to take professional pride in selling her favourite jumper to her ex-lover.

'I hope the lady likes it,' she said in her primmest shop assistant voice.

'The lady is my mother.' Again, he looked as if he wanted to say something else. 'I'm sure she will.' He shrugged. 'I hate Christmas.' The silence stretched out the implicit invitation.

She steeled herself. 'Yes, I'm sure it's a difficult time for a vet. Will that be all?'

'It seems that way. Happy Christmas.' He turned to go.

'Thank you. And you,' she said brightly. He left without a backwards glance. Hate Christmas, hate. And it wouldn't even suit his mother, who'd probably put it in a drawer 'for best' and never wear it. If it was for his mother of course. He'd lied to his wife often enough; he was probably lying now. Probably did want a present for his new girlfriend but had lost the bottle to say the words. The cheek of the man! She supposed she should feel flattered that at least he knew where to get a classy present, but flattered was not how she felt.

By four o'clock the sky was dark and the streets rowdy with boozy celebration. Five boys swayed to a halt outside 'Helen's Handcrafts' and pushed their faces against the shop window. Helen stared back, bemused, as noses and tongues were pushed into gargoyle shapes against the glass.

229

A tall one, wearing a shiny black jacket with elastic rib cuffs and collar, noticed Helen and started doing the sort of dance Helen had only seen performed by a randy gibbon. The accompanying noises added to the likeness and Helen just stood still, not so much watching as unable not to see. Her still presence seemed to aggravate the youth, who turned to his mates.

'Let's see what the bitch can show us, boys.' With a walk that was more stagger than the intended swagger, black jacket came into the shop, followed by the others.

'What handcrafts can you do, Helen?' slurred the boy, grinning at his friends and ducking his head from side to side, never once looking directly at Helen. 'S'wha it says on the shop – Helen does hand jobs.' He grinned again, checking that everyone had got the point, and the others made slurping noises and gave thumbs-up signs. It should have been funny. They were fifteen? Sixteen? Seventeen at most. All mouth and no trousers.

'Bugger off, boys,' Helen told them cheerfully and half-turned to pick up some patterns and leaflets. She found herself grabbed, her arm twisted and a beery mouth close, far too close to her face. A bit of spit landed on her cheek as black jacket spoke.

'Oh bugger off, boys.' He gave a mocking version of her accent. 'We're not boys, Helen.' He looked to his friends for encouragement. 'We're men.' There were supporting nods and one or two muscular arm gestures.

Helen couldn't help it. 'Yeah and I'm Santa Claus.' She could feel the adolescent blackness gathering over her head.

'Thinks she's funny. Can we show her something funny?' Black jacket's invitation was lost in the chaos caused by two distractions. A lad in a football sweatshirt had doubled over and suddenly loosed a stream of vomit over one of his mates and part of Helen's window display.

230

At the same time a woman's voice yelled, 'Mike! I thought it was you. I told you to stay away from that lot. Now get yourself home. And you wait till I see your Mam, Justin Rees. And you Walkie.' To Helen's amazement black jacket let go of her, turned into Mike, said 'Yes, Mam' and slunk out of the shop.

'Christ, you smell like your Dad,' said his mother sociably as Mike passed her in the doorway. She included Helen in her survey of the shop interior. 'Bloody disgrace they sell booze to kids. Shops'll do anything for a profit. And then the police pick up the poor kids, too pissed to know their own names.' Her tone sharpened. 'Get yourselves home, and for Christ's sake have a wash.' The remaining boys shambled towards the shop door. One of them obviously felt some kind of gesture was needed to retrieve the situation and he paused, looked meaningfully at Helen and said, 'Get this.' He then dropped his trousers, fumbling a little over the technicalities of zip and belt, but ensuring that Helen had an uninterrupted view of young male buttocks. Having apparently regained the upper hand, he gave a one-finger salute and followed his friends.

Shaking, Helen sat down. You couldn't always guarantee that someone's mother would turn up in time and what if . . .? They were only kids. Weren't they? You had to laugh at someone who considered a sixteen-year-old bottom to be the ultimate weapon. And yet.

Helen locked up early. She decided not to open up the following day, Christmas Eve. Town would be heaving with drunken men and it was always possible that Mike and co. would pay a return visit. She started mopping up the sick. It was Christmas again.

The doorbell woke her next morning and she hastily grabbed her dressing gown and answered the repeated ring.

'You're lucky it's got here,' said the postman, handing

231

her a parcel. 'Only posted yesterday but there's hardly any mail today so yours has got through. People have got the message about posting early for Christmas – you tell your friend that.'

Helen was still half asleep and merely muttered an obedient, 'Yes, sorry, thank you,' as she took the package and retreated indoors, echoing the postman's 'Merry Christmas' without enthusiasm. She ripped open the brown paper, vaguely assuming that one of her friends had bought her something to cheer her up. If she had been more awake, she would have guessed what it was from the size and softness of the parcel, but it wasn't until the olive and gold jumper fell out of the tissue in which she had so carefully wrapped it, that she realised. A Christmas card with a donkey on the front was enclosed and Helen found herself unable to throw it away with the others she had received, without reading its contents. Underneath the card's Christmas platitude, Dai had merely written 'from Bogart'. Helen noted the 'from' not 'love', the brevity of the message, all that was not there, and read into it sadly. Perhaps she had subconsciously hoped that the donkey would keep something open between them because she now felt the finality of this gift as a body blow.

She slipped on the jumper and looked in the mirror, trying to ignore the red-eyed misery of the face which looked back. She sighed. Better not to look in mirrors but just to feel the rich texture of the yarns and look down at the intricate motifs cabling up from the welts. She would wear her new Chrismas jumper, watch old films on television and survive the festive season once more. There had been worse Christmases.

It cost Helen nothing to tear up the cards which enabled her parents, and her sister, to salve their consciences. She could imagine the relief with which they informed their

232

friends, in suitably solemn tones, 'We try every year to get in touch with her but she doesn't want to know.' Their friends would be suitably sympathetic, saying, 'She always were difficult, your Helen. You couldn't have done more for her.' And Helen could remain gloriously, defiantly, miserably alone, even five years later.

Christmas Day spent on her own, wearing the jumper she had designed with love, given to her by the man she had loved and left, was in the fine tradition of Christmases past. At least she was able to switch off 'Mary Poppins'.

14

One can of beer was Dai's Christmas limit, as he had volunteered to be on call, foreseeing little joy in the day. He had suffered a traditional dinner with his parents, then retreated to the cottage. There had been a sprinkling of snow on the hills, prompting Meatloaf to jump excitedly for the snowballs Dai scraped together and fired at him, while the little Jack Russell shivered and looked disdainful. Although the dogs had moved in with Dai, the superior scraps at Brynglas always put a bounce in their step and they left reluctantly, tails low, until revived with play and irresistible smells en route. It was comical to watch three black noses competing for the same blade of grass, presumably graced earlier by a fox if Dai's less sensitive nostrils were any judge.

There had been a few days of looming snow clouds which had let loose occasional flurries, but today's sky was sharp and clear, pure blue and sparkling to sear the eyes. The snow had crisp, frosted edges, crunching as Dai walked. However often you saw the magical transformation worked by snow, it would always catch your breath. Trees shook white fringes in a light breeze and the hedges were neat piping around square cake-top fields. Even the council housing estates glittered under iced roofs in the distant villages down the valleys. It would last a day or so and prove that a white Christmas was possible, but there was not enough for children's games. The coastal areas had probably had nothing. Dai could predict the exact level of the snow line, finishing abruptly as the road dipped on the long slope down to Llanelli, where people would look with disbelief at the melting snow on his car. Llanelli, where Helen was. How she would love the views today. She sometimes spoke nostalgically of Yorkshire winters, their guarantee of coldness and clarity, and he teased her about the effect the city's landfill sites and phosphorous output must have on the Leeds air. She had talked and he had teased.

Sod's law operated without mercy and, just when Dai was longing for something to take his mind off Helen, the entire animal population spent an entirely healthy Christmas Day, as far as he could judge, for there were no calls. He even telephoned his emergency transfer number to check the phones were working, but a cheery 'Happy Christmas – no, no calls, enjoy it,' confirmed his freedom. He visited Bogart, penned in a stable in case the weather worsened and suitably appreciative of a fresh carrot. Dai had been tempted, for one mad minute, to take the donkey some Christmas pudding. As if he didn't know the stomach problems that followed Christmas treats from sentimental – and lonely, he reminded himself – pet-owners. Still, there was something about a donkey at Christmas. He stroked the long ears and bony nose, informing the enigmatic animal that only a donkey could appreciate the true meaning of Christmas. Dai was rewarded with a double huff of warm breath and some nuzzling at his hand in search of more food.

Talking to a donkey was one thing but Dai, like Helen, drew the line at watching *Mary Poppins*. He went out on restless walks, confusing the dogs until all but Demi, the sheepdog, gave up accompanying him and stayed by the fire. He flopped in front of the hearth, contemplating unfinished walls and unpainted coving. He lit an open fire which sparked quickly and raced greedily up the ash logs cut from the overgrown hedging trees. The flames warmed his face, leaving his back cold, making his body seem oddly two-dimensional. He stood with his back towards the fire, roasting in its warmth. He paced some more. He even wondered whether he should have tried to make more of his marriage with Karen, but then he remembered what coming home to her had really been like. He looked absently around the room and remembered he wanted to put a shelf up in the little hallway, as a telephone stand.

A glance at the clock later on showed him an unexpected eleven o'clock. Bedtime had finally caught up with him, covered in wood shavings amid little piles of nails and screws, television pictures unrolling in the background. He stood back and looked critically at the shelf, which was crooked. He went to bed.

He was woken by the insistent ringing of the telephone and it was with some irritation that he padded downstairs to answer it, wondering why calls out only came at the most inconvenient moments. Sleep vanished at the unprecedented sound of his father's voice, slow and expressionless.

'Dai? There's bad news . . . it's Dad, your Grandad . . . he fell in the night. It's too late for you to do anything so don't rush up, but it would ease your Mam's mind if you saw him, you being medical. To be honest Dai, if I thought

235

there was a chance you could do anything, I wouldn't have phoned you. He deserves his peace now.'

'You mean he's dead?'

'That's what I said, isn't it?'

'I'll be there now.' Dai hung up, dressed quickly and automatically took his bulging briefcase, which meant driving the short distance up the lane rather than walking across the field. The road was icy but the four-wheel drive barely registered the shifting grip.

Will was looking out for him, and Dai followed his father to the foot of the stairs where Gwen was sitting, crying and holding the hand of a tiny husk of a man, his spirit finally gone. A pillow had been placed under his head and his eyes closed. There was no need to check the pulse but, mindful of his father's words, Dai pulled a stethoscope out of his bag and ostentatiously spent long minutes listening to the silent chest before pronouncing his Grandad dead and giving professional authority to what his mother needed to hear.

'Death was instant. He felt no pain. His body was so fragile the lightest blow would probably have had the same effect, particularly on the head.'

Dry-eyed and drawn, Will spoke. 'It's a release for him Gwen. And for you too. And don't think I don't know it.'

She looked up, stricken. 'How can you say that at such a time!'

'Because it's true. And no shame in it.'

Still holding the old man's lifeless hand, she murmured through the tears, 'I loved him. What will I do now with the time?'

'He'll be missed,' her husband said quietly, 'but there's others to . . .' he ducked the word 'love' and ended lamely 'look after'. Dai, sensing the raw spots in his parents' marriage, stooped to hold his mother briefly, disengaging

236

her hand from the dead grip and holding it in his own warm clasp.

'Dad needs a cup of tea,' he told her, giving her a job to do and reminding her at the same time that her husband needed her. Her own need for comfort made her turn to Will and put her arms round him as Dai deliberately stepped back, out of reach.

'I'm sorry, cariad.' Her words were muffled in his chest. Will stood stiffly, managing no more than a clumsy pat on her back in response, but his voice was choked as he replied, 'Cup of tea would be nice.'

While waiting for the doctor, Dai heard his mother's account of what had probably happened, with some terse interventions from his father. It seemed that Will had been in the kitchen – 'got up early,' – and Gwen was lying awake, when Lloyd had presumably got up and tried to go downstairs alone. He must have missed the steps, hit his head and had no chance of saving himself with what little strength was left in his wasted body.

'I can't understand why he didn't wait for me to get him up as usual. He's been too shaky for months to even get to the bathroom on his own without some help to start him off. We were going to get a handrail and one of these stair lifts but they're so expensive. If he'd been in hospital he'd have cost them a fortune, but when you look after someone at home they give you nothing. Grants, that's what they tell you. Well there's no grants without Grandad signs the forms to say he's weak and useless. How can we do that to him?' Then she remembered again. 'He won't need to sign any forms now.' Her eyes filled up again.

'He died a man, at home with his family. You couldn't have done more,' Dai soothed.

'But why would he want to come downstairs? If he hadn't, he'd still be alive.'

'There's always an "if only" about a death, Mam. There's nothing you can do.' Death on a particular occasion could always have been prevented, with hindsight, but death itself was inevitable. Like the paradox of Achilles and the tortoise, Dai thought, but wise enough to spare his parents the insight. Instead he offered a comforting answer. 'Perhaps he felt stronger, capable of getting himself a drink downstairs, and he died feeling independent again.' Or desperate to talk to the son he knew was pacing the kitchen after another sleepless night. Who knows?

'If I'd known, I'd have said something more . . . important . . . than "good night"!'

Dai thought back. What had been the last words he'd said to his Grandad, now given undeserved significance? Surely he could have done better than 'Merry Christmas'. At least he had not been tempted to add a Happy New Year to the banal irony. 'He knew we cared. That's all that mattered.' Will nursed his mug of tea and his eyes were empty.

The doctor's visit provided Gwen with another chance to relate events, and relieved Dai of his fears that an inquest might be necessary. The death certificate triggered Will into his now undisputed role as head of the household and he set the rituals in motion. 'Leave the curtains drawn, Gwen, for people to know. We must make arrangements. There'll be a nurse on her way already after the doctor's visit. I'll call Davies Undertaker's.' The body, for such he was becoming to them, was covered in the Welsh tapestry blanket which had been on Lloyd's bed for years, and Davies arrived promptly.

Although accustomed to the old ways, Dai was relieved to spend the night back in his own cottage, leaving his parents to their murmuring vigil in their bedroom above the parlour where the district nurse had carefully laid out the

238

body. The four days leading up to the funeral saw a procession of neighbours and relatives visiting Brynglas to pay their respects. Word of the death spread via the milkman and the travelling baker, as well as the official announcements in local chapels and the personal column of the *Llanelli Star*. Will and Gwen, stiff and awkward in their best clothes, were by now able to offer a word-perfect narration of the story of Lloyd's death. As they balanced fine china teacups, brought out of their cabinet specially for the occasion, and ate fresh *bara brith*, the conversation followed its traditional course. Compliments to Gwen on her baking were punctuated by solemn head-shakes and vaguely philosophical pronouncements such as, 'Puts things back in perspective' or 'Makes you wonder, doesn't it', to which there could be nods and assenting noises. The reminiscences had begun and would reach a climax in the gathering after the funeral.

As was proper, Dai was with his parents by day, receiving the stream of visitors, when he was not replenishing the stores of food and drink or ensuring the day-to-day business of the farm continued according to his father's instructions. He also answered the seemingly endless phone calls, protecting his weary parents from well-meaning callers when necessary. He helped his mother to maintain her careful list of well-wishers so that she could write her thank-yous at a later stage, in the meticulous schoolgirl's script that he found somehow touching.

There had been concern in case the ground should freeze again, delaying burial, but the post-Christmas thaw continued, leaving the ground sodden but workable. Davies had steered the family through the necessary decisions, most of which were predetermined by tradition. Will carried out his time-honoured duty, treading in the footprints of his father before him and leaving the tracks to show his son the way, when his own time came. It was to be a men-only funeral, of course, in Capel Sion, the chapel attended by the Evans family, where Dai's great-grandfather had laid the foundation stone in 1882. There was a family plot in the small graveyard around the chapel, situated on its own small hill and visible from the houses in the surrounding village. Lloyd was to be buried here, joining the inmates whose memory was cherished by Gwen's regular visits to tend the grave and place fresh flowers there.

Bearers were chosen; six of the village rugby team, which had started its days on a field loaned free by Lloyd, who had kept up an interest in their matches while his health lasted. The volunteers were well matched for height, avoiding the difficulties that Dai had witnessed at other funerals, where a short man had to hold the coffin at muscle-wrenching arm's stretch while it rested on the others' shoulders. There were advantages to a mixture of heights, however, when it came to negotiating the inevitable steps into a chapel. Two short men in the lead could avoid the back-straining stoop to accommodate the shifts that occurred when the group had to mount the chapel steps. There had been much debate as to whether the coffin should be left in the foyer, as was unavoidable in some chapels, but Will insisted that it was possible to get the coffin through either of the two narrow entrances and up an aisle so it must be done, as it had been done before. The bearers would just have to shuffle into a clumsy single file as they manoeuvred the coffin up the narrow aisle.

Davies asked about the number of cars required, happy to oblige as this time of year saw few weddings. Death was a serious business to Davies, though his image was flawed by his one famously comic gesture; his hearse was instantly recognisable by the grim humour of its numberplate; U L B

1 2. It was difficult to imagine where this sense of humour was kept hidden when you saw Davies in the full splendour of his bowler hat and funereal black with matching face. Everyone agreed that you couldn't do better than Davies for a tidy burial and so it proved to be.

The cars came at exactly ten o'clock and Lloyd left his farm for the last time, followed by Will, Dai and Will's brother-in-law in the leading mourners' car. Gwen watched the slow exit, wheels churning mud spots over the gleaming black bodywork, then she wiped clean hands on her apron and returned to the kitchen to make ham sandwiches and funeral conversation with the aunts, nieces and female neighbours. The proverbial drowning man's review of his life is nothing compared to the audit conducted while contemplating a coffin in a hearse. In the eternity before the cars reached the village, each man was lost in his own memories and regrets.

As they rounded the end and saw the first ribbon of houses, they saw the people. The cars slowed to a suitably staid pace, and the bearers had caught up with the hearse to accompany it on foot past the small groups of women and children who were lining the route. The cars imposed silence as they passed, leaving the ripple of noise to spread behind them again as they moved on. They bore their silence to the chapel itself, where knots of dark-suited men in black ties and white shirts ground out their last hasty cigarettes and stretched their legs quickly as rumour of the cars reached them and they vanished into the echoing pews. Whispers carried along the seasoned wood, rousing wonder and worry in equal proportions. 'Who'd have thought Hefin would still be here . . . Eric's away I've heard, something wrong if a man is away at Christmas . . . not so many from our class now . . . ten pints is here, see, at the front . . .' Then the coffin spreads silence like a wave. The bearers

241

struggle to maintain their dignity while turned sideways on. Behind them the grieving family carry the stillness to the front right pew – so much so that the minister's voice comes as a relief. As the bearers sink into the front left pew, you can see their shoulders sag with relief that Part One is over with no major mishap. All eyes are on the coffin with its simple floral cross, the only flowers in the stark chapel.

Now it is the turn of the ministers, who have argued their allotted place and time in private beforehand but will extemporise to make the most of their slot. Clearly the Capel Sion minister had pride of place, and gave the longest speech in memoriam, reminding the congregation that Lloyd had been 'a character' (technical religious term for someone of whom the minister disapproved strongly) 'with a sense of humour (technical religious term for someone who disapproved of the minister) who would be 'welcome at the pillars of heaven' (presumably joining the past pillars of the community). His colleagues from other local chapels had to make do with brief eulogies and announcements of the hymns. The third minister took his place at the lectern with an expression of distaste more likely to spring from his inferior role than from the occasion itself. In compensation, he not only announced the hymn, 'Mae d'eisiau Du pob awr' ('God is needed every hour') but read three verses, in sonorous tones, before the congregation were asked to give their rendition.

All of this was part of the pageant to which Dai was accustomed. He had attended his share of funerals, even acted as bearer, and he would have been shocked at the suggestion that there was anything unusual about the ceremonial involvement of so many men in the death of someone they hardly knew. You didn't get a full choir

242

nowadays unless it was a member's funeral, but even so, the singing lifted the heart and brought tears at the same time. Five old men, in their choir blazers, stood together and forced their voices through the old harmonies, carrying other singers with them.

After the chapel service, the burial, preceded by an awkward exit in reverse; the sideways-slinking bearers, the grieving family and the congregation trekking across the muddy ground. The freshly piled earth was clearly visible in the middle of the graveyard, like a slag heap in a valley. From the bearers' point of view, the grave could not have been in a worse place; they had to lift the coffin again from the trolley and carry it across the treacherous ground while showing respect for the silent tenants. Men squelched across the grid-lines between graves, splattering their newly polished best shoes and suit trousers.

Two bearers stood on the makeshift wooden planks, one either side of the grave, and with the assistance of the others taking the strain, like some macabre tug of war, they slowly lowered the coffin using the two straps. Again the ministers took turns to speak, still holding their cane-handled black umbrellas like a badge of office, but this time nothing was said of Lloyd, the individual. This time he was Everyman, dust to dust, ashes to ashes, awaiting the resurrection with his head to the east. Dai felt something was expected of him but he didn't know what or even by whom.

Then it was over and the men walked back to the road, where they surreptitiously wiped their shoes against hedges, standing on one leg like nervous schoolboys. Handshakes and brief parting exchanges separated the onlookers from the main party. A coach parked discreetly round the corner would carry a contingent to the working men's club where they would 'get them in' in Lloyd's honour. Davies' cars led

243

the elect on their way to the reunion with the women at Brynglas.

The familiar surroundings of his childhood home merely increased Dai's sense of unreality. His jaw ached from the set expression he'd assumed without being aware of it.

Dai moved through the groups of people, picking up snatches of conversation which had started in the hushed tones but were rapidly increasing in volume and ribaldry. He watched the stranger who was his mother picking up each of the 'In Sympathy' cards from the mantelpiece, reading the verse aloud and explaining the history and relationship to the Evans family of each sender. Women of her own age stood around her in a semi-circle, nodding appreciatively, repeating the lines of verse and adding their own snippets of information to each name mentioned or blushing modestly as her own card was displayed for approval.

'Do you remember Kevin's birthday lock-in at the Three Crowns?' one of the men was saying.

'Don't I just,' someone else joined in the reminiscing. 'One in the morning and going strong when the local copper, Bendit was it?' – he appealed for confirmation.

''Course that, PC Bendit. Well there's a name I haven't heard in years.'

'No guesses on how he got that name!'

'Now what was his real name?' No one seemed to remember.

'Anyway, there we all were, caught in the act, and Bendit says in his best policeman's voice, "I'll be back in an hour boys," and looks meaningfully at Ron the barman. Ron near wet himself, says "Come on boys – if you're not out before he's back, I'll lose my licence for sure. He won't give me two chances." Bit green was Ron, see. So Lloyd stopped mid-pint in order to educate him. "You daft bugger," says Lloyd, "he means he'll be off duty in an hour and he'll be

244

back for a pint with us then!" And then everyone settles back down to some serious drinking.'

'Lloyd was a boy all right.' A moment's pause for solemnity.

'No one could waggle their ears like him and balance a beer mat on his head at the same time.'

'Stan could waggle his ears.'

'Not as much, he couldn't, and not do the beer mat at the same time.'

'Maybe you're right.' Another pause and some thoughtful drinking.

In lower tones, looking sideways at a man in the far corner of the dining room, 'I'm surprised old Ceri turned up.' Significant glances exchanged.

'It was a long time ago.'

'If it happened.'

'Come on, man! No one believed that story about her car breaking down and Lloyd just passing and a convenient storm so they couldn't get home. And a glow on Edith for weeks that she never got from Ceri. '

'Lloyd's wife believed him.'

''Course that. How else could she have stayed Lloyd's wife! She always believed him.'

'What a boy!'

Dai absorbed the descriptions of a man, his grandfather, from all the conversations around the room, but he could not join in. He felt as much of an outsider as the cousin's nine-year-old son – or was it second cousin? – who jabbed his elbow into a small girl's face and made her cry. Putting down the plate of butterfly buns which he had been carrying around like a waiter, Dai went outside. The dogs complained, scratching the barn door, but he couldn't let them out with so many best clothes to spoil. Instead he walked further away from the house until the dogs quietened. His shoes and trousers were already so muddied that he didn't hesitate before crossing the small field to the right of the farmhouse.

At the far end was a small copse, officially 'not worth levelling and reclaiming', unofficially a natural haven for wildlife and for Dai as a small boy. He had lain invisible in the hollow, watching the wind quicken the branches over his head, listening to his mother call him for a meal and savouring his power to stay hidden. His parents had always maintained the illusion that they had no idea where he was, and he had thought his hide-out to be outside even his father's domain. When he walked through the first trees he was taken aback to see the figure seated on a fallen trunk, smoking. There was no mistaking the man, like himself wearing a dark suit and white shirt. It was his father, like himself wanting to get away.

At the foot of an old hawthorn tree was a crooked wooden cross which had looked hundreds of years old to Dai as a boy. It was at this ancient fixture that Will waved his hand, still holding a cigarette.

'Best ratter I ever had. Twm we called her. Right from a pup she'd stare at a bale of hay and you knew there was something there. No chance of getting away from her, better than any cat, a Jack Russell.'

Dai sat down beside his father on the log and got up again as quickly. 'That's sopping wet, Dad!' Although the air was mild, the damp was bone-chilling.

'Bit of wet won't hurt.'

'I always thought that had been there centuries, maybe a foal I thought. I used to come here you know, as a boy.'

His father showed no signs of surprise. ''Course you did. If I hadn't known you were here, how could I have gone to such lengths not to find you?'

'So you knew?'

246

"Course you came here. We all did, you, me and your grandfather.' The tone was so matter-of-fact that Dai felt for the first time that he wanted to cry. 'Perhaps your children too one day.' Dai's head hurt. 'When you're young, you think death is a calamity, a one-off that you'll never survive, but you do. And then you have to go through it again. And then you realise death is not a one-off, it's always and everywhere. You even wish everyone you cared about was dead to get it tidy and over with. Or that you were.'

Dai said nothing because he had no idea what to say. He hoped to God that listening was helpful because he was incapable of anything more.

'I'd better be getting back. We don't want your mam to worry.' He stubbed out his cigarette and stood up wearily. 'There's enough ham sandwiches there to feed all the starving of Africa and if there's food left over, she'll worry it wasn't good enough.'

Dai swallowed painfully. 'If it's all eaten, she'll worry she didn't make enough.'

'That's women for you.' Father and son returned to the funeral party and made heroic, carefully judged inroads into plates of sandwiches and cup cakes. If one or two platefuls disappeared to the barn and some grateful canine stomachs, Gwen was none the wiser.

That night, Dai found it difficult to get to sleep. When he tried to recall his grandfather his mind went blank. When he tried to sleep, images of his Grandad chased his young self, acting out photographs and overheard anecdotes, as well as real memories. Every word seemed to come to mind in his grandfather's voice, and they all now seemed newly invested with the authority of legacy. From the specific, Dai's restless mind roved to the universal – life, death and love – returning inevitably to the specific; this time, Helen.

There was no time to waste. He must decide immediately

247

on all that he wanted to do with his life and do it. Top priority, he must make contact with Helen and make her realise she was necessary to him and therefore she must be with him. He must pursue some field research to prevent brain rot. And he really must finish decorating. It was vital to get these things done before death caught up with you, so he must act now, tomorrow. Or if not tomorrow, the day after that. Exhausted by so much planned activity, Dai slept.

Perhaps his good intentions would have gone the way of most New Year resolutions, had not his grandfather's words, echoing in his imagination, given him an idea of how he might reach Helen. It seemed so obvious to him that they ought to be together, that to be frustrated by what he saw as mere barriers of her mind, was an insult. There were potential problems of course. She was likely to throw away any missive from him, without reading it. It might not work, but he would be no worse off, he reasoned. Apart from losing his most treasured possession of course, but that was a risk he was willing to take.

Helen was wary of the mail after receiving her jumper as a Christmas present, but the brown padded envelope looked innocuous enough with its formal, typewritten address and Llanelli postmark. She was expecting some floppy discs and a manual from her college computer course and it would be typical of the tutor to mail it to her home, assuming everyone had a computer and was desperate to try out new software. Helen could now see the benefits of computer design and would be more than happy to use one in her business, if someone would only donate the necessary capital. Given the current state of her business, buying anything out of the profits – what profits? – was out of the question.

She opened the package, pulling out the contents and

248

recognising Dai's handwriting too late to avoid reading the opening words of his letter. 'Helen, my grandfather has died and taught me something.' Buying time, Helen stooped to pick up whatever had fallen onto the floor. Nonplussed, she identified Dai's passport, complete with the inevitable lowlife mug shot that could have been almost any Caucasian male with short, dark hair. Most feelings can be mastered individually but add curiosity to the cocktail and it would take a stronger woman than Helen to throw away that letter without reading it.

Helen, my grandfather has died and taught me something which I can only explain to you in person, but which is meant for you as much as for me. Meet me at Paxton's Tower on Saturday at two o'clock. Grandad also told me what a man's most treasured posession is so I've enclosed it for you to keep. I want to take you to France so I can face your demons – you owe me the chance, don't lose my passport. I love you. Dai

It was preposterous. She wasn't going of course. Even if she wanted to go it was virtually impossible to get to Paxton's Tower without a car. How typically thoughtless of him! There were only four days, and then the non-meeting would have come and gone and she could forget about it. *Why Paxton's Tower?* she wondered. It wouldn't hurt to find out a little more about the monument. She might as well understand the message fully, having read it. It was always interesting to find out a bit more about the area she lived in. And it wasn't as if she was going to meet him there, or indeed anywhere.

15

How typical of him to be late! There was a bitter wind cutting through Helen's layers of wool and waterproof as she paced about Paxton's Tower. Early January was not the best time to see 'the splendid panorama of the Tywi Valley where the river meanders lazily through the Golden Grove or Gelli Aur as it is called in Welsh'. There was no sign of 'a patchwork of fields' and certainly no chance of spotting Dryslwyn Castle, 'the next interesting sight travelling west along the river valley'. Helen could hardly see the corner of the folly known as Paxton's Tower because fog crowned the hill so thickly. The eerie change from the usual grey drizzle of Llanelli to this disorientating veil had surprised her into silence on the drive here. She had commented to Neil on the stark line cut across the higher ground by the fog, above which only past experience suggested that the road and village continued. Entry into the whiteness was momentarily terrifying, confusing the senses you most relied on. Helen had wondered why fog was routinely described as a blanket; it seemed to her more like the filaments of a cocoon in which you were isolated, wanting to break out and only fighting your way to more and more soft wisps which weren't there when you tried to touch them. When the road dipped down briefly below the fog-line, Helen gulped in all she could see and hear before they vanished once more into the timeless zone.

The car park and National Trust sign indicated the position of Paxton's Tower, but Helen had to take it on trust that there was a tower – or indeed anything – up the slope. The footpath petered out, and she just had to keep walking up the wet grass and assume she would reach something. It probably wasn't that far on a summer's day, following a path worn by visitors' feet, but Helen was beginning to regret leaving Neil waiting in the warm car by the time the stone façade came into view. She had read all that she could find in the library and its tourist office, but her theories about why Dai had chosen this particular place remained tentative.

Also known as Nelson's Tower, the folly was built by the wealthy Sir William Paxton to celebrate Nelson's victories at sea. Was Dai hoping for victory? Another story was that Paxton spent thousands wining and dining local dignitaries to secure a seat in parliament. Despite promises of support for his campaign, Paxton was not the prospective parliamentary candidate elected in the constituency of Carmarthen. In bitter disappointment, he erected a monument to remind the people of Carmarthen of their betrayal. Did Dai feel betrayed? Was he telling her that she was his campaign and he would never get over failure? Or was she his 'folly' and this conversation planned as the final parting?

The building itself was disappointing, a square tower which might well look like a romantic castle from a distance but without hidden passages, its only mystery created by the shifting fog. It was hard to imagine it as 'an ideal picnic site'. Helen closed her eyes and tried to imagine the summer view of cattle in distant fields by the meandering glitters of the River Tywi. What came to mind instead was a view from a very different folly, also created in bitterness and pride, a view across black tiled roofs and spires with cast-iron weather vanes, a view which also had a river running through it. The River Lot at St-Geniez was nearer to the mountains, running fast and shallow, whereas the Tywi at this point often overlapped its flood plains in slow, middle-age spread. At the same time that Marie Talabot had made her gesture of defiance to the bourgeoisie of St-Geniez, who had refused to accept the former maid,

251

Sir William Paxton looked down on the middle class of Carmarthen and built his own, less elaborate but equally expensive, memorial to folly.

Just as she told herself she would keep Neil waiting no longer, the fuzzy edges of a human shape loomed to her left. She must have turned slightly because that was not the direction from which she was expecting him to appear. You could be here forever in this weather, all sense of direction lost. When she had lived in Leeds, a neighbour had died in the annual Three Peaks Run on the Derbyshire hills. He had collapsed in exhaustion right beside the footpath but although the mountain rescue team searched day and night, no one found him until the mists cleared and it was too late; he died of exposure. They must have passed within five feet of him, again and again. Helen shivered and the voice from the fog made her angry with relief.

'Helen?' The familiar Welsh accent.

'I don't know why I'm here so you'd best say your piece and get it over. I don't want to keep Neil waiting.'

Dai gave the same old infuriating grin which made difficulties disappear – and caused you more of them. 'Neil's gone. I saw him in the car park and told him I'd take you home.'

Helen was lost for words. The nerve of the man! She retreated into cold formality. 'I prefer to make my own decisions, thank you.' The tone lapsed into retort. 'And if you hadn't been stupid enough to suggest a meeting place that only pigeons can get to, I wouldn't have had to ask Neil a favour in the first place!'

The answering shrug was only marginally less infuriating than the grin.

She remembered part of the reason she'd come. 'I'm sorry about your Grandad.'

A modified shrug. 'We'll miss him but it's kinder so.'

When he spoke again, he was more hesitant. 'A death makes you think, you know. About what matters. Grandad put so much into living, and into loving.' A mischievous smile played across his features. 'At least so I gather from the conversations of the old boys at the funeral.'

'I can imagine.'

'I've practised this, but I still don't know if I can say it.' Helen waited in the artificial silence of the fog, watching his face as he stared at the ground. If she'd reached out she could have traced a line from the muscle in his temple along his cheekbone to his mouth and he would have caught hold of the adventurous hand and kissed each finger, singly. She clasped her hands together. He spoke again. 'You are the love of my life. If we can work through your feelings about the past, we could share the future. I know you haven't been back to France. I thought perhaps we could go together?' This time it was he who waited.

'Revisit the scene of the crime you mean? I hadn't heard that generally helped anyone but the police.' She couldn't help the bitterness. If a raw spot was rubbed, then it hurt.

'Please can we try? That's if you haven't destroyed my passport of course!'

'I meant to bring it. I'll post it to you.' She could feel the numbness of despair creeping over her again, wrapping feelings in layer on layer of clinging white tendrils, too wispy to fight.

'It'll get lost in the post.'

'I'll send it registered delivery.'

'It won't be accepted.' His determination was wearing her down without reaching her. As if he sensed this, he reached out for her hand but she flinched and backed off.

Quietly, he continued, 'My grandfather's death has reminded me of something I'd forgotten, his message for you. People grieve in different ways at different times but

253

everyone needs to grieve. Perhaps you'll think it's patronising of me to say this, but I'm speaking from my own loss and that of my mother and father. I think you know everything about guilt and nothing about the grief that heals.' The fog thickened and Helen could neither move nor speak. 'I thought we could plant a rose garden at the cottage. In memory of Rebecca.' He looked straight at her as he said her daughter's name, as if it were something that could be said without lightning splitting the skull.

She opened her mouth to speak but instead gave an animal groan that shocked her. Why couldn't she just cry? She sat on the wet grass and put her head in her hands until she could speak.

She had to repeat the words for him to catch the muffled response. 'It's not as easy as that. I can't grow spider plants never mind roses.'

He pushed further. 'Do you think roses would suit Rebecca?'

She thought of the tiny buds at the funeral. She remembered Becky, laughing at play. 'Yes, roses would suit Becky.' She pulled a handful of grass and bent it until it broke.

'I'd like you to tell me what she was like.' Dai put a steady arm underneath Helen's to help her stand again, and he left the support there as she leant against him.

'She was a little girl.' Helen shrugged her way back into control without leaving the sheltering arm. 'Prince Rainier of Monaco made a rose garden in memory of his wife.'

'I know.'

'How would you? Oh, of course, film star wife.'

'I remember seeing a picture of it in the Sunday supplement. Big walled park with a statue and hundreds of different roses. I'd imagined something a bit smaller, perhaps one bed and you choose four or five bushes.'

'I wouldn't have to say? To your parents or anything?'

254

'Why would you? Just because we plant a few roses.'

'This is crazy. It's all going too fast. You're confusing me.'

'Take your time. It's pretty unpleasant up here. Shall we go back to the car?'

It was so easy to walk beside him. 'I'd like the roses. But it doesn't mean you and me . . .'

'France?'

'Maybe. I don't know. Perhaps in the spring, I'll see how things go.' She could feel his sigh but he didn't push her any further. 'Anyway, why did you choose Paxton's Tower? Was it anything to do with Paxton himself ? Or Nelson?'

'Who was Paxton and what's it got to do with Nelson?' Helen told him.

'Well I've lived here all my life, but I've never thought about it. That's why I need you.' He squeezed her hand. 'Purely educational reasons. I just thought you'd like the view.' He gestured ironically at the expanse of white. 'Down there is the Tywi Valley, over there are the Brecon Beacons and that way, on a clear day,' he turned her to face another direction in the blinding fog, 'you can see as far as Ireland.'

'You're having me on.'

'Honest to God.' She could hear the smile in his voice. 'You come back with me on a fine day and I'll show you.'

'You don't change!'

'No,' he agreed smugly and she wasn't sure whether to be glad or sorry when he dropped her at home with a brief kiss, a serious look and the request that she phone him when she was ready.

That first meeting set the pattern between them, a curious mixture of intimacy and caution. Months apart had imposed physical abstinence which electrified the air between them in the unspoken agreement, 'Not yet'. Helen was wary of

255

this old-fashioned courtship, but no amount of sarcasm could breach Dai's impeccable, patient courtesy. Her life was suddenly, literally, a bed of roses. She could have resisted bouquets for herself but, from the moment Dai showed her the circle of dormant earth in front of the cottage, her imagination bloomed in memoriam. With all of her skills for blending colours and textures, she chose roses for Becky.

It was difficult to believe that four thorny sticks of blackened wood, branching at knobbled arthritic joints, would ever carry 'delicate pale blush-pink blooms in large clusters', but Dai assured Helen that this was exactly what happened whenever his mother treated herself to a rose bush. February might be a good time to buy and plant but it took a leap of faith to collect six dead bundles of twigs, in their containers, and pay a fortune for them at the garden centre checkout. Dai's unshakeable belief in the ordinary, annual miracle of spring, freed Helen to dream the rose bed. She had instinctively and impossibly wanted bud roses. No rose is a bud forever, Helen thought heavily as she tried to find some echo of her daughter in the named variety pictured on the small tag attached to each bush. She found it not in the plastic perfection of the hybrid teas, nor in the blowsy display of the large floribundas, but in the fragile, diminutive beauty of the patio roses.

On a frost-free day, Helen directed Dai in the planting of the little twisted stumps, which looked even more naked out of their pots. The central feature of the bed was a miniature standard rose tree called 'Tear Drops' which would be 'festooned in pure white blooms.' Like children dancing around a maypole would be the five small shrubs with blooms in pink, red or white, their names an elegiac song; 'Festival', 'Gentle Touch', 'Melody Maker', 'Robin Redbreast' and 'The Fairy.' Helen read aloud the descriptions to Dai while he was digging and then tamping down the surrounding earth, until Becky's garden glowed with 'blooms of light vermilion with a beautiful silver lining' despite the grey February light.

The cottage itself had come as a revelation to Helen and she couldn't help repeating, 'But it's exactly as I imagined it!' as she followed Dai in his proud tour. She couldn't resist the invitation to supply the missing element and tell him what wallpaper to get, what paints, what finishing touches. Sitting in front of the fire, companionable, it became understood that Helen would go to France with Dai in April. They made plans in a careful, factual manner, retracing whatever steps in her past Helen felt 'necessary' – Dai's word – and allowing 'room to change our minds' – Helen's contribution.

Inbetween times with Dai, which were usually once a week but not fixed, Helen planned the next steps of her life. She congratulated herself on being able to enjoy these last two months in Llanelli in Dai's company, before she left both to start again, probably in London, certainly in a city. She had been a romantic fool to think she could run a design business in this backwater. The best she could negotiate with her bank was an overdraft spread over the coming year, on the understanding that she would be completely re-thinking the business. She had given notice on both the shop – March 31st – and the house – the end of April. There were no assets to cash in unless you could count the small amount of stock she had maintained along with the yarns themselves. She would use all that in her new city business, where she would save money by renting shop and accomodation combined, in some downmarket area. She was investigating a catalogue – perhaps mail order would give her more security. The computer course had opened up another possibility but at the moment she couldn't afford a computer.

She had been a romantic fool in many ways but at least there would be a tidy ending. She would know that somewhere in Wales was a rose garden for Becky, an idyllic country cottage and a nice man with a donkey. Leaving them would be like every other time she had designed her heart into a garment and sold it to someone else to wear. The visit to France would neatly mark an ending. This well-intentioned trip merely confirmed her knowledge that Dai would never understand her. He had not repeated his declaration of love and she believed, with a little selfish regret, that his passionate words were merely transferred emotion from his grandfather's death, and would as easily warm someone else when she had gone.

So it was that Helen found herself once more being driven south on a French motorway, with a map on her lap and a man at her side. She deliberately sought the quietness in the back of the car where her daughter had once been, but the empty space she tried to imagine refused to appear in the four-wheel drive with its cheerful clutter of holiday gear and unidentifiable veterinary essentials which Dai had forgotten to take out.

'We'll probably get done for drugs,' she predicted gloomily.

'If you can get high on sheep wormer it's the first I've heard of it,' he responded cheerfully. 'Anyway, there's laws about drugs, so that's about the only thing you won't find in the back.' He glanced quickly at the piles of stuff and added dubiously, 'At least, I don't think so . . .'

'You're impossible!'

'What's the next turn-off?'

'You mean apart from your untidiness,' she muttered as she returned to studying the map.

It was so easy to play at being married, perhaps even easier for Helen with the knowledge that she must make the most of the fortnight and then make the break. Living for today allows difficult questions to be postponed indefinitely. If Helen wondered at the wisdom of confronting her past while planning to run from the present, she quickly justified both. Returning to France would break the taboo and possibly allow interesting holidays in some future she could not imagine, but Dai's naive belief in some kind of cure for her guilt was not one she shared. It would be easier to live with that alone, once this fortnight was over. Helen's major preoccupations were actually far more basic; money and sex. Lack of both was a matter of some concern.

Typically, for someone earning 'good' money – is there any other kind? – Dai had offered to pay for Helen's holiday and cheerfully accepted her insistence on paying her way, without any realisation of how difficult this would be for her. Having realised all her assets, folded the shop and arranged a loan against her business plans, Helen had a little money in the bank. It was, however, all earmarked for her future survival and at an unpleasant rate of interest. At first Helen had inwardly groaned every time they stopped at a sevice station, wasting a jumper's profits on coffee and cake, but she had too much pride to tell Dai that she could not afford the little extras. He was already paying for all petrol and motorway tolls, on the grounds that it would have cost him as much without her. An overnight hotel break in northern France had made clear what the total for the holiday was likely to be and Helen had given up thinking of a financial tomorrow. She was likely to spend two computers and the day of reckoning would have to be settled from future business profits. It was better not to think too much on predictions based on past business performance, so Helen didn't.

The overnight stop in St Omer had also highlighted Helen's other concern. It had seemed natural for Helen to make the booking and practise her French. She had turned to Dai and, expecting contradiction, had queried 'two singles?' and been surprised by his assent. She had kicked herself for asking the question at all and yet she felt the awkwardness left by their separation had created the need to ask. He had been relaxed and friendly throughout the meal, kissed her briefly, and without even throwing her a lingering look of regret, had left her for his own room. There had been no visit in the night, although Helen had lain awake, restless and hopeful. Twice she had thrown on her dressing gown and padded barefoot to the door, intending to slip into her lover's bed. Twice she had pictured him asleep, unconcerned, and she had returned to bed, tormented by her body's unequivocal declaration of need.

Her sullen responses at breakfast had not touched his good humour, and she was puzzled as to what she should do. Pride prevented any direct approach, and she could draw on no similar experience to help her. She had no reason to think he didn't want her, and he made no move which showed he did, no intensity in his eyes nor quickening of breath, nothing. When she thought of their past hungers and satisfactions, she was at a loss. She was also extremely uncomfortable and irritable but there was no way she would make the first move. They were indeed playing at being married, but the sort of marriage, she thought bitterly, in which passion was only a type of fruit you discussed buying in the supermarket. If her brightness became brittle, there was no sign of Dai noticing.

'How far's St-Geniez now?' Helen looked at the map, tracing the route of the motorway through the volcanic landscape of the Auvergne. Waiting for the answer, Dai

260

glanced over at her. 'Is the map the right way up? You know I'd never say anything about women navigating but . . .'

She ignored his well-meaning attempt to distract her from all that St-Geniez meant. Before leaving Wales, they had talked about where to go, what they would do, in this bizarre combination of therapy and vacation. She had decided to go back to the village where she had been happiest, with Becky, and even with Tony. She would re-visit some of the tourist sights with Dai then they would head north, stopping at the campsite where the accident itself had happened. Not so much like feeling an ulcer with your tongue to check it still hurt, as like stabbing an open wound, Helen thought, and with someone watching. Yet again she wondered what this was supposed to achieve. At least she was back in France and in good company. How superficial! She concentrated on the red autoroute. 'Probably an inch and a half,' she replied.

Dai had quickly grown accustomed to her map-reading and converted into kilometres. 'Motorway?'

'No, I think we go right soon and wiggle along the river for the rest of the way.'

Whatever Dai thought about 'going right' off a motorway and 'wiggling along the river' his expression was firmly under control as he gave his opinion. 'That should take about an hour and a half then.'

'That's what I thought,' she said smugly. 'So it's an hour to an inch.'

St-Geniez came on her unawares, the signpost appearing by a straggle of houses on the outskirts of the village. While Helen was deliberating the most likely route to provide a bed for the night, Dai noticed a 'logis' sign and pulled into the parking courtyard.

The receptionist greeted them with professional charm. Helen trotted out her requirements, sighing inwardly when there was no contradiction from Dai to the 'two single rooms'. Dai took the bags up to the rooms, ignoring Helen's protest that she could carry her own. The plain, black rectangular suitcase seemed an odd mate for the loud sports carryall, topped by an escaping sock. Helen explored the storage space and neatly placed unpacked clothes on their allocated shelves; Dai rummaged through his bag for some clean clothes to wear for dinner, placing a random pile on the nearest shelf and ignoring the oddments which had spilled onto the carpet and under the bed. Both of them freshened up, then met up again in the small restaurant at the back of the hotel. Already the holiday had established its own routines, its own time zone outside the limits of the working week.

Eating out was always a treat for them; eating out in France was an adventure. Although the hotel was 'only' a two-star the standard of cuisine and service was impeccably French. There were far more than five stages to the ceremony of the five-course set meal and Helen relished each moment, even savouring the formality imposed on her relationship with Dai. It gave her the same frisson as looking at Renoir's 'Déjeuner sur l'herbe', the juxtaposition of the naked and the formal but in reverse situation. As she read and translated the menu, and shared opinions on the hors-d'oeuvres, she was aware of his forearms resting lightly on the white linen. She leaned towards him, brushing his warm skin under the excuse of pointing out items on his copy of the menu.

Even the set meal allowed choices, and in their imaginations they sampled every item on the menu, not just the Roquefort salad and *pâté de maison* which appeared before them. Neil had warned Helen about the French habit of keeping cutlery throughout a meal and she laughed as Dai, less prepared, faced eating a main course with his fingers, all other implements having vanished with his plates. She was willing to ask the waiter for replacements – at a price – but Dai rejected all attempts at blackmail and caused even more laughter by miming to the waiter his frustrating attempt to eat. Inevitably, the waiter contemplated the mime and responded in English, 'Sir would like a knife and fork. Of course,' leaving Dai with his panache a little bruised. A few well-chosen words of Welsh, which Helen felt needed no translation, righted matters, and the meal progressed at a leisurely pace. The waiter concluded his duties with the restaurant's latest techno-logical aid, a miniature battery-operated vacuum cleaner with which he cleaned the table of crumbs, maintaining a serious frown of concentration throughout the exercise. Helen contained her giggles until they had left the restaurant and then lost control, hiccupping into a pleasantly alcohol-induced state of wellbeing.

Her hand had somehow found Dai's as they went up to their (adjoining) rooms, and her growing certainty that she would not sleep alone was rudely dispelled by the words 'Sleep well', the familiar kiss on the cheek and a hand somehow helping? pushing? her into her own, empty hotel room for another restless, irritable night.

Helen surfaced from sleep the next morning heavy-eyed and resentful, even more determined that the first move must come from Dai but really doubting and for the first time whether that would ever happen. Wilfully, she brought all her memories of St-Geniez to mind, lingered over remembered snippets of conversation and outings with Rebecca, reminding herself of all the reasons she had to be unhappy. Her equally wilful subconscious confused things by presenting heartchurning images of lovemaking with Dai which were only banished by the spontaneously recalled memory of the previous evening's laughter and its causes. The day insisted on bonhomie and she gave in, joining Dai in his attempt to turn a bread roll, jam and a *pain au chocolat* into a breakfast.

Dai was happy for her to plan some sightseeing, re-tracing her steps with what struck her as appalling nostalgia. She felt what she should not and did not feel what she should: who was there to forgive her?

'Are you all right?'

You either said everything or you said nothing. 'Fine. Let's walk across the bridge, along other side of the river and we can look at the church then I want to show you the monument of Marie Talabot. There's a story that goes with it . . .'

Helen had realised that the weather would be different in April from her previous summer experiences, but it didn't prevent the shock to her senses of the fresh wind and grey skies. How could France have anything but sunshine and blue skies, the eternal holiday snap? She had destroyed all actual photographs of St-Geniez but had been haunted by the picture postcard brightness of one with Becky in the middle, her unchanging smile a rictus in Helen's imagination. It was dislocating to be confronted by clouds which reminded her of Llanelli.

'Look at this!' Dai called her over to one of the narrow houses bordering the river. Halfway up there were marks on its façade indicating the heights reached by the Lot in two flood years. 'It makes you wonder how anyone can carry on living here.'

'I suppose it's what you get used to – like you having one leg shorter than the other to live up the Mynydd.'

'At least there's no chance of getting flooded. Unless I've been diddled by the plumber.'

'I've walked past this loads of times without seeing it,' said Helen in amazement. 'The campsite's just along the river bank and across the next main road, so I always came this way and then cut up to the church. I can't believe I didn't notice.'

'See? I do have my uses.' She bit her tongue on the various responses that came to mind and turned away from him, heading for the broad sweep of steps in front of the grand, classical entrance to the church. She pushed open the heavy wooden door, which moved easily despite its appearance of antiquity, and blinked at the gloom inside. The French idea of a 'parish' church seemed to be closer to an English cathedral, with an ornate altarpiece and saints' statues in their various niches. St Christopher seemed far more approachable than the figure of Christ, and Helen felt an instinctive reproach looking at his sheltering arms around a child, 'So where were you when . . .?' It was easy to lapse into childhood ways of dealing with God and his entourage, asking for what you wanted and calling it prayer, passing on the blame for what went wrong. If there were adult forms of religion, Helen had never found them, and she settled for the aesthetic pleasures of her surroundings.

'It gives me the creeps. All that money going to line the fat pockets of the church. All that power directing the way ordinary people live, from birth control to education. Just look at all that gold!' Startled, Helen looked at the altarpiece again, considering Dai's words.

'There speaks the chapelgoer. Surely all art has a price. You wouldn't worry if we were in an art gallery, not a church.'

'But it pretends to be religion, not art.'

'Who says? If you were a medieval artist, then you'd have to express your creative flair through religious subjects.' She imagined the constraints. 'But then it's the same for me.'

'What, you mean Bambi and Baloo are the modern icons?'

She smiled. 'I guess. I was thinking more of being given a commission and the art being in the interpretation of a given theme or form.' She became self-conscious. 'Sorry. I know most people don't see what I do as being art at all. This must all sound very pretentious.'

'I think you're very creative. I couldn't do it. But don't expect me to understand theories of art.'

'As long as you know what you like . . .'

'And as long as I like what you do . . .'

'Come on. I think you'll like this monument. It's got a good view and you owe me a trek up a hillside to see a folly.' Even the sunless grey of daylight was startling after the dark interior of the church. Once her eyes had adapted again, Helen realised that the weather was worsening and visibility unlikely to be good. However, she was keen to see Marie Savy again and she climbed the steps with enthusiasm, remembering her worries last time about leaving the buggy and how slow the climb had been with Becky beside her. Instead of the expected pain, her memories seemed distant and burdened with her marriage to Tony, leaving a tingling lightness of foot and spirit. She could not help being glad at the easy adult company, the pleasure of a man at her side, with her in a way she had never known before Dai. She did remember telling Becky stories about the village while they went round the sights, but she had never been able to linger and muse on what she saw. Now she enjoyed the freedom of looking, thinking and sharing, without having to keep a toddler occupied, and she realised how much she had missed on her previous visits to St-Geniez. The backlash of guilt flicked her without its usual force, muffled by her interest in Madame Talabot (as Marie Savy became) and Dai.

'What was he like, do you reckon, Mr Talabot?' Dai had listened to Helen's version of Marie's life-story, rags to riches and forever defying the contempt of her home town.

266

Helen consulted her tourist guide, translating from the French. 'It says here she worked as his cook.'

'I bet her cuisine was nouvelle. Perhaps I'll advertise when we get back. "Financially secure, intelligent vet requires imaginative sustenance from nubile female." Ah, the good old days, when it was easy to get what you wanted.'

'You've never seemed to have a problem. Anyway, Monsieur Talabot wasn't financially secure, he was rich. He was also the engineer behind most of the railways in southern France, Portugal, Italy, Algeria . . .'

'I wonder what she did while he was away all the time?'

'Don't judge others by yourself. She probably went with him, or ran her salon in Paris which was "frequented by talented artists" like the guy who built her monument, the famous Denys Puech.'

'See. She must have spent a lot of time with Denys. When she wasn't visiting St-Geniez in a posh carriage to show off.'

Helen shook her head. 'It wasn't like that. She just wanted to see her home.'

'She married Paulin for his money and learned that she couldn't buy everything.'

'She didn't. She loved him, I know she did.' Helen felt ridiculously vehement, as if her own integrity had been challenged. 'Just because someone's got more money than you, doesn't make them better, or make it wrong for you to love them and share their money.'

'Hey, hey.' He threw an arm round her shoulder. 'I'm sure you're right and she loved him. She was certainly a good patron for old Denys. This must have cost a bomb.' They circled the severe figure of Marie Talabot, sitting in judgement over her fellow citizens.

'She looks the kind who wouldn't allow a pretty serving

267

girl into her house,' Dai observed, 'not as if she wore clogs herself once. Show me this marvellous view.' They walked across the grass surrounding the monument to the point which overlooked St-Geniez. The roof tiles shone black with damp, angling steeply downwards. Mist shrouded the river and curled upwards towards the steps they had just climbed.

'The panorama extends from the river villages of St-Geniez and St-Hilaire to the mountains of the Aubrac on the right,' Helen improvised, pointing at the swirling white distance.

Dai grinned. 'You're having me on. It looks exactly like the Tywi Valley, with the Brecon Beacons and Ireland in the distance.' They walked back down into the village, following one of the tourist routes recommended in Helen's guide.

Just beside the cloisters, on a busy shoppping street, was another church known as *l'église des penitents*. There was no impressive entrance this time, merely a side door through which Dai and Helen slipped unobtrusively.

This time it was the wood which caught Helen's eye, carved and gilded representations of the Wise Men, the Virgin and various relics.

'This is more like it!' Dai's voice summoned her. He was looking at a painting on two screens, the figures a little like those Christmas card reproductions of works by Bruegel. At first Helen could only make out lots of men all grouped around one small one in some kind of church setting. Then she noticed the Japanese cartoon-style drops of bood and the knife and . . .

'Oh!' The exclamation was involuntary. 'I don't believe it!'

'Well he was a Jew, you know. And they didn't have the high quality circumcision tools we've got today.' Dai seemed to be taking a professional interest in what seemed to Helen to be an odd representation to find in a church.

'Such veneration of a bit of male skin! Yuk.'

Dai considered the depiction of the scene in the temple. 'A bit of veneration doesn't go amiss from time to time. Without the knife and the audience.'

'How about a coffee? My feet are killing me,' said Helen.

'I thought you couldn't get enough sightseeing,' Dai teased.

'Well, I've had enough now. Let's go.' They descended the hill to the small square by the bridge, and were just turning towards the Café du Pont when Helen noticed the large Phildar sign in the shop opposite. Dai followed her glance and groaned, 'Oh no.'

She frowned at him. 'I'll only be a minute. I'd just like a quick look. I'll join you at the café.'

'It's all right – there's no fighting the call of the wool-shop. Naked instinct at its most animal. I'll look round the square first, then wait half an hour in the café for you.'

'I won't be long,' she murmured, already distracted. Phildar was the most popular brand of continental yarns and she was interested to see if there were any new trends. She also wanted a closer look at the hand-knitted examples in the shop window. They were well worked and in tasteful combinations but were merely literal reconstitutions of the patterns beside them, lacking individuality. She went in, smiling at the customer warning bell which reminded her of her own shop, her ex-shop she corrected herself.

Her glance ranged professionally over the wools shelved by shade, ply and texture, lingering on a fluorescent section which would appeal to those sorts of fourteen year old who wore zipped rib jumpers in black, lime green or shocking pink as dresses. She contemplated a Sixties collection, pop art, zips and early Avengers styles, but dismissed the idea. Grey angora clouds drifting across cubist rooftops on a

269

long, long tunic; a fit-and-flare evening dress in metallic black two-ply gathered into a gold fleur-de-lys at the dip of a deep V neck; a scoop-neck loose summer top with a bold, full-blown poppy centring on the neck and a drift of scattered petals across the body. Helen stroked the big Pingouin mohair balls with the back of her hand as she dreamed designs.

'You bought that jumper in Paris?' The question uttered in harsh French had to be repeated before Helen responded. Dark, bright eyes assessed her from behind the counter, where the knitting needles continued to click.

One professional to another, Helen replied, 'No, I'm English. I designed it and made it myself.' She was wearing a cream cotton top with a patchwork effect where she had inserted crocheted rounds and other textural signatures created by drop-stitch patterns. Like you I run – ran – a wool shop, but I use my own designs.'

'You find our company patterns boring?' The question was shrewd and Helen hesitated, seeking a tactful response and settling for honesty.

'Yes, I do. But if they sell and your business is doing well, that's what matters. After all,' she added bitterly, 'I'm broke.'

'We do well,' the woman conceded. 'And we have the tourist markets in the summer. But we too are bored. My daughter is like me – we can see what is beautiful but we can only make what the instructions say. I hoped she would have the art as well as the craft but . . .' Here there was an expressive shrug and shake of the head. Her body could have been any shape under the black blouse and long skirt. Her face, wrinkled and weather-beaten, contrasted with the fine dexterity of her hands as they plied their craft. Madame Lefarge indeed.

'Are you looking for work?'

Taken aback, Helen played for time. 'What sort?'

Two gold fillings showed briefly. 'Shaping, making. What other kind is there for a real woman?'

Helen felt as if she'd stumbled into Gypsy Rose Lee's fortune-telling tent and was at a loss. 'I'm only here on holiday,' she mumbled lamely.

'You would have to talk to my daughter, Amélie, but I think we should see some more of what you can do.'

'I couldn't knit for you. I have to go back home,' said Helen stupidly.

Again a flash of teeth. 'See what Amélie says. Perhaps we could have an arrangement. You show us some of your designs, some you have made up too, and we could test out a designer range. But of course we must talk more and see each other some times in the year. Amélie has some idea about computers, but you must talk to her.'

'But you've only seen one thing I've done,' said Helen, convinced that if you looked a gift horse in the mouth long enough it would turn back into a toad.

'I am getting old. To be really succesful you must take a risk, the right risk. If you can show us that there is more to you than one jumper, you are the right risk. Have you never looked at someone and known the right moment? It is so in business too. Think about it. Come back any day this week and Amélie will be here to talk to you. She speaks good English so she can tell me your stitches. These,' she spread her hands, still keeping her grip on the needles, 'must speak for me.'

'I'd better go. My friend is waiting,' said Helen bemused.

'I am Madame Voudoir. You are?'

'Helen. Helen Tanner.'

'Helen Tanner English Designer Knitwear. For us there is chic about the word "English"; for the tourist we say "made in France" – both are true, it is only a question of marketing. Think about it. Au revoir.'

271

Helen didn't notice the tinkling of the bell as she left the shop, but even through her abstraction she could see the thunderclouds hanging over Dai as he sat under a parasol in front of the Café du Pont. The coffee cup in front of him was empty. She gulped and rushed over.

'I'm really sorry. You'll never believe it but . . .'

He cut her short. 'Even for you, that's a bit much. Do you know how long I've been sitting here.'

'You've had your coffee?' It was not the best time to state the obvious.

'I've had two coffees and I would have had the waitress too if I could communicate with her. I've certainly had the time.'

Helen opted for deference, submission and more deference. 'If you can face another coffee, I'll get you one – or perhaps a beer? – but if you'd rather move on now, whatever you want . . . even the waitress.'

He eyed the long legs and shapely rear view bending over to wipe down a table near them. He took his time to reply. When he said, 'Too skinny,' she knew she was forgiven and ordered some drinks, defying the clouds to break. It was part of being on holiday to watch the world go by and listen to the waitress passing the time of day with customers. She didn't see any need to tell Dai that what he had taken for unfathomable French was in fact deeply accented but perfectly comprehensible English.

16

Helen could not believe that after all the closeness and flirtatious sparring of the previous day, she had again spent a solitary night. She asked her mirror, 'What is wrong with me?'. It whispered in return, 'Everything', and she turned her back on it, despondent. This trip was not going to plan at all. St-Geniez with Dai was a different place, overlaying her memories with new ones. She could no longer recall telling Becky the story of the marmot without also remembering Dai's concern, on being told the same legend, at not knowing the anaesthetic requirements of marmots. He would check up on marmots when they returned, but in the meantime he would have to think guinea pig and increase dosage in proportion to weight. She smiled. It wasn't surprising that memories of Becky and Dai had become interwoven, when you considered their determined and unintentionally funny pursuit of personal agenda. Yet he was a good listener, too. If she told him about the strange offer of work, he would let her talk through her doubts. She dismissed the possibility, regretfully. If she wanted to discuss her future, it would mean telling him that she had folded up business in Llanelli and was moving. She couldn't do that. She hadn't envisaged telling him at all. In her imagination she had just seen herself somewhere else, while he stayed in his cottage and found happiness. She had even used that phrase to herself, to see her leaving him as a corollary to him 'finding happiness'. He seemed happy enough at the moment, but he certainly didn't need her physically. She sighed and went down for breakfast.

Sunlight spilled over the checked plastic cloth, making a still life of the French bread, coffee and posy of fresh flowers in a glass jar. Dai was poring over a map but looked up as she joined him.

'I thought we could go for a drive today, given the change in weather. You said you haven't seen the Aubrac and we could stretch our legs in the mountains.'

Stretching legs sounded like torture. Helen could out-walk Dai round a town any day but give him an open space and he could cover more inches on a map than Helen thought healthy.

'How on earth could you have come here without exploring more?' he muttered, more to himself than to her. She remembered the outings while Tony was fishing, the shopping and cooking, a rare drive to another village along the river. That younger Helen would have felt it immoral to book a coach trip and go out without her husband; not being there when he expected her to be would have caused unbearable friction. She saw now that she wasted so many opportunities.

'Mountains sounds good. But I'm only up to a short walk.'

'That's what I said,' he murmured abstractedly, tracing out a route. 'Check your guide book for me and give me any sights we should pick up on.'

The way he took her for granted gave her a curious ache. He too expected her to be there, but it was different. Perhaps the difference was just that she wanted to be there too. No, her freedom was given, not just taken; her freedom was also taken for granted, not some wonderful concession on which he congratulated himself and for which he would later reproach her. He really didn't think about treating her as his best friend; she just was. She rummaged in her shoulder-bag for the guide book which was already dog-eared and bent.

'There's a ski station up there.' She reconsidered, 'Do you think it's safe for us to go? I mean if they're skiing, there's snow.'

'Weather conditions are good and we've got a four-wheel drive which I take out in all conditions – it's my job.'

'It's not Mynydd Molehill you know – these are real mountains.'

'The roads on the Mynydd are as challenging as anything on your real mountains, believe me. Look, I'm the last person to risk a mountain rescue. I hate it when there's some damn tourist or ten boy scouts lost on the Brecons in

274

predictable bad weather, and some poor sod has to risk his own life for their stupidity, but it's a beautiful day, we're not even going that far. If the weather changes, we'll stop at the nearest auberge. OK?'

It was indeed a beautiful day. Through the restaurant window Helen could see the twisted trunk of an old wisteria drooping its trusses of lilac flower-cones across the door and lower windows of a shuttered three-storyed house. 'OK.'

As they drove, St-Geniez was quickly replaced by St-Eulalie which kept its *village fleuri* promise with tubs of spring bulbs, fluttering lemon, white and purple. The road rose until the river was only visible in shimmering glimpses at the bottom of a shrubby valley. Occasional mailboxes with names like 'Belle vue' or 'Didier' hinted at cottages along pitted lanes but the only village they passed through was tiny, with no more than four houses and a farm. Where there were fields, they were grazed by cows fresh from starring in TV butter advertisements, big brown liquid eyes and tan bodies. Helen thought them pretty but a little undernourished. She didn't invite Dai's observations, fearing an extended professional disquisition on the state of their health.

Across the valley Helen could see the silhouette of the opposite hillside and above that the blue skies she associated with France. As she admired the light and clarity of the sky, she noticed three specks moving fast and high towards their side of the valley. Neil had trained her well and she reached for her field glasses, shouting, 'Stop!' Dai obediently braked, looking for the hazard on the perfectly clear road. 'What ?' he started to ask but Helen was already jumping out of the car. He watched in amazement as she walked along the verge with a total disregard for oncoming traffic, binoculars fixed on the sky. 'If you can't beat them,' he muttered to himself, manoeuvring the car across to a comparatively safe parking spot up on the grass.

'I thought they were buzzards,' she informed him, without losing her concentration.' Two are, but I think the third might be . . .' she tailed off. Dai shielded his eyes, following the direction of her focus. The three shapes were clearly outlined against the sky, the fantails and fringed wings of the large buzzards, circling higher than the hills opposite, reducing the river valley to a food trough. Could they really see that far? Dazzled, Dai looked down again. When he took another look, one buzzard had dipped away from the sun so that its mottled undercarriage and the white patches which close up would look like crescents made from golf balls, were clearly visible.

'It's got to be,' pronounced Helen. 'It's bigger than the other two and they're pretty big buzzards. It's got the long-fingered wings, which made me wonder if I was wrong but when the light catches it you can see it's all brown and there's no mistaking that beak. Same sort of flight pattern though. I wish Neil were here, but I'm sure that's an eagle.' She passed the binoculars to Dai.

'Longer tail perhaps. My Dad always said, "People who just look with their eyes see nothing." Your eyes are better trained than mine – I'm sure you're right.'

Helen was relieved that he sensed her impatience and passed the binoculars back quickly. They both sighed as air currents or whim carried the birds out of sight.

'What type do you reckon?'

'Golden, I think, but that's probably because I don't really know others which might come this far north now,' Helen replied. 'And the sheer size.' She quoted:

> *Man flung me from his leather glove to hang*
> *between the freedom and the flight to circle*
> *over cliffs and green-bed valley to drop*
> *and drink the rabbit's scream.*

276

My rock they name this, little men
as if there were a high place
worth the name, not eagle's.

'What's that from?'
'Something Neil wrote. It still makes me shiver, sort of puts people in their place.'

They headed once more for the high places in the laborious land-limited way of mere humans. Just after the tiny village of Condamines, they turned right and the road started climbing steeply.

Drifts of wild narcissi in open grassland quickly gave way to first patches, then even layers of snow dazzling in the sunlight. Dai took it more slowly but the four-wheel drive ignored the snow packed and gritted on the road, gripping like the safari vehicle from which it had originated. One of France's wildernesses, the rolling moorland on the Aubrac heights, rose and fell into the distance like a white sea parted by the dirtier, lumpier road. They stopped twice more en route, once to see the ski station of Brameloup, where the nursery slopes were studded with the primary colours of padded jackets and salopettes, ringing with shrieks of both fun and fear as the lift groaned and lurched, tiny human legs swinging over the distant drop as they headed for the start of the run. Helen, shivering in the extreme change of climate, fancied the clothing, but not the activity. Their second stop was by a small reservoir, partly iced but thawing in the sun, snowy edges melting into the water. Helen reached again for the field glasses at the sight of a rocky island in the middle where three herons posed, statuesque and intent. Their stillness made them difficult to spot against the grey rock poking through white snow, but the distinctive shapes of their heads stood out clearly. It was an impossible camera

277

shot and Helen didn't even try it. She just wished she could have captured the whole scene for Neil as a present.

'Three seems to be the magic number for birds today,' observed Dai.

'It's certainly magic. I wonder if I've seen these same herons at Penclacwydd.'

'What, on their holidays? They'd have to be mad.'

Helen smiled. 'No accounting for taste. I mean, they love wetlands after all.' Dai insisted on inspecting the engineering of the barrage before they returned to the car. Helen regretted wearing her trainers which were now soaking. In the short time they had been standing by the lake, the sky had turned grey and threatened more snow, which arrived in a flurry as they regained the warmth of the car.

'They say the weather changes quickly in the mountains but this is ridiculous,' muttered Dai as he switched the wipers onto their fastest speed while flurries accelerated to a snowstorm. Helen bit her lip, doubting whether Dai could see anything though the blinding assault, and wondering whether they were even on the road still, but she kept quiet. Within what seemed to be hours but could only have been minutes, with her icy feet sending chills up her entire body, Helen glimpsed part of a road sign through Dai's window. Thank God, Aubrac.

'Thank God, Aubrac,' echoed Dai, adding ruefully, 'I might have underestimated mountain weather. Are you all right?'

'I will be when I've changed these shoes! I never thought it could be so cold!'

'No, even when you know there might be snow at the top, it's difficult to really remember what that means when you're walking around a village in spring sunshine. Come on, let's get you warm and dry.' Holding his coat over her head, despite her protests, Dai rushed them both round the corner from where he had assumed there was legal parking, to l'Auberge Fleurie. 'We're staying here,' he told Helen, 'at least for tonight. It'll probably clear but there's no point taking chances and you need to get warm and dry.' Helen had no quarrel with that and meekly booked two rooms, ran a hot bath in hers and dropped thankfully into it while her shoes and socks steamed on the radiator.

A tactful knock woke her later from a warm, comfortable snooze and Dai appeared with a pair of large hiking socks. 'They're not very elegant but they'll do as slippers until your footwear dries out, and if we want to go out for a walk' – Helen groaned – 'you can borrow these. They were in the back of the car,' he said, holding up a large pair of wellies.

'That doesn't surprise me at all,' she said drily, remembering the random debris which travelled everywhere with Dai. 'Thank you.' There was a pause as he stood at the door to her room and she waited for him to ask to come in, to ask . . . something, anything.

'Do you fancy a coffee?' Not quite what she'd had in mind but it would have to do.

'Do you think they'd send up?' She pointed at her bare feet, which were now redder than usual, having recovered from the blue phase. 'I'm not sure these meet the dress code here.'

He looked a little crestfallen. 'Sorry. I can manage to get two coffees but if I start trying to say "Could we have them in our room?", we're likely to get thrown out for an indecent proposal I didn't know I'd made. Anyway,' his face brightened, 'I've explored downstairs and it's the sort of small hotel which takes walkers and climbers. Just go down in your socks . . . or rather my socks.'

'You're joking!'

'Why not?' Which is how Helen found herself sitting in a restaurant eating strawberry tart and drinking coffee, wearing nothing on her feet but large purple tweed hiking socks. The room struck her as gloomily Germanic in its dark wood panelling, hunting trophies and ceramic tankards but brightened by the poster-size photographs of summer Aubrac scenery, including one life-size portrait of a typical local cow. The receptionist, doubling as waiter and presumably in most roles in the small hotel, maintained formality until he saw Helen's socks, when his features twitched into a broad smile.

'Sore feet, huh? Long walk here?'

'Short walk, big snowstorm, wrong shoes – wet feet,' Helen replied in telegraphic French.

'It is so easy to think the mountain's smile will last but she is untrustworthy, as you have found. For me, it is good for business.' He gave another broad smile. 'You have come on just the right day. Tonight we have a special music night, traditional songs of the Aubrac, and I cook a traditional meal for you.'

Helen rightly interpreted 'for you' as meaning for all the skiers, walkers and mad sightseers looking for a night out; sales pitches were not so different in the wool business from the tourist trade. Even so, they were here for the night anyway and there was always the possibility of real local flavour surviving the hype.

'What's he saying?' asked Dai while the hotelier hovered. Helen translated for him. 'Oh well of course we'll try it; we're here anyway. Book a couple of places and ask when it starts.' Dai dismissed the matter and raised a far more serious issue, judging by his expression. 'Can you ask him about that cow?'

Helen stifled an inward groan. 'What exactly do you want to know about that cow?'

'Everything.'

The Frenchman's smile had been fading as he looked from one to the other, trying to follow the exchange and wondering if he were still required. The beam returned in response to Helen's query and the torrent of French suggested that this was his favourite subject. Helen nodded and smiled, desperately trying to take in all the facts hurled at her.

'Salar,' said Dai. 'He said "Salar", didn't he! I knew it!'

'Oui monsieur, Salar', the hotelier enunciated clearly for the foreigner, 'la vâche la plus belle du monde.'

'Oui, belle, belle,' said Dai vaguely but with acceptable enthusiasm. Too much enthusiasm, thought Helen suspiciously. He was up to something. 'Well?' he asked her eagerly when new customers had distracted their patron.

'He said that's an Aubrac cow, but you won't see them on the mountain until the end of May. Come back then and you'll see the trans-something-or-other,'

'Transhumance – mountain-style farming where they take the herds up to the lush mountain pastures for the summer and back down to the lowland fields in the winter. They do it with sheep in the Pyrenees – or they certainly used to. Go on . . .'

'That's about it really. You got the rest. They're the best cows in the world, they come from all over to get cows here, they make the best milk, butter, cheese and meat etc etc. Oh, I remember, and there's big cattle fairs in spring and autumn at Laguiole and Nasbinals. He just about told me how to make the damn cheese or cantal – apparently that's what we're eating tonight, only it's called l'aligot. Sounds like something Grandpa gave Heidi to bring out the country roses in her cheeks.'

'Be good for you then,' said Dai abstractedly. 'Dual-purpose, that's got to be the answer. Pretty too.' Helen considered wryly that the waitress had been no real

281

competition; now she was in trouble. No contest, she silently informed the ruminant's big brown eyes, you win every time.

'I'll just see if it's still snowing. You wait here.' As if, she thought, inspecting her cosy toes, she were likely to skip down the street in her socks going 'moo', or whatever it took to recapture his attention. She waited while he took a snow check, returned to the table, went to check the weather again and told her, 'I've got to make a phone call. There's probably an international box in the square. I won't be long.' She ordered another coffee while she waited, considering the offer made to her while Dai had waited with his coffee the day before. She found a pencil in her bag and started idly sketching on a serviette, wondering if there would be any market for large knitted wallhangings depicting herons, rocks, snow and a belltower in the distance.

Will answered the phone, as Gwen had started cooking the evening meal. He was surprised to hear his son's voice, 'Dad, it's me, Dai.' He was so clear he must be back in Llanelli, which meant that something had gone wrong.

'Beth sy'n bod?'

'Nothing's the matter.'

'Where are you?'

'France. Listen, I've got the answer for you. Salars. Get some Salars.'

'Dai, don't phone when you're drunk. Sailors indeed. If they opened up all the docks from Llanelli to Carmarthen, I still don't think we'll be seeing sailors on the Mynydd. What do you think? That your Mam will dance the hornpipe for them? Go and sober up, man. You can't even remember your Welsh.'

'There isn't a Welsh word for Salars, Dad. It's a breed of cow.'

282

Gwen called through from the kitchen, 'Who is it?'

Will spoke slightly off mouthpiece but clear enough to Dai, impatiently waiting. 'Our Dai. Drunk he is. At least he'll throw up on someone else's staircase.'

'All the way from France! Tell him to save his money and not to stay on too long. And tell him it's not cheap rate the same as home.'

Dai didn't wait for the distant buzz of his mother's voice to cease. 'Dad, I'm not drunk. Remember when you first got the Charolais and everyone said you were mad, but you were right. Be right again. The cows here are Salars, dual-purpose, milk and meat, beautiful honey-coloured beasts and I've read about them. It only came back to me when we saw the cows but there were some articles saying Salars were catching on in Wales. I know at least two farmers in Pembrokeshire are starting up herds.' Silence. 'Dad are you still there?'

'I'm here. Say the truth now, you are sober.'

'Stone cold.'

'Flimsy creatures, are they? Like sheep – a hint of hurt, decide they're gonners and die on you out of sheer stupidity.'

'They've been bred to trek up these mountains for hundreds of years and they're used to free grazing over rough pasture, no sheds all summer, wintering down in the valley. They've got to be tough enough for the Mynydd. Believe me Dad, they're right, everything fits.'

'I'll think on it. Mam says watch your phone bill and it's time we saw Helen again.'

'Got to go,' Dai evaded the implicit question. ''Bye.'

As the pips went, Will yelled to the listening kitchen, 'He says they'll be round as soon as they're back and they're having a good time.'

''Bye son,' he told the dead line. 'Thanks.'

283

Pleased with himself, Dai returned to the Auberge. What he'd told his father was true, although at the time he had read the articles he had dismissed the experimentation with new breeds as a compromise, acceptable to continental standards of milk and beef but not to British. His father's problems of sustaining the traditional beef herd, other farmers' difficulties with milk quotas, the BSE disaster and the scrubby grazing available on the small Welsh hill farms, had all made him re-think. After all, it was merely a jingoistic belief in British quality which had prejudiced him against the dual-purpose cattle. Surely that quality came from the farming – and the vet care of course – and would tell just as much in the newly imported Salar as in the older Charolais and more traditional English breeds. He was tempted to put his theories into practice himself, visit a French market with his father and invest with him in a likely starter herd. Partnership money would be a strong inducement to his dad to take the sort of risk that made him a good farmer, and between them they'd know good animals when they saw them, that was for sure.

His full attention returned to Helen, who shoved a few serviettes into her bag as he rejoined her.

'Get through?' she asked curiously.

'Yes. I phoned home.'

'I guessed. There aren't that many people you can phone who will appreciate the true beauty of a cow.'

'How did you know?'

'Something about the way you looked at her.'

He just laughed at her, then stared seriously at her face. He reached across the table and carefully pushed her nose flat. She shook him off. 'What do you think you're doing?'

'I thought if you had a nose job, so it was broader, flatter and preferably brown, you could snort more attractively.' He added suggestively, 'I could make you low like a cow.'

284

'Thanks but no thanks! I want to perfume my socks before dinner so I'll meet you back down here at half-seven, OK?' He let her go, wondering if he'd imagined a wistful look as she turned to go upstairs.

The restaurant was fairly full for dinner without being crowded and, as far as Dai could hear, no one around them spoke English, so the other tourists did not break the holiday spell, despite the jollity of a group of eight friends who felt that their loud enjoyment was a valuable contribution to the clientele as a whole.

The main dish, l'aligot, turned out to be the most filling soup Dai had ever known, with tomme de cantal, the local cheese, melted with mashed potato and seasoned with garlic.

'This is supposed to have sustained the shepherds and cowherds for centuries,' Helen informed him.

'Like a miner's snap.' He swallowed another spoonful. 'How'd you put it in your sandwich box?'

'You wouldn't. Those stone igloos across the Aubrac – see that one in the poster?' she waved her spoon in the direction of the wall – 'are the burons, winter shelters for cows and cowherds' huts, where they made the cheeses. I bet they did a bit of campfire cooking in the buron.'

'If you say so. Good soup though.'

'I don't think they see it as soup. It's part of "the cure" that they come from Paris to sample.'

'City folk! Phone me up to tell me a sheep is giving birth in a field without an obstetrician!'

They ate in companionable silence for a while, then Dai plucked up courage. 'Have you had many of those nightmares?'

'No,' she said, then thought about it as the realisation dawned, 'no, I haven't had any since,' she swallowed and spoke so quietly he could hardly hear her, 'since the one before you left.'

He certainly didn't see what had happened as 'him leaving' but the last thing he wanted was to argue. He commented quietly, 'I thought that this . . . trip . . . might have sparked off more nightmares.'

'No,' she said, closing the conversation. Clapping and encouraging whistles announced the arrival of the folk singers, two men and one woman wearing red waistcoats, lightly embroidered, over loose white shirts and black trousers. One of the men sported a battered leather broad-brimmed hat. They settled, one man sitting and strumming a few chords on a guitar, the others standing and smiling at the clientele before launching into a simple ballad. Dai liked the sound but, for himself, would have been tempted to plug in the guitar and add bass. However, he cheerfully tapped his knee along with the beat, and was pretty sure he could recognise the chorus each time in what were clearly traditional folk songs. You didn't have to understand a word to guess that the lyrics portrayed a lover and his lass, the call of the king's shilling (or the comrade's franc), the maid's ruin and the country calendar. Dai hoped one of the songs, which brought a very personal involvement from the man singing, was about his hopes for a fine herd of cattle, but he didn't risk asking Helen for a translation. When he did glance across at her, he was horrified to see tears streaming.

He reached for her hand. 'What?'

Under cover of the clapping at the end of a song, she told him, 'I've been re-visiting something that's not there . . . and now I'm missing what's here and good . . . and I'll come back in five years and now will have gone too and it's all in the songs.'

At a loss, Dai asked, 'Have they been singing Cabrel?',

286

thinking he had missed some deeply significant lyrics with shared memories attached. She shook her head.

'No, I don't know any of the songs. And I probably won't ever see the octagonal belltower at Prades d'Aubrac and I'll get back home and I'll always wish I'd seen it. That's the kind of person I am.'

Nonplussed, he offered, 'If it's not too far we'll go there tomorrow.'

'The belltower's not the point,' she sniffed. 'If it's not that, it would be something else.'

He tried to follow her line of thought and wondered if she was upset that she hadn't found and faced up to the memories of Becky.

As gently as he could, he asked, 'Do you want to go on, to the next campsite sooner then we planned. Get the worst over with?'

She turned her tear-stained face towards him. 'Don't you see?' she said, 'I don't need to any more. It's become irrelevant and that's the hardest thing of all.'

He didn't see at all. He only wished he knew if this was a good development or a disaster. A psychology degree would possibly have helped, but – not for the first time – he thought ruefully how much easier animals were to deal with than women, particularly this woman whom he loved very much. He ordered, and drank in one mouthful each, both the gentian liqueur and the strawberry liqueur (local specialities which had been offered as a choice) then bravely kept to The Plan.

'Come for a walk.' He didn't wait for her assent but stood up, saying, 'Give me your key and I'll get your coat and wellies.' Helen's trainers had still not dried and, much to her chagrin, her feet were still clad only in purple socks. She had slunk to a corner table in the restaurant and tucked her feet firmly out of sight during the meal. Now she

287

meekly handed over her key, saying only, 'My coat's in the wardrobe.'

They closed the heavy wooden hotel door on the warmth and noise, and caught their breath in the sudden chill. It had stopped snowing earlier, and Dai felt hopeful when he saw how clear the stars shone in the night sky. He braced himself, Gregory Peck shooting a rabid dog, the deerhunter, showdown – one shot was all he'd get. They crunched through the fresh snow, backtracking down the road they'd driven along earlier.

'Can we slow down?' Helen pleaded, struggling in Dai's wellies. He tried to adapt his pace but if he didn't concentrate, he found her lagging behind. An interior glow in the village church suggested a welcome pause and they walked down the steps to the side entrance, set back from the road. Dai watched Helen explore the building, which was much plainer than others they'd visited, but with a long, modern mural of a nativity scene, more French peasant than Jewish.

Helen called him over. 'Look!'

There was no mistaking the animal observing the baby's birth; it was an Aubrac cow, golden brown and painted with love.

'It's almost as if the cow is the centre of attraction rather than Baby Jesus,' Helen observed.

'At last – people who get their priorities right.' Dai nodded approval. 'Quite a narrow face on that one.'

'Come on,' Helen tugged at him. They were right at the edge of the village, which offered little light from the shuttered windows to interfere with the breathtaking panoply of the sky.

Dai found his bearings but stayed silent for a minute, marvelling. Helen shivered and he moved behind her, slipping his arms round her.

'I wish I had a torch.'

'Why?' she asked.

'It would be easier to show you the stars.'

She laughed. 'I can see the stars. And that,' she pointed,' is the moon.'

'OK,' he persisted, looking at the moon in the west, 'see that row of three stars, below the moon as we look?' He would never, as long as he stargazed, get used to the idea that it was three-dimensional infinity he was map-reading in two-dimensional terms.

'I've got them – sort of horizontal line.'

'Yes, that's Orion's belt.' What would it be like just to stand here, holding her, for the time it took the light from Orion to reach earth? But human life was of the moment.

'Overhead is the Sospan, the Plough, the Big Dipper.'

She looked up obediently. 'I know that one. Seven stars shaped like an ice-cream scoop sideways on. Don't you find something else if you follow the long handle?'

'Polaris, the sailors' steering star.'

'It is an ever fixed mark,' Helen quoted.

'Neil?'

'No, silly – Shakespeare on the theme of true love.'

Dai mentally crossed his fingers. 'That's unbelievable, look at that.' He turned her to look north and slightly west, at a low angle in the sky.

'There's loads of stars. I can't see anything exciting – apart from the fact that they're all good.'

'It's not a star – it's a comet,' said Dai his voice breaking with excitement. 'It looks like a cone shape because it's trailing two tails of gas and dust. Funny really – it's all just debris but that's what makes it special... beautiful ... all that dead matter it's picked up through time and space.'

'So trailing dead matter makes you special ...'

He picked up on her tone and squeezed her. 'Very

special. Do you know how rare it is to see a comet as bright as this and without a telescope.'

'What about Haley's Comet?'

Dai shook his head. 'Not as bright or clear as this. There's been nothing like this for over four hundred years and this particular comet last visited us in 2,600 BC.'

'I suppose you even know its name!'

'Yes actually – it's Hale-Bopp, named after Mr Hale and Mr Bopp who discovered it at the same time during telescope observation in America.'

'How do you know all this stuff?'

'I read an article that said there was a chance of seeing it and gave some details.' Given that everyone in Wales who wanted to see the comet had been watching it and reading about it for the last month, there had been a fairly good chance of seeing it in any clear sky over Europe. It was typical of Helen that she had noticed none of the media hype nor even Llanelli chat.

'Just think,' he left a dramatic pause, 'a once in four thousand year chance and we're here.'

Her imagination was fired. 'If we hadn't come out we'd have missed it. We're so lucky!'

He buried his face in the back of her neck, breathing in her perfume, tightening his arms around her. 'If I hadn't wanted to buy a jumper, I'd have missed you. I can't wait four thousand years for my next chance; one lifetime I've got and I want to spend it with you.' She twisted in his arms and he wasn't sure what she would do next until he felt the pleasurable shock of her hand between his thighs and her mouth hungry on his. He sank into the kiss then broke off and held her gently at arms' length, firmly preventing her hands from arousing him any further. His breathing gave him away but he congratulated himself on his marvellous control and tried desperately to imagine being packed in ice at the centre of the comet, an extreme substitute for a cold shower.

'That's lovely, but it's not enough,' he told her, 'I've got to know you'll marry me.'

'What!' She looked at him round-eyed. 'Are you seriously telling me you won't have sex with me unless I promise to marry you?'

'I wouldn't put it as crudely but broadly speaking, yes.'

'Why?'

'Because I want you to be there when I wake up in the morning.'

'I could be there anyway.'

'I want to know that it's legally required.'

'You stole that from a film,' she said suspiciously.

'I did not,' he lied.

'You're a vet. You wake up at all times of day and night and I most certainly won't always be there.'

'Well at least I'll know you'll be back,' he pursued gamely.

'I don't know. Nothing's changed and I've been through this decision before. I've sold up. My flat's up at the end of the month. I should move on. There'll still be nightmares. I know nothing about gardening, even less about cows and your parents don't like me.'

Dai swallowed hard, horrified at how far she had discounted him, elated that she was seriously thinking about changing her mind, and confused as to which of the ridiculous obstacles she had put in the way to counter. He'd given her a comet in a starry night on the mountains of the Aubrac and he'd run out of romantic persuasion. He said simply, 'Take a little risk.'

Helen felt an absurd impulse to follow Dai's example and phone her parents. She imagined her mother answering the phone, shrieking, 'Dad it's Helen.' She would tell her

Mum, 'I'm phoning from holiday in France to say I'm engaged.' What she'd said would be repeated word for word to her father before Joan's reproach, 'We've been so worried,' her Dad's intervention – 'Your Dad said not to worry, you've phoned at last,' – and the inevitable 'What's he like?' Would it really be possible? And what was he like, this man? He was persistent, that's what he was like. And it was a very bad idea but she loved him. He made her want a future. She had travelled all round the world, or at least to France, to find that home was best and that home was with him.

'I suppose so,' she said grudgingly. 'Now can we go to bed? Please?'